Incident at Indian Cave

Jim had his gun out but we decided to wait for whomever the sheriff's office was sending. As we waited, Jim kept scanning the area, the woods, the house, the barn and greenhouse, the garden and field beyond it. I liked the fact that he was not focused on me.

Many times I have wished I was a less attractive woman. I look like my mother and my mother is gorgeous – tall, big busted, small waisted, shapely hips, long legs, thick blonde hair, and a perfect face with big blue-violet eyes. She dresses in elegant tailored suits which still cleverly reveal her figure. Mother has developed a cold, aloof deportment which discourages familiarities of any kind, unfortunately not only with impudent men but also with Dad – and me, even when I was small. I dress to cover up but I still get far too many leering stares and unwanted advances. However, I do try to maintain some balance and not repel everyone.

As we waited, Jim asked casually, "Can you make any guesses as to who that masked man might be?"

I said, "None at all." Jim was looking at me and I realized he was evaluating whether I was telling the truth or not. I could hardly blame him. Most people are not attacked by total strangers appearing out of nowhere. "I've been thinking but I can't think of anyone."

Jim regarded me solemnly and then gave a small nod. I knew he believed me.

When the sheriff's car arrived, it came with lights and siren. Jim stowed both his gun and phone, while still scanning the area. "If our perp is still around, that'll scare him off," he commented.

We moved out of the woods as the deputy exited his car with his gun drawn. It was Roger Springer.

I thought to myself, *This is definitely not my day!*

Books by Mary Cambron-Collard

The Points to Ponder Series

Family Secrets
An Odd Soul
Survivor's Guilt
Incident at Indian Cave

The Bigfoot Tales

McDugal's Kirk: Book 1
Redemption: Book 2 of the Bigfoot Tales

Coming Soon

Feud: Book 3 of the Bigfoot Tales

OHP
Ozark Heritage Publishing was set up to publish books reflecting Christian morals and values but often containing non-traditional elements.

E-mail: ozarkheritatepublishing@gmail.com

Dear Readers,

When someone experiences a major tragedy, some recover and go on to live a normal life and some don't.

Why? Is it more the nature of the tragedy or is it the person?

Why do some veterans suffer more from PTSD (Post Traumatic Stress Disorder) than others? Is it what they experienced, the kind of help they get, or the person themselves?

Where is God in all of this?

Come with me to Indian Cave Farm where two people with past traumas meet and find themselves working together to deal with present mayhem.

Mary Cambron-Collard

DEDICATION

I dedicate this story to two black girls
who at different points
in my young life befriended
a hill country white girl
trying to cope with an unfriendly new school.

I give these two girls credit
for demonstrating that
black people are human, intelligent, compassionate,
and sometimes God's agents.

Incident at Indian Cave

Mary Cambron-Collard

Blessings,
Mary Cambron-Collard

This is a work of fiction. Any resemblance to actual persons, living or dead, is completely coincidental.

Copyright © 2019 Mary Cambron-Collard
All rights reserved.

Cover Photos
by Diana Collard
Ozark National Scenic Riverways

ISBN-10: 1729784151
ISBN-13: 978-1729784150

OHP
OZARK HERITAGE PUBLISHING
723 North Ninth Street
Poplar Bluff, Missouri
E-mail: ozarkheritagepublishing@gmail.com

Printed by CreateSpace, an Amazon.com Company.

> But Joseph said to them,
> "Don't be afraid.
> Am I in the place of God?
> You intended to harm me,
> but God intended it for good"
>
> Genesis 50:19,20a (NIV)

Part 1
Indian Cave Farm

❧ Chapter 1: The Invader ❦

Faith

 Monday mornings, even in May, are normally quiet at a greenhouse business so I was working on my computer at my other job, editing a manuscript for an aspiring writer. The novel was supposed to be an historical romance set in the Civil War, the one war I knew about, so I had initially approached the project with enthusiasm. Now, a third of the way through the book, I was having to force myself to trudge on. It was long on explicit love scenes and short on history. The author had asked only for corrections to punctuation, spelling, and flagging for possible grammar errors but I was struggling even to do that much.

 A flagrant instance of historical inaccuracy had me so absorbed that I was slow to focus in on the noise I heard at our front door. Normally our dog, Lassie, would have been barking but she had disappeared yesterday. When I heard a board creak, I knew someone was in the house. My grandmother had died six weeks ago and my son was in school.

 Whoever it was in my house did not belong here!

 I didn't go look and I didn't wait.

 The room I use for an office has a door onto the back porch and I went out as quietly as possible. I ran, not for the barn or the greenhouse, but for the woods and the creek where we have a small dock and a 16 foot jon boat. I heard the intruder come out a back door and pound across the back porch and down the steps after me. I still didn't waste time looking back. I knew the average home invader could run faster than me in my sandals and the path was mostly downhill so I concentrated on watching where my feet were going.

 If I fell, he would have me!

As I approached the curve in the path just before the final drop to the creek, I could hear him behind me. He was gaining. I would not have time to start the boat motor. Could I push the boat off the dock strongly enough to be out of his reach? It would have to be untied.

I was not going to have enough time!

As I rounded the curve in the path, I was watching where I put my feet and only when I was almost to the dock did I see the canoe coming downstream. It had only one man in it with his gear weighting down the front end.

I shouted, "Help! Help!" and dived into the creek which because of recent rains was more like a small river. I am a poor swimmer but the adrenaline in my system helped. Because of my splashing, I could no longer hear my pursuer. I was catching glimpses of the man in the canoe as I was trying to get as far from shore as possible. He was looking at me and I yelled again, "Help!" and got a mouth full of water.

He redirected his canoe to bring it closer to me and then he yelled, "Catch this."

A cushion flew into the water. His aim was good and I had no trouble grabbing it. He had run the mooring rope tied to the back of his canoe through the cushion's handles so he could tow me behind him. Hanging on to the cushion was not easy and I swallowed more water but I didn't turn loose. I bobbed up and down as the man paddled urgently. I could not see my chaser but suddenly I heard a loud pop. It was followed by another one and I heard something hit the aluminum canoe. Only then did I realize that my home invader was shooting at us.

As I was running, I had been silently praying and now I added, "Oh, God, make his aim bad!" Then I realized we were drifting. The man in the canoe was no longer paddling. Had he been hit? "Father God," I prayed, "please help us."

With the canoe slowing down, I was managing to keep my head above water. I worried about getting shot. *What should I do?*

Then the man sat up and started paddling again. "Hang on!" he told me. "Once we're around this bend, we'll be out of sight."

We went around the bend and the man said, "I can't pull you into this canoe while it's on the water but I'll go to shore and you can climb in."

Then I heard a boat motor start and I recognized the sound of our jon boat. Whoever had been chasing me was not stopping.

Ahead was another bend and beyond that was a bluff. In that bluff was a good hiding place.

"Keep moving," I shouted. "Go around the next bend. Stay as close to the bluff on the right as you can," I told him.

I dropped off at the right spot and started climbing. Using the well-placed hand and foot holds in the rock, I went up quickly. When I reached the crevice, I scrambled into the hole at the back on my hands and knees.

The canoeist had moved on and I didn't dare stop to look. I crawled until I came to where the ceiling was higher and reached to the right where my searching fingers found two kerosene lanterns and the small waterproof container of matches. As I lit a lantern, I heard our jon boat pass the entrance of the cave. Cautiously, I crawled the short distance back to the entrance leaving the lantern burning behind me. I risked putting my head out to look but because of how the crevice which held the cave entrance was shaped, I could not see downstream, but I heard the boat as it abated and went to shore. Not far downstream was a place with a sloping bank and I speculated that the canoeist had put in there.

I listened and after a few minutes, I heard a splash and several shots, followed by another splash and more shots. It was quiet for a minute and then I heard shots that sounded like they were hitting the aluminum canoe.

Was I listening to that man in the canoe being murdered?!

After what seemed like a long wait, I heard our jon boat coming back upstream slowly. I scooted into the small cave entrance backwards. After I heard our boat pass, I risked a peek from behind the plants growing on the upstream side of the crevice. The man was all in black, completely covered, even black sunglasses, and he had a black handgun. He was moving slowly searching the creek banks but he never looked up the bluff. I told my thumping heart to be quiet while I tried to estimate his size but that wasn't easy. After he went around the bend, I thought about the size of our boat and guessed he was maybe six feet or so tall, muscular but not fat.

I heard the boat stop at our dock and the motor go off. I managed to scoot back into the cave entrance where I collapsed, shaking and crying. I couldn't even focus my mind to pray.

I don't know how long it was before I heard, "Psst! Ma'am, are you still up there?"

I froze.

Then I heard small sounds and the voice said, "That perp sank my canoe. Is there room up there for me too?"

It was the canoeist! He had not been shot. He was climbing up. I waited. I was happy he wasn't dead.

His face appeared over the edge and he said, "I see you found a hole. Do you think he'll come back? That hole doesn't look big enough for both of us."

The canoeist had a long, gaunt, homely face which reminded me immediately of a portrait of Abraham Lincoln without a beard. He was tanned with wet dark hair which was trying to curl and hazel eyes, an odd combination of green and brown with streaks of yellow. He had paddled the canoe easily, looking strong and co-ordinated like he was used to physical activity.

I tried to stop crying and tried get up but I was too shaky.

"Are you hurt?" he asked, and I heard concern in his voice.

"Just sca-scared to-to-tally out of my wits," I managed to stutter out.

"Who was he?" he asked. He sounded calm and that helped.

I shook my head. "I d-d-don't know."

"Maybe we should introduce ourselves," the man said. "I'm James Willis – call me Jim."

"Faith Johnson," I told him, managing not to stutter.

"I'm on vacation," he said. "I live in Springfield but I'm from Ellington."

"I was praying," I told him, "and then there you were."

He smiled. "Well, I don't think I've ever been anyone's answer to prayer before."

He had a nice smile, wide with even teeth and his eyes twinkling. He wasn't handsome and somehow I liked that.

My 15-year-old son, Job, is turning into a very handsome young man and it worries me.

I got up on my hands and knees and managed to back into the hole. "You can come in," I said. "This is the entrance to a cave."

He followed me in to the place where the lit lantern waited. I huddled with my back to a wall, my arms around my bent legs. I was still shaking.

He looked around and asked, "How many people know about this cave?"

"Everyone local knows about the cave but not about this entrance. There's another one near our house. My son and I found this one and we never told anyone except my grandmother and she's dead now. Do you mind if I ask you to keep it a secret? The cave has pictographs and other Indian artifacts. I don't want treasure hunters in here."

"Do you think you can tell me what happened?"

I realized he had been giving me time to recover. I still felt weak and shaky but I could talk. "I was on my computer and I heard someone break in the front door. I didn't wait to see who it was. I just ran. I heard him behind me but I didn't look back. I had to watch where I put my feet. I knew if I fell, he would get me. I ran for the dock. I was hoping I could use the boat to get away but I could hear him behind me and I knew I wasn't going to have enough time. Then I saw you and I just dived in the water. I'm not a good swimmer but I was terrified."

He had listened, still and focused. I stopped and he was quiet for a minute and then he asked, "Did you ever get a look at him?"

I took a deep breath and said, "Yes, when he went back by in the boat, I peeked. He was searching the banks but not looking up. He was all in black, even gloves and a ski mask and wearing sunglasses. I tried to judge his size. I think he was bigger than average, taller and filled out but not really fat. I can't get any closer."

"Physically fit?" he asked.

"He was gaining on me as I ran, so yes." And then I added, "He had a gun."

"What kind?" he asked but I don't know guns. I told him it looked like what I had seen police use in TV shows and he nodded.

"You're actually an accurate observer," he told me. "I hid but watched him throw my stuff in the water and sink my canoe. I take it you were home alone."

"Yes," I said. "My son's in school."

"So everyone who knows you would know you were home alone?"

I nodded and he asked, "What do you think he wanted?"

He waited while I pulled myself together enough to answer.

"Rape?" I heard the tremor in my voice.

He nodded and said, "Thieves wait until everyone is gone and don't need such an elaborate disguise. Have there been other rapes around here recently?"

"I haven't heard of any," I answered. "We have a greenhouse business but we never keep more than a hundred dollars in cash on hand. My son drops it to the bank on his way to school. If someone wanted money, they'd intercept him on a Monday morning after a busy weekend but it's never enough money to be worth the risk."

The man, Jim Willis, was silent and I could see the wheels turning in his mind but whatever he was thinking, he didn't comment. Instead he finally asked, "Which way is out?"

I led the way. When he stood up, I found he was extremely tall. I'm 5 foot 10, tall for a woman, but he towered over me, 6 foot 4 at least. He had good shoulders and the long, lanky build of a professional basketball player. His size made me uneasy but as we moved through the cave, he never crowded me or brushed against me.

Along the way was one long tunnel requiring crawling and Jim was bigger than me. It took us quite a while to get out. I was still shaky and also barefoot, having lost my sandals in the water, but was wearing long sweat pants which gave my knees a little protection. He was dressed in camouflage and his trousers also were long which helped. When my son and I came in here, we normally brought knee pads and gloves.

When we came out of the cave, we were up a bluff overlooking the house, barn, and greenhouse but only the greenhouse was totally visible. The house and the barn are surrounded by large old trees, mostly oaks, but the greenhouse and kitchen garden and the open field beyond them lie in the sun. We watched for several long minutes but saw no movement so we ducked down the path and were quickly hidden in the woods. At the bottom of the bluff, we crossed the tiny brook on stepping stones and moved through a belt of trees.

I stopped out of sight of the house and said, "I wish I had my Track phone."

The man asked, "Who do you want to call?"

"The sheriff," I answered and wondered who he thought I might want to call. "I don't want one of my neighbors coming in and meeting that man with his gun."

"I have a cell phone in a waterproof case," he told me and pulled it out. "It even takes pictures," he added, "but when that perp was sinking my canoe, I was not really well hid. I was afraid if I moved to get my phone out, he would see me." He paused and then said, "I also have a gun."

"Do you?" I told him. "Good."

I called 911 on his phone and eventually got the county sheriff's office in Eminence. Janice Dunbar was their dispatcher and I told her that I'd had someone break into my house. I told her I had run and someone in a canoe on the creek had helped me escape. She said she'd send a deputy.

I sat down because I still felt weak but I chose a spot where I could see my front porch through a screen of shrubbery and weeds. The invader had propped the screen door open and the inside door was also standing open. As we waited, our calico mouser, Cheshire, come and cautiously peered into the open doorway. Then she went inside. I told Jim, "No one's in the house right now. That cat doesn't like strangers. She always hides."

Jim had his gun out but we decided to wait for whomever the sheriff's office was sending. As we waited, Jim kept scanning the area, the woods, the house, the barn and greenhouse, the garden and field beyond it. I liked the fact that he was not focused on me.

Many times I have wished I was a less attractive woman. I look like my mother and my mother is gorgeous – tall, big busted, small waisted, shapely hips, long legs, thick blonde hair, and a perfect face with big blue-violet eyes. She dresses in elegant tailored suits which still cleverly reveal her figure. Mother has developed a cold, aloof deportment which discourages familiarities of any kind, unfortunately not only with impudent men but also with Dad – and me, even when I was small. I dress to cover up but I still get far too many leering stares and unwanted advances. However, I do try to maintain some balance and not repel everyone.

As we waited, Jim asked casually, "Can you make any guesses as to who that masked man might be?"

I said, "None at all." Jim was looking at me and I realized he was evaluating whether I was telling the truth or not. I could hardly blame him. Most people are not attacked by total strangers appearing out of nowhere. "I've been thinking but I can't think of anyone."

Jim regarded me solemnly and then gave a small nod. I knew he believed me.

When the sheriff's car arrived, it came with lights and siren. Jim stowed both his gun and phone, while still scanning the area. "If our perp's still around, that'll scare him off," he commented.

We moved out of the woods as the deputy exited his car with his gun drawn. It was Roger Springer. I thought to myself, *This is definitely not my day!*

Roger Springer and his wife split up last year. She caught him with another woman. The word around town was that no one was surprised. He had asked me out a number times and I had said no every time. In my opinion, he was a macho jerk. But right now, he represented the law so I moved out to meet him with Jim Willis following me.

I said, "I'm pretty sure he's gone but you might check the house anyway."

As he moved into the house, he was imitating the dance he had seen TV cops do, standing at the side of the door and jumping in with his gun pointed. I thought it was silly but I was still too shook-up to find much of anything funny. We followed him inside and watched as he treated every doorway like there was a shooter in the next room. Cheshire had disappeared. Smart cat.

As we came to the kitchen, I was suddenly thirsty and got a glass of water. Jim said, "Good idea. It helps with shock. Drink as much as you can." He also took a glass and filled it.

At Jim's suggestion, they checked the barn and greenhouse. When they returned, I was sitting at the kitchen table. Roger Springer asked to speak to me alone and Jim said, "I'll wait on the front porch."

"You could just go ahead and leave," the deputy said and I could hear an edge in his voice.

Jim shrugged with his hands out, palms up and said, "Sorry, no transport. That perp shot my canoe full of holes and sank it."

I was wondering what Roger Springer was thinking. Our old pickup truck was in the carport attached to the barn but he could plainly see it was the only vehicle around.

Roger said, "I thought you were here visiting Faith."

I said, "I never saw Mr. Willis before he happened to be passing by our dock at the right moment. Without his help, that man would probably have gotten me." My use of *Mr. Willis* was my way of denying a prior friendship. It was absolutely none of Roger's business but the suggestion that I had been entertaining a man with no one else here was a sensitive issue for me.

Jim nodded to me and headed for the front door. I didn't like being left alone with Roger but I knew this house and with the front door open, what was said here in the kitchen would be audible on the front porch to anyone near the door.

So I said to Roger, "We can talk here." He asked for coffee and I got up to make some. I was a irritated by his demand for hospitality but tried to tell myself I was being unreasonable. Many people keep a pot of coffee on all the time.

Instead of starting on what had happened, Roger asked, "What's all that computer stuff about?"

My office was in a room off the kitchen which originally had been a bedroom. I said, "I work over the internet."

He said, "I thought you ran that greenhouse."

"I do but it doesn't provide income year around. I have a business editing manuscripts which I do over the internet." I decided not to mention the children's books. Instead I said, "Do you want to hear what happened?"

I could hear the challenge in my voice but he just shrugged and said, "Okay, what happened?"

As I moved through the story, I mentioned a crevice in a bluff where I hid but said nothing about the cave. At the end of my story, I said, "When he came back by and was past me, I tried to get a look at him. He was dressed all in black, even gloves and a ski mask and sunglasses. He was taller than average, maybe your height, but thinner. He had a handgun."

"Could the two men have been working together?" Roger asked.

"No," I said. "Definitely not. Mr. Willis was as surprised as I was. He got a much better look at the man than I did. He watched him throwing his stuff in the creek and sinking his canoe. I think he knows what kind of gun the man was using. He can tell you more."

As I said this, I heard my son, Job, arriving on his scooter. I checked the clock. It wasn't even noon yet so it was no where near time for him to be home from school. I went to the front door. He was asking Jim Willis, "Where's my mother?"

He saw me and asked, "Mom, are you okay?"

I could hear the anxiety in his voice and I wondered who told him. I said, "I'm fine. Just wet and dirty." I gestured to the man on our front porch and said, "This is Jim Willis who just happened to be going by our dock in a canoe at the right time. Jim, this is my son, Job."

Jim held out his hand and Job shook it saying, "Thanks, man." But I had seen Jim's quick surprised glance from Job to me to Job. Job is already as tall as me and people often think he is grown. And he looks nothing like me. He has rich mahogany colored hair and big, thickly lashed matching eyes. Girls were already admiring his looks and I knew he was going to be a very handsome man.

Job looked at me and said, "Mom, I should've told you. When Lassie didn't show up yesterday evening, I went looking for her. Someone shot her. She was here when we left for church but we didn't see her the rest of the day. Someone came while we were gone and killed her. I should've told you."

As Job stopped speaking, Roger Springer came out on the porch. Instead of joining the circle of people in a natural manner, he stepped sort of halfway behind me and he put one hand on my shoulder. I jerked away from him and moved closer to Job. He looked irritated and I said, "You need to get Mr. Willis's story."

Jim Willis said, "I smell coffee. I wouldn't mind a cup." His request smoothed over the awkward moment.

I moved through the door with Job behind me. I didn't look back but crossed the living room to the kitchen where I poured coffee into a large mug. Jim Willis had come through with Roger Springer behind him and I asked him about cream and sugar.

I said, "I'll leave you two here to talk," and moved back to the front porch with Job following me.

Job started to say something but I motioned him quiet. I wanted to hear what Jim Willis told Roger Springer. I stood on one side of the door and Job on the other. We heard Roger ask, "Have you got any ID?" It was confirmation of my assessment of how he felt about Jim Willis.

After a brief pause, I heard Jim say, "My gun is in one of my pockets. Do you want me to get it out?"

After a moment Jim said, "I'm here on vacation. My family lives at Ellington – Willis Electric."

Roger Springer asked his occupation and Jim said, "I work for Guardian Security in Springfield."

"Security guard," Roger said and I thought, *That explains the calm, professional way he's handled all this.*

"How long have you known Faith?" Roger asked.

I could not believe Roger's obstinate insistence on misreading my relationship with Jim Willis. "About an hour and a half," Jim answered, sounding calm and unruffled. "I was paddling down Indian Creek and suddenly she appeared running for that small dock they have. When she saw me, she yelled for help and dived into the creek. The man who was chasing her was running hard and was catching up with her."

Jim moved on with his story. Like me, he omitted any mention of the cave so I think he was listening when I talked to Roger. Jim told him what kind of gun the man was using, saying it was the same as his own and similar to Roger's. He finished with, "I got a good look at him while he was throwing my gear into the creek and sinking my canoe. He was about six one or two, decent physical shape, but he had a sore right arm. Under the sleeve of his hoodie was a bandage. It might be why his aim was bad when he was shooting at us."

Then to my puzzlement, I heard Roger moving into my office and then back to the kitchen. He asked Jim for the name, address, and phone number of where he worked in Springfield, and the name, address, and phone number of his family's business in Ellington.

I thought to myself, *I can't believe Roger's one-track mind. He's treating Jim Willis like he's a suspect!*

I heard Jim ask, "Have you had any other house breaking incidents around here? Any rapes?"

Roger responded with a belligerent, "We do our job!"

"Yes," Jim said diplomatically, "that's why I'm asking you if there's been any similar incidents."

"Nothing at all!" Roger stated emphatically. I heard him scoot out his chair and I motioned to Job so when Roger emerged, we were sitting in two chairs away from the door looking bland. As he came through the door, he said, "I think it was just a random event." He moved out onto the porch and looked at me. "Faith, if you're really scared, I'll come spend the night."

"Job will be here so it isn't necessary," I told him.

The deputy then said to Jim, "Since you don't have a car, I'll take you back into town with me."

I spoke up, saying, "Mr. Willis needs to retrieve his canoe and other belongings out of the creek. Job and I will help him."

Roger didn't like that idea. In the end, he stayed, supposedly to help, but actually all he did was watch and try to tell everyone what to do when he wasn't too busy trying to talk to me. He asked me out on a date again and again I refused. I tried to be tactful but he kept trying to pin me down and I finally had to just flatly say no. I could tell he was miffed.

Jim and Job both swam well and they recovered Jim's gear and located the canoe. I got in and helped them with the canoe, joking about needing to wash the mud off me anyway. Roger just stood on the bank watching and ogling my body when my wet clothes were sticking to me.

It was Job who suggested, "If we used duct tape, we probably could tow this canoe back to our dock." When Job and I started to go get the tape, Roger wanted to go. I said, "Well, then you go with Job and I'll stay here. I don't want him going alone."

Roger didn't like that idea either. He wanted to be left alone with me and and I didn't like it. I was beginning to feel really irritated with him.

Job saw it too and said, "Mom, I'll just be quick. I know exactly where it is. You tell Deputy Springer about Lassie." And he started the motor and was gone.

I told Roger about our dog not being around yesterday evening and Job finding her shot. Now he was thinking maybe our home invader had killed her. But Roger dismissed the idea, saying, "I expect it was just a rabbit hunter."

Jim asked, "Do you want bullets for evidence? I think I can find some in my gear."

It was clearly something Roger had not considered but he agreed and Jim found two for him. I suggested having a look at Lassie's body and trying to find a bullet for comparison. Roger didn't think it was necessary.

Jim was saying almost nothing.

When we got the canoe back to our dock, Roger Springer tried again to take Jim Willis with him but Jim said, "My brother's coming from Ellington to get me and the canoe."

Roger called me aside. He tried to take my arm and I pulled away and said, "Roger, I don't like being touched." I was fed up with him and decided it was time to protest.

He looked irritated and muttered something I didn't catch. I didn't bother to ask for clarification.

He said, "I don't like leaving you here alone with Willis. He's a stranger. What was he really doing here?"

I took a deep breath and tried to sound calm and reasonable. "He was canoeing. If he was going to do anything to me, he had plenty of opportunity. It was even his phone I used to call the sheriff's office. He was truly helpful and I'm not here alone. Job is 15. That's almost grown. You can leave."

After he was gone, I said to Job and Jim, "I don't like that man."

Both of them looked at me sharply. Job said, "I didn't like how he as looking at you. Did he ask you out again?"

I nodded.

Jim asked, "Have you ever gone out with him?"

"No. Last summer he and his wife split up and he asked me out before it was even a definite split. He kept on and I started dodging him. Still, he's asked me out at least a dozen times and I've said no every time. You'd think he'd get the message."

Jim said, "He's the kind that doesn't take a hint. You need to get blunt."

"I told him I wasn't looking for anyone. He tried to take my arm and I told him I didn't like being touched. Was that not being blunt enough?"

Jim smiled. "Normally yes, but with some men, no. And it may be more than that. Some men like a woman who fights. It turns them on."

It hit me like a bomb and I felt faint. No wonder I didn't like Roger. He reminded me of something in my past.

Jim said gently, soberly, "I'm sorry. That scares you, doesn't it?"

I remembered that Roger and his wife had fought for years. Gossip said it got real physical sometimes but she went to the doctor somewhere besides Eminence. She had finally left him because she caught him with another woman, not because of the fighting. Maybe Roger liked fighting. It gave me the willies.

"Yes, it scares me," I said. "Any suggestions?"

"Avoid him as much as possible. Keep Job handy. A 15-year-old son is a great inhibitor to romance."

Job looked disconcerted. Jim smiled.

I asked Job, "How did you know something had happened?"

"Someone at school. We aren't suppose to use cell phones at school but some of the kids do it anyway. Someone said the sheriff's office had got a call to send someone out to our place. As soon as I heard it, I thought about Lassie and I came straight home. Mom, I really am sorry I didn't tell you. I thought it was probably some trespasser hunting rabbits and decided I needed to check our boundary signs."

Job looked away and I saw the tears hovering in his eyes. He had just turned 15 and Lassie was 13. She had been here as long as he could remember. I said, "I understand. Did you bury her?"

He said, "Not yet. It was already pretty dark when I found her and I knew you would miss me. I wrapped her body in plastic and put it in one of those old feed bins in the barn."

I said, "We'll bury her later. We'll have a small funeral for her."

Jim asked if I had a digital camera. He photographed my front door and then said, "If you don't mind, I would like to have a go at recovering a bullet from that dog. I could tell you two were really attached to her so if you show me where, I'll do the deed. Then we can bury her where you like."

Jim

Job showed me where he had stored the dog's body and returned to the house. I had seen the tears hovering in his eyes. I remembered my own dearly belovéd dog, Sheba, and the day she was hit by a car.

As soon as Job was gone, I pulled out my phone. It was no accident that I had been paddling down Indian Creek this morning. I had been asked by a friend, Vernon Chilton, who was a Missouri State Trooper, to investigate a rumor he had heard about a marijuana patch. The location was supposed to be on the north end of Indian Cave Farm near a small spring. I had found the place and trash left over from parties but no marijuana. However, I had seen an open area concealed by trees which had been cultivated in the past but then had been burned over. It appeared the burning had happened some time in the past, probably last year. Maybe local law enforcement had found the patch and destroyed it without reporting it officially. When a grower had local influence, it did sometimes happen. When Faith Johnson had appeared screaming for help with a man all in black in hot pursuit, I had assumed it was drug related.

I called Vern and said, "Vern, Buddy, you landed me in the middle of something." When I told him what happened, he was sure it was over the marijuana but I told him, "If she's being targeted because of marijuana, she doesn't know it. She thought the man was a rapist."

"Threats over marijuana are often delivered with violence."

"I know. I'm going to make sure she's got someone here to protect her before I leave." Then I changed the subject and asked, "Do you know anything about a deputy sheriff named Roger Springer?"

Vern snorted and said, "Met him, have you?"

"He's in hot pursuit of Faith Johnson who doesn't like him at all. He's a bit of a jerk. Demanded to see my ID and I showed him my concealed carry permit as well. He actually held his gun on me while I got my gun out of my pocket."

Vern said, "Sounds like him. Everyone says he beat his wife and she finally left him. He applied once to be a State Trooper but didn't make it. Never heard the reason but it wasn't hard for me to think of some."

I got off the phone and thought about the deputy, Roger Springer. I knew his type. They are drawn to law enforcement but they often are eventually fired. Their "I'm the law around here" attitude leads to overstepping their authority and Roger Springer had been right on that line today.

I also thought about Faith Johnson. At some point in the past, she had been the victim of a violent incident, probably rape. Her running without looking might have been provoked by involvement in marijuana growing but the degree of past trauma revealed when I asked what she thought the man wanted was all too clear.

I knew my immediate impulse was to protect her. I had two younger sisters and I had been very aware of both her terror over the masked invader and her irritation with Springer. I had seen him ogling her body when her wet clothes were sticking to her and I had also seen that she had been very quick to jerk loose the clinging fabric of her long, loose, high necked smock which had obviously been chosen to conceal her figure. Faith Johnson was a beautiful woman but that did not justify Springer's behavior.

I also knew that just because Faith Johnson was clearly terrified and couldn't name her home invader, did not mean I should let myself get involved. However, if the best local law enforcement could produce was Roger Springer, then the woman did need help.

♈ Chapter 2: Boys Will Be Boys ♋

Faith

We buried Lassie at the edge of the woods where Grandma and I had buried Lassie's predecessor and a few cats over the years. Each grave had flowers and I planned to put Columbine on Lassie's grave. Columbine grows wild here in the Ozarks and it's a beautiful flower with attractive plants. We had a small simple funeral. I told Jim, "Grandma got Lassie when Job turned 2. She was part of our family. Grandma died only six weeks ago. It's really hard to lose Lassie right on top of that."

Job said, "Lassie was my playmate. She went everywhere with me. Once I stepped on a copperhead snake and Lassie killed it. It's like a friend dying and someone murdered her."

I read from the beginning of Ecclesiastes, Chapter 3, "To every thing there is a season, and a time to every purpose under the heaven: a time to be born and a time to die." I prayed, "Father, it seems to us that it was not time for Lassie to die but you allowed it so we commit her spirit into your hands and look forward to meeting her again on the other side. Thank you for the time you let us have her. Amen."

I noticed that Jim Willis did not fidget. He gave no sign of thinking our sorrow was too much, prayer silly, or belief that animals also go to heaven stupid. Instead he asked, "Do you mind if I pray?"

When I said okay, he began, "Father God, we don't know who killed this faithful companion but you do. We don't know who that man in black was but you do. We ask for your help with this and I ask most specifically for protection for Faith and her son, Job, and over their house and property. I ask that you reveal the identity of this man and bring him to justice. In Jesus name, Amen."

Jim Willis was a true believer. The thought hit me like a Roman candle exploding across the sky on the Fourth of July. I think this is the point at which the small seed of trust which I had in Jim, spouted and began to put down roots.

Back at the house, I put frozen french fries in the oven and did hamburgers. None of us had had any lunch. Jim's brother was in the middle of something but would come when he finished. Jim said, "I didn't tell him what happened, only that the canoe had a hole in it and I needed for him to come get me."

While I cooked, Jim and Job unpacked Jim's gear in our back yard under the trees. It had all been done up in two waterproof bags but our perp, as Jim called him, had shot the bundles full of holes so they took on water. They hung things on our clothes lines and set up Jim's pup tent to dry. Quite a few things, including the tent, had holes in them. He took pictures. He retrieved more bullets. He had put the two he took from Lassie in a baggie and he asked for another one. I gave him two sticky address labels.

With only the screen doors closed and our windows open, I heard their conversation while they worked. Job loved it when my father was here and I knew boys need male role models. Dad knew it too and he tried to come as much as he could. In general, Job got on well with people and he had been tactful with Roger Springer, even though he didn't like him. But as I watched, I saw that Job liked Jim, chattering freely with him about camping, camping gear, canoeing, Jim's family in Ellington, and then in response to Jim's questions, about school.

Jim had done four years in the army and had been deployed to Afghanistan. Job was interested and I knew why. I had told him his father died in the middle-east wars. I had said his father and I had been planning to get married as soon as I finished high school. I said his father had graduated and joined the military but just before he shipped out for the middle-east, we had let things go a little too far and Job was the result. I told him his father had been trying to get leave to come home and marry me when he was killed in action. I wanted Job to feel wanted and loved and secure.

We ate and on their way back out, Jim asked about the family portraits on our walls and Job took him on a tour. The earliest ones predate the Civil War and Job knew them all. The picture parade ended with the wedding portraits of my dad's sister, Lois, and of my parents. I wondered how long it would take Jim to wonder about Job's father but if he had questions, they didn't show.

Jim had asked Job where he found Lassie and they had looked at tracks. Jim told me, "Your Lassie didn't make it easy for whoever got her. He had to shoot her four times. That perp had a sore arm and Lassie might be the reason. If you had any idea who he could possibly be, we could check."

I shook my head. I didn't know. I had really tried to think but even thinking about it scared me so bad I was short of breath and could hear my heart beating.

To get my mind off it, I asked, "Job, did you tell the school where you were going?"

"Not really," he said. "I told my friend, Jacks, to tell them after I was gone. I knew they'd want to call the sheriff and check on the story before they let me go and it would waste time." Because we live so far out with no other students nearby, Job has permission to ride his scooter back and forth to high school in Eminence.

I checked my phone for messages and realized the phone was dead. I told Jim and he went looking. The line had been cut.

Jim said, "Faith, I don't like this. Someone is targeting you. He'll be back. We need to do something."

Only later did I think about his use of "we." At the time, I just said, "What?"

He asked if I had a gun. Grandpa, dead since Job was a small baby, had had a rifle for hunting and a shotgun. We had never had a handgun. Jim inspected the two weapons and asked when they had last been fired. My dad routinely took them out each fall, fired them a few times, and then cleaned them. Jim said he'd check them out. Job knew how to use a rifle but had never used the shotgun. Jim said, "This shotgun is actually a good defense. It scares people because you don't have to be a good shot but loaded with bird shot, it's only fatal at close range."

Jim also made another suggestion. "You've got an extensive computer system. Have you considered surveillance?" His job in Springfield was actually mostly installing and repairing surveillance systems. His family's business in Ellington had started selling them too. He said, "It's amazing how much prices have dropped in the last few years on electronics and country people are finding themselves targeted more and more by thieves."

When Jim's brother arrived, I was surprised. They didn't look a thing alike. His name was John Willis and he was handsome with straight pale blond hair and clear blue eyes. He was above average in height, six feet or a bit over, but shorter than Jim and more stocky, a totally different kind of build than Jim's long-boned physique. They may not have looked like brothers but it was immediately clear they were good friends.

John regarded the canoe and the ventilated pup tent and said, "Okay, Bro, what'd you get yourself into this time? Another meth lab?"

Jim shook his head and said, "I was just peacefully paddling down the creek when this lady came running down to her dock screaming for help. She was being chased by a masked man all in black. You can see the results."

"Did you catch him?" John asked.

"Unfortunately, no," Jim said. "There's good reason to believe he's targeting her. Someone shot her dog yesterday and we found her phone line cut today. She was home alone. If he'd just been a thief, he could have easily come when she was gone. We've been discussing surveillance."

John nodded. "Good idea." He looked at me and said, "If you can't afford it, we can work out a payment plan."

John looked around and then he and Jim discussed options. They got on the internet and ordered what was needed. I learned businesses get special prices and everything was being delivered to Willis Electric in Ellington. John totaled it all up and I offered a credit card but he said, "We'll wait until everything arrives. Sometimes things don't and we have to order somewhere else. Bro, are you going to do installation?"

Jim nodded. "Your perp may very well be local. It's better if this surveillance system is a secret." He looked at Job and said, "Don't even tell your best friend. The perp could be his uncle or cousin or even a sheriff's deputy." He looked at me and then said, "That Springer is the right build and height but your perp was missing the beer belly. Do you have anyone who can come stay a few days or can you go stay somewhere else?"

I said, "Because of the greenhouse, we really can't be gone this time of year. It's not just the customers. The plants need constant attention. My parents live all the way over in Fredericktown. My father teaches high school and next week is the end of the school year so it would be very hard for him to leave right now." I didn't add that my mother would object.

Jim asked if the sheriff's office could provide someone other than Roger Springer for protection and I shook my head, explaining that Shannon County didn't have a lot people and so the Sheriff's Department was small.

We started discussing other options but everyone I could think of had a job, small kids, or both. Job said, "What about Mrs. Voden? She was Grandma's good friend and she was always here a lot. I know she couldn't fight anyone but she could make a phone call."

As we discussed the possibility of the elderly neighbor, Jim suggested diffidently, "I'm on vacation. I could stay a couple of days and if your grandmother's friend was here too, no one could make accusations of improper conduct."

I protested he would miss his vacation but he said, "With my canoe full of holes, I can't go canoeing." He paused and looked around at the trees and hills and then said, "John tells me the forecast for the next few days is for rain." Then he looked at me and smiled. "Probably all I have to do is be seen in order to scare off an intruder."

After more discussion, I agreed to Jim staying but only if I paid him. He suggested a very modest amount, saying, "For me, it'll be like staying in a guesthouse." He grinned. "I get to laze around and somebody feeds me." I knew he was making light of it to help me relax. But someone who killed our dog and cut our phone line was not a random vagrant. He might very possibly try again.

I used my Track phone, which number I never give out, to call Mrs. Voden and then my father. He would come Friday evening. I downplayed what happened because I knew if I told it all, Dad would drop everything and come immediately.

While I was on the phone, Job helped Jim and his brother load up the canoe. Jim kept part of his gear but sent some of it home with John including the tent. I saw him give the two baggies with bullets to his brother. Job told me later Jim knew someone in the state police who could get them processed for him but his own examination with a magnifying glass suggested they came from the same gun.

In the process of our conversation, I learned John had a wife and three children with another one on the way. When John was leaving, I asked John if his wife liked plants and what was her favorite color? I went into the greenhouse and brought out a hanging basket of violet New Wave petunias. I stuck in a card with directions for care. John smiled and said, "Esther will love it!"

Jim went with us to pick up Mrs. Voden. He had propped a chair to hold the front door closed and I locked the other doors. We had a prominently displayed sign and buzzer for customers. Jim checked and the buzzer had been disabled. He shook his head. "No doubt whatsoever."

I felt a chill go up my spine and I told him, "Normally I keep the front door locked and that other door onto the front porch is not only locked but has a bed blocking it. I only lock the two back doors when I'm gone. I think I should start locking them when I'm here too."

Jim and his brother, John, had shook their heads over the impossibility of securing my house. Not only did each room downstairs have an outside door but our doors were not designed to keep out human housebreakers. Both front doors and the one from the kitchen had glass panes. The house had a generous number of long old-fashioned windows. The four rooms upstairs all had windows opening onto the roofs of the porches. It was a good arrangement in case of fire but no good at all for keeping out unwanted intruders. We had no air-conditioning so in summer the windows were only closed when it rained and even then, the ones under the porch roofs were open.

Jim had asked John not to tell the rest of their family what happened. He said, "They'll just stew. Take the canoe somewhere else for repair and say I'm camping for a few days, which I'm doing here at Indian Cave Farm."

I said, "I wish I knew where we could get another dog like Lassie. She knew what was normal for customers to do and when they did anything unusual, she would bark at them. Once a man and his wife got into an heated argument and Lassie broke it up barking and growling. She never bit anyone but you think she bit our intruder?"

Jim said, "I noticed that perp had a bandaged arm. He might have gotten it somewhere else but we could see from the tracks that he'd had a scuffle with the dog back behind the barn."

Mrs. Voden lived in a little granny house beside her daughter on a farm closer to Eminence than us. I introduced Jim and told her what happened. I told her Jim worked for a security company and he was staying a few days as a security guard until my father could come. I said, "I want someone else there so no one can say I'm keeping a man."

Mrs. Voden laughed and said, "Maybe you need to find one you can keep." While Jim was putting her bag in back of the truck, she asked, "Is he married?"

"I don't know," I told her. "His brother came after his canoe and they talked about the brother's family but no wife was mentioned for Jim." It crossed my mind that he might not be attracted to women but the careful way he kept his eyes off my body made me think he was aware of me as a woman but respectful. And his interaction with his brother had been the typical male joshing covering affection with no odd undertones. And Job liked him. I trusted Job's instincts.

When we went after Mrs. Voden, we had found our sign out on the county road had been turned from Open to Closed. When we came back we left it Closed. Jim and Job fixed the buzzer and the cut phone line. Jim knew about electronics and Job liked learning. I heard them talking while they worked and it sounded like Jim enjoyed teaching him.

We showed Mrs. Voden and Jim the cellar deep under the house which oral family history said had been dug during the Civil War. Locally during that war, law and order had been non-existent. Official military units and semi-official local militias from both sides had "requisitioned" supplies from farmers and drafted any man they saw of suitable age. Boys as young as 14 had been forced into military service. Local grudges had been settled with violence and immunity. Robbers had freely looted and women had been violated. Families had been left with insufficient provisions to carry them through the winters. The Johnson family had stored supplies in Indian Cave and it's easily defended entrance had been manned at all times. When trouble appeared, everyone but two elderly women, a baby, and three children under six had hid in the cave. If they couldn't make it up to the cave in time, then they retreated to the cellar which had been dug so deep they hoped it's occupants would survive even if the house was burned over their heads. But the house had not been burned and most of the Johnson family survived the war.

I'd not used this wonderful hiding place this morning because the trap door to the cellar was hidden in the closet under the stairs in the living room. Now we told Mrs. Voden if there was trouble, she was to immediately go hide. She had a cell phone and I told her, "Hide and then phone."

That night we all were tired and went to bed early. It started raining. I put Jim downstairs in what had originally been a second parlor which my grandmother had used as a bedroom. I apologized to Mrs. Voden as I took her up to her room saying, "I'm sorry to make you climb the stairs but you know yourself people will ask you later about our sleeping arrangements."

Mrs. Voden had answered, "I understand. And anyway, if he's here as a guard, he needs to be downstairs."

I had nightmares. I had known I would. I was up early and did bacon, eggs, biscuits and gravy for breakfast. We normally ate a bowl of cereal. During breakfast, Cheshire appeared. Mrs. Voden had been here enough that the cat knew her but I was surprised she was not hiding from Jim Willis. But then Cheshire is a smart cat and the smell of bacon is pretty enticing.

As forecast, it was raining off and on. When Job left for school on his scooter, it was just drizzling but picked up again later – not good canoe weather and I felt less guilty about Jim staying.

We e-mailed all the photographs we'd made to the sheriff's department. Jim needed a report for insurance purposes. I called Janice Dunbar to make sure she got them. She said, "What's all this? Roger said it was a domestic disturbance situation, that you had two men fighting over you." She stopped and I was so shocked I couldn't think what to say. Janice went on, "Now that I think about it, that doesn't sound like you. And you called in about an intruder. What happened?"

I told her. I was so mad, I wanted to spit. I told her, "That Roger Springer keeps asking me out and I don't like him. If I ever call in again, don't send him!"

Janice said, "I was going to send Carl Cunningham but Roger volunteered to go."

Janice asked me all the details and said she would write up a report but I would need to come in to sign it and Jim Willis as well if he wanted a copy.

Jim was working on the front door. My grandfather had had a workshop out in part of the old barn and Grandma had never gotten rid of his tools. She had used them some herself and my father used them when he came. He was teaching Job who had started making birdhouses and cute signs which we sold to our plant customers.

Mrs. Voden and I went out to the greenhouse and she mostly talked while I worked. Grandma and Grandpa had once had two greenhouses. When he got sick, Grandma had let one of them go and was considering shutting down the other one when I moved here before Job was born. She had kept it, saying that the two of us could handle it and I was going to need an income. Her social security wasn't all that much but she owned the land and house and a pickup truck free and clear so she didn't need much. Over the years, I had built up my manuscript editing business which was all done over the internet. I had also written some children's books, illustrated with Job's help, which had been published by a major textbook publishing company. As Grandma got older and less able, Job got bigger and we could keep the greenhouse going. I liked it and it provided exercise.

It also provided income. Local people all knew we were here. We were in the phone book and even on the internet. I also supplied plants to the Bestway grocery store in Eminence. Now in mid-May, we could expect customers so Job had changed the sign on his way to school and the rain was intermittent and light. We started getting more people than usual. Two women Mrs. Voden knew slightly came first and she entertained them with the tale of my home intruder as they picked out some bedding plants and a yard sign.

Several more local people came and then a couple I didn't know who had seen our sign and asked did we have tomato plants? They took several big ones. They picked out a hanging basket of the new yellow petunias and a large pot of Black-eyed Susans. The husband told me he was red-green color blind but he could see yellow.

I had been shifting plants, closing up the gaps which always developed next to the isles. Jim had been helping me and had gone on working while I dealt with customers.

When they left, Jim asked me if it was possible that my

intruder had been here as a customer recently. It would have been a good way to scout the place. I thought and then said, "We seldom get total strangers like that last couple. I can't remember any man by himself I didn't know and the only other strange couple who've come recently were older."

"Could he have been someone you know?" Jim asked. "Maybe that's why the disguise."

I told him, "I considered that but I can't think of anyone the right size. Like you said, Roger Springer has that belly. I would say by how he moved that the man was under 40. I can't think of anyone. Now I'll be checking out every man I see, looking for one the right size."

While we talked, a van arrived and I knew when I saw it coming that it was Simone Oliver. He had not grown up here but had appeared three years ago and opened a shop in Eminence. He called himself a decorator and sold artwork, décor items, furniture, custom made draperies, and other odds and ends. His customers were mostly tourists and wealthy people with country retreats in the area. The locals watched him like they would have regarded an elephant had it appeared in their town. He was openly homosexual and the sheriff had had to make it clear that it was not illegal any more.

He was a good customer but I wasn't sure what Mrs. Voden would do with him so I moved to help him and Jim went back to shifting plants. Simone said, "I've come for some birdhouses and I'd like some white bedding plants." I was pointing out choices but then realized he was distracted. He was watching Jim work.

Simone asked me directly, "Is he yours?"

"He's here as a security guard," I answered. He walked over to Jim and said something I couldn't hear as his back was turned.

Jim looked at him and looked across at me then back to Simone. "Sorry but you're not my cup of tea," he told him but smiled and didn't sound disturbed.

Simone turned to look at me and commented, "She is really very decorative."

I didn't know if to laugh or be offended.

After he was gone, I asked Jim, "Do you often get that sort of proposition? You were so cool about it."

He shook his head. "It happens sometimes. I once asked my brother, John, *Why me?* He's much better looking than I am but he never has it happen. He said it was because I'm graceful. I started trying to move more like a klutz."

He paused and then said, "I think also it's partly my mixed ancestry. Homosexual men move on the fringe of society and so do lots of people with scrambled racial backgrounds." He looked at me and said, "You did notice that John and I don't look anything alike. We had different biological fathers. Mine was black."

I looked at him in astonishment but now that I knew, I could see it. He said, "I hide it and pass for white when I'm in this area because the rest of my family is white and it makes things a lot easier." I don't know what Jim saw in my face but he gave me one of his smiles and said, "Your customer probably saw it straight away."

I didn't know what to say.

Jim said, "Maybe it's that sort of incident that gives me an idea what a really beautiful woman like you deals with."

"I wish all of them were as polite as Simone," I commented.

He asked, "Does Job know about him?"

I answered, "Everyone knows which I suppose is a point in his favor. Job says he makes him uncomfortable so he disappears whenever Simone comes but Simone has never actually said anything to him like he did to you today."

Jim nodded. Then he said, "I'd appreciate it if you didn't talk about my ancestry. Ellington's not that far away."

I nodded. "I won't tell Mrs. Voden. She's a sweetie but she does talk."

Jim asked if I minded if he looked the whole place over so he would know what was normal. He said that included the bedrooms in the house. I told him to go ahead; I thought it was a good idea.

Then as he started to move away, the phone rang. Grandma had put an extension in the greenhouse long ago and many customers always called to be sure we were open before they came. I answered and it was the school, asking me to come. Job had gotten into a fight. "Is he hurt?" I asked.

The secretary wouldn't tell me anything except that they wanted me to come. "Job never gets in fights," I told Jim. "Never has before. Why wouldn't they tell me anything on the phone?"

Jim said, "I'll come with you if you want but it might be better to take Mrs. Voden."

Job has always been a good kid, diligent about helping out at home. He had played basketball this year at school but had told me he didn't think he'd play next year. He had said, "I'm pretty good at basketball but you've seen how little Coach has let me play. I think he's mad at me because he wants me to play football and I said no. Coach seems to think that all we're here for is winning football games."

Not only is Job already 5 foot 10 but he's still growing rapidly. And he's broad shouldered and strongly built. He'd be good at football but I was glad it didn't appeal to him. I didn't want to think about why.

At the school, I went straight to the Principal's office with Mrs. Voden in tow. I didn't see Job anywhere. When I asked if Job was hurt, his secretary said, "Mr. Fields will see you immediately."

In the doorway of his office I stopped. Roger Springer was sitting in a chair in the office. I looked from him to Mr. Fields who had stood and was saying, "Ms. Johnson, please come in."

I looked back at Roger Springer who was in his uniform and said, "What are you doing here?"

Mr. Fields said, "Ms. Johnson, please have a seat and we'll talk about this."

I looked at Mr. Fields and suddenly I was not only scared but angry. "Why is Roger Springer here? Has he arrested my son?"

Mr. Fields heard the anger in my voice and made soothing motions with his hands. "No, no, no, Ms. Johnson. When boys get in fights, we normally have the parents of both boys in to talk about it."

"So Job got in a fight with Springer," I said looking at Roger. "What over?" Roger's son was Roger, Junior but as he got older, he had objected to being called Junior so the other kids at school called him Springer. He was two years older than Job and bigger. He was the star of the football team. I looked back at Mr. Fields and said, "And nobody will tell me if Job is hurt."

"Oh," Mr. Fields said, "it's only a few scrapes and bruises, nothing serious."

"So what was the fight over?" I demanded.

"Well," Mr. Fields was still making his soothing motions, "we aren't really sure. Neither of the boys will say." He sighed but I could tell it was a dramatic gesture, not a true expression of emotion. "I expect it's over a girl. It usually is when they won't tell us. Boys will be boys."

I just stared at him and then said, "Where is Job?"

Mr. Fields said, "We need to talk about consequences. Boys will be boys but we can't have them fighting all the time. Your son threw the first punch so I think it's necessary to suspend him from school for three days."

I looked at him and said, "Where is Job? I am not discussing anything until I talk to my son."

Roger Springer spoke up. "Faith, everyone says your son slapped Junior and started the fight."

Instantly I knew what it was about. Janice Dunbar had said that Roger had said the event out at my place had been two men fighting over me. I looked at Roger and said, "Roger, right now you are just another parent in this office, same as me, and not an officer of the law."

I turned to Mr. Fields and said, "Did anyone tell you what Springer said just before Job slapped him? I am willing to bet it was something derogatory about me." I turned to Roger and said, "I already heard that you been saying the incident out at my place yesterday was two men fighting over me. It's nothing but jealousy making you think that."

I then turned to Mr. Fields and explained, "Yesterday a man dressed all in black including a mask pried open my front door. I ran out the back and down to the creek where by the grace of God, a man was going by in a canoe. He helped me get away but in doing so, that invader shot the man's canoe and his gear full of holes. Fortunately he missed the man. That invader killed our dog and cut my phone line. I have no idea who he was or I'd be having him arrested. The man in the canoe was a total stranger from Ellington."

I paused, looking at Mr. Fields' shocked face, and then said, "Now I will talk to my son."

Job had a busted lip, a cut over his eye, and the eye was bloodshot. He had blood all over his clothes. I looked at him and decided on a little humor. "What does Springer look like?"

He smiled and then winced because of the lip. "Not as bad." Then I saw that his arm was wrapped in a towel. I asked to see it and he was reluctant. I insisted. I was astonished. "He bit you!"

Job shrugged. "Yeah. He was shouting insults and using bad

language. I shoved him up against the wall with my arm across his mouth and said right in his ear that his father was a liar."

I nodded. "I already heard this morning that his father is claiming the incident out at our place yesterday was two men fighting over me." I paused and then said, "You're lucky you didn't get Roger Springer for a father."

Job laughed. He said, "Mom, you do think of things. They told me I'm getting three days suspension. I need to talk to Mr. Jenkins. I'm going to miss a test on Friday." Job had told me he was glad PE was credit/no credit because he thought Coach who was also his PE teacher would have ruined his straight A grade record.

He went to find Mr. Jenkins and I went back to the office. Roger Springer and his son were in Mr. Fields' office. I had breezed past his secretary and Mr. Fields did not look happy to see me. I took a quick look at Springer. His shirt had a lot of blood but I suspected some of it was Job's. He had a busted lip and his nose had been bleeding but I didn't see any other cuts. Considering Springer's size, Job had made a good showing.

I said, "How many days suspension is Springer getting?"

Mr. Fields said, "Well, he didn't start the fight."

"So he's getting off with nothing? He was insulting me to my son and he bit my son. I think you need to do a little more investigating." I turned and walked out.

Mrs. Voden had been waiting in a chair in the office of Mr. Fields' secretary. Now I told her, "I think we're ready to go."

I took Job to our doctor. I asked them to take photos and then the doctor put two stitches in Job's eyebrow and more than a dozen in his arm, although he said the bite wasn't deep but he wanted to minimize scarring. So much for Mr. Fields' description of a few scrapes and bruises. They took more pictures of the stitches and I watched as they e-mailed all the pictures to me and to the school. I called the school secretary to make sure they got the pictures and that they didn't get deleted. She gave me the e-mail addresses of several school board members and we sent them copies along with a note explaining what they were.

Back at home, Jim was waiting for us and I liked the feeling. He had fixed the front door. I noticed that Cheshire was treating Jim like she did us. She was not an under-your-feet cat but did like petting and cuddling. She was only skiddish with strangers.

Jim told us, "I found where our perp has been watching your house. I wanted to keep an eye on the house so I didn't follow his trail but he was using a small motorcycle to come and go."

Jim pointed to a rock outcropping up on a hill and told us to keep an eye on it and if we saw movement or a flash of light up there, to let him know immediately. He also said, "Try not to show that you noticed him or he'll be gone when I get there."

I nodded and said, "I was thinking that with Job here, you don't have to stay."

Jim said, "My canoe is still being repaired and I was thinking I might work with you and Job on using those guns. I could also give Job a few pointers on hand-to-hand combat but if you prefer that I go, that's fine."

I admitted, "Today when we were headed home, I definitely liked knowing you were here so I was not going to find that masked man waiting for me. And I do need to know how to use the shotgun."

Jim said, "I don't mind staying. I don't want to scare you but from the tracks I saw, I think your intruder has been back to his watching place today. I wondered if he followed you when you left to go into the school."

I looked at him and said, "Please stay."

He said, "Don't go anywhere alone. Keep Mrs. Voden or Job with you."

"I will," I promised.

He smiled at me and I noticed again how his homely face lit up when he smiled. "I don't mind staying," he said.

Jim asked me how much land we owned. I told him, "All together we have 898 acres but it's in three tracts. Here where the house is located is part of the original farm. It's 640 acres and the family got it way back in the 1850's. At one time, they farmed about 80 acres but grandpa only farmed 40 acres. The rest was left in forest and in the late 1800's when the lumber companies were all logging this area over, the family refused to let them log their land.

"After the logging companies left, the family bought the 160 acres on our south side. The cave runs under that land and they bought it to protect the cave. It's mostly not flat and only a small area had ever been farmed. The family let it grow back up in woods.

"Then in the 1930's during the Depression, the family on the farm on our north side wanted to go to California. They owned 98 acres. Our family gave them a car and some provisions and enough money for the trip in exchange for the farm. There's a 30 acre field that's still being farmed. For years, we've rented it to Cleve Dunbar but last summer he had a stroke and one of his grandsons took over. There were some problems so this year, we haven't rented it to anyone. Job wants to try farming and my dad said he'd help him.

"Our east boundary is Indian Creek and our west boundary is the county road. Both of them twist around so the width of our land varies a lot. From north to south, it's a little over a mile and a half."

"Is it posted?"

"Yes," I said, "and I was thinking we needed to check our boundaries and maybe put up some more signs."

"With Job here," Jim said, "I could do that tomorrow."

When things slowed down a little, Mrs. Voden sat in the greenhouse crocheting on a baby blanket while Jim gave Job and then me gun lessons. Job had gone deer hunting with my father since he was 10 but they had always used the rifles Dad brought with him. Neither of us had ever used a shotgun.

Then Jim gave Job some hand-to-hand combat lessons. Jim told me quietly, "Don't worry. He's already bruised and I'm not going to do anything very strenuous but I can show him a few things to help him defend himself." He paused and then asked me, "Have you ever had any lessons in self-defense?"

I nodded. "The summer Job was two, my dad paid for me to attend a self-defense camp for women. It was four days and most of it was what you might call dirty tactics but our instructor said we would not be engaging in duels of honor but defending ourselves against disgusting perverts and any tactic which worked was fair."

Jim smiled. "So that masked man might have gotten a surprise if he'd caught you."

I shook my head, "I don't know. I was shaking because I was so scared."

Job asked about Jim's handgun and he got it out and taught him how to use that too. Handguns are really mostly for scaring people and desperate up-close situations. They are easily fatal which Jim was careful to emphasize. He said a shotgun loaded with bird shot was better defense and less likely to get you stuck with an excessive force charge.

That evening, Job and I introduced Jim and Mrs. Voden to a game called Rummicub. Job teamed up with Jim and I took Mrs. Voden. She was a sharp old lady, which I already knew, and Jim is a quick learner. It was a fun evening and took our minds off masked intruders, murdered dogs, and salacious gossip.

I slept better that night, maybe because I had slept so badly the night before, but also another day with Jim Willis had confirmed my assessment of both his competency and his politely pleasant social behavior.

In the morning, I checked Job's bruises. He had a real shiner and purple spots in several other places but the worst wound was the bite. He was shrugging it all off and said, "I'm getting a free vacation. I'll go put the Open sign out and we can work on greenhouse stuff."

Customers started arriving for the greenhouse and Job stuck with me. What surprised me was these people were really coming to find out about the rumors going around about me, the incident with the intruder, and the fight at school. They were being nice but they were clearly wanting to know what happened. After the first bunch of curious customers left, carrying away hanging baskets, assorted other plants, and a yard sign, Job suggested putting a bandage over his arm. He said, "All these stitches look like Frankenstein and I can tell people are shocked."

I told him, "Leave it on display. It gives us a good opening for refuting all that gossip about me having men fighting over me."

Mrs. Voden said, "I can't believe anyone would believe that."

I said, "Roger Springer is a deputy sheriff and people like shocking gossip. Some people enjoy passing it on even if they know it isn't true."

More people arrived and we were busy. The day developed into the equivalent of a Saturday with people coming all day for garden plants, bedding plants, and hanging baskets. They were all checking out the rumors.

Jim fixed a strap on the shotgun so Job could carry it across his back. We had programmed our numbers into our cell phones. Jim was going to check our boundaries. I packed "No Trespassing" signs, violet "No Trespassing" tape, violet spray paint, a hammer and some roofing nails into a small backpack along with water and sandwiches. Jim added a few things and we showed him where the path ran along the creek. He was going south and planning to circle the entire property.

When he was gone, Job said, "I feel safer when he's here."

I said, "Yes, he does give off an atmosphere of being able to cope with trouble that's reassuring."

Job said, "And he's nice. No sneaking drooling looks at you when you're busy."

Last summer we'd gotten a rather horrid man at the greenhouse one day and Job had surprised me by saying quietly, "Mom, why don't you go in and send Grandma out?" I had not realized he was old enough to see what the man was thinking.

Today I made Job laugh by telling him about Simone Oliver.

We were busy all day. People often phoned to be sure we were open before coming so when the phone rang again in the middle of the afternoon, I was surprised to find the school principal, Mr. Fields, on the phone. He was calling to tell me Job's suspension had been reduced to one day so he could return to school tomorrow. I was so disconcerted, I just said, "Thank you," and hung up.

When I told Job, he said, "Drat! I was kind of looking forward to a break."

Job had always liked school so in surprise, I asked, "Why?"

Job looked around. We had a couple of customers but they were at the other end of the greenhouse. Job said, "Mom, some of the kids have been razzing me about not having a father. Springer had picked up on it but he isn't the only one."

I looked at Job and I felt tears in the back of my eyes. I said, "Job, I'm sorry."

Job reached out and hugged me. "Mom, it's okay. Some kids feel like they always have to have someone to put down. It'll blow over. And the comment you made about Springer's father's true. I could have some fun sharing it with my friends but I kind of feel sorry for Springer. No father at all is better than having a jerk like he's got."

Job's mature attitude and compassion warmed my heart and I told him so.

Mrs. Voden volunteered to cook so I didn't send Job out to turn the sign until almost 8 o'clock. I still had customers and was glad when they finally left. Supper was on the table and Jim had returned. I teased Mrs. Voden, "This is really nice. I could get used to having a cook."

We told Jim about Job's suspension being shortened. He said, "You getting that doctor to take pictures and then sending them all around was a smart move." He looked at Job and said, "You got a smart lady for a mother."

Over supper we asked Jim about his trek and he asked about the north field. He'd found our new gates open with the padlocks broken and trash back by the small spring near the creek.

We told him about last summer when we discovered Cleve Dunbar's grandson, Jerry Sutter, had broken the gate we had at the back of the field and was having parties back by the spring. There was more to the story but I didn't want to talk about it in front of Mrs. Voden.

Jim also told us he had found where our watcher had been driving a vehicle, probably a pickup truck, off the road at a place where it was hidden behind trees and shrubs. He was unloading a small motorcycle which he was riding to the place where he had been watching us.

After dinner, we sent Mrs. Voden to watch TV and Jim helped Job and I with the dishes. The talk had moved on to Job's plans to try farming that north field. When we finished the dishes, I went to work on my editing job and Job took Jim out to the barn, still talking about farming.

Jim

I didn't plan to get involved but I did. Once I was sure the dog had been killed by our masked man and he had also cut her phone line, I was certain Faith Johnson needed protection. I was also sure that Roger Springer was not the answer. She and her son needed some training on protecting themselves and it was all too clear to me that Faith had been traumatized by some past incident.

But at the first opportunity, I told her about my ancestry. Faith is attractive, both physically and in other ways. I knew I was protecting myself from any possible romantic involvement.

When I called Vernon Chilton and told him I would be staying at Indian Cave Farm a few days, he said, "It's perfect. It puts you in position to look for more marijuana patches."

I said, "I might also be in position to get shot full of holes like my canoe."

"Oh, Abe, don't to that," Vern said, using the nickname I'd been given in the military. "Your family would kill me."

So I set off to check the boundaries of Indian Cave Farm with the double agenda of looking for marijuana patches. I did hang more No Trespassing signs, string violet tape, and locate where Faith's intruder had been leaving the road and unloading a small motorcycle to get to his perch.

I also found a marijuana patch. It was near the southern border of the farm. I installed a high quality trail camera and hoped my growers didn't spot it and also that the card would not be filled up by a curious raccoon or other wildlife.

When I called Vern to report on the marijuana, he said, "Really! So your masked man in black is linked to marijuana growing!"

I told him, "I'm not sure. What I do know is that Faith Johnson doesn't know about the marijuana."

"How about her son?"

"No way," I assured him. "He's a straight A student and very busy at home helping his mother with the greenhouse. He's not absent from the house enough for it."

Then at dinner Job was talking about farming the north field. I wanted to ask him about his fight with Roger Springer's son out of earshot of his mother so I let him take me out to the barn to look at farm equipment.

∽ Chapter 3: My Baby ∾

Faith

I heard Jim and Job return and Job came wondering in to where I was working and asked, "Mom, can I talk to you about something?"

"Sure," said, jotting down the time, hitting save, and closing the laptop I used for editing which would put it into sleep mode. It took a password to get it going again.

Job said, "It's serious so can we go outside?"

I was puzzled but our old house is not reliably sound proof so we made our way to the greenhouse which has some comfortable chairs and lights.

Job started, "I been talking to Jim and he said I should talk to you." I waited and he finally went on. "In my computer class, they had us all do an exercise where we looked up our birth records and our family genealogy. I never told you because the first thing I found out was you were only 15 when I was born. Of course, I wanted to know about my father so I researched the name on my birth certificate. There isn't any such person."

My heart dropped and I felt total dismay. I had always known that someday I was going to have to tell Job something but I had thought it could wait until he turned 18. What could I say? I sat frantically trying to think. I finally said, "I didn't want you to feel like you were unwanted."

"I know, Mom, but I been thinking about it. Whoever it was, I expect he was someone you didn't want to raise a child with and I can understand that. But now at school the other kids found out I didn't have a father and they been razzing me about it. Some of them have started calling me *Bastard* all the time."

"Have the teachers not said anything?" I asked.

"Mr. Jenkins heard it one day and he did but Coach has heard it over and over and he just sneers. One of the worst has been Springer and Coach thinks the sun shines out of his hiney." Job's use of our usual childhood euphemism was endearing.

I debated. He had already guessed that his father was no-good but should I tell him how bad it was? I said, "Job, you've been the best the thing I ever had in my life. You're a great kid who doesn't even use crude language. You're turning into a good man and that's all I want."

He said, "You don't have to tell me about my father. I'm sure you have your reasons. But when I told Jim about the other kids calling me Bastard, he thought I should tell you about it."

Job went in and I sat in the warm greenhouse thinking. Finally I got up and went into the house. Jim was doing something on his smart phone. I said, "Maybe I should talk to you."

Job had gone upstairs and Mrs. Voden was watching TV. She's a bit deaf so I took Jim into my office to talk. "Thank you for telling Job to tell me about the kids at school calling him *Bastard*. I didn't know he'd found out that the story I told him about his father isn't true."

"Did you tell him about his father?"

I shook my head. Jim waited and I said, "No, it was bad and I don't want him to know." I stopped to pull myself together and then went on, "When I 14, I was kidnapped and raped."

Jim had this look on his face and I knew he found what I had just told him distressing. I said, "They never caught the guy. I never talk about it because I don't want Job to know. It's bad enough that he doesn't have a father. I don't want him to know he's the result of rape."

When I did not say anything else, he said, "When you told me you ran without looking to see who was in your house, I suspected you'd had something happen before. And as shook up as you were, I suspected it was rape." He paused and then said, "You could have gotten an abortion or put the baby up for adoption."

"When I realized I was pregnant, I knew my mother would insist on an abortion. Our church had made quite an issue about abortion and when I finally quit denying to myself that I was pregnant, I thought it over. That rapist had not given one thought to fathering a child. I decided that even his sperm had been trying to hide from him and my baby was my baby, not his. That may sound like a weird way of looking at it, but it's what I thought."

I hesitated but then explained, "My parents are an odd couple. My father's sociable, a warm sort of person, an involved parent. Even when I was small, I was much closer to him than to my mother. She's somehow remote, aloof, concerned with status, and hyper-sensitive about reputation. Mother worked and Dad's a teacher. He often taught summer school. I always spent my summers here with Grandma and Grandpa. When I finally faced the fact that I was pregnant, I asked to come stay with Grandma. Grandpa was dying of cancer and Mother hadn't wanted me here that summer but with everyone talking about my abduction and rape, she agreed.

"We didn't tell Mother I was pregnant until Job was born. She was appalled and I've never been back to her house. She's been down here exactly twice. She didn't even come to Grandma's funeral.

"Grandpa died in the summer after Job was born in the spring. Mother felt obligated to attend Grandpa's funeral but was mortified when we took Job with us. Then about a month later she came down here without Dad and did her best to persuade me to put Job up for adoption. She accused me of sleeping around. Somewhere she got the idea that no one gets pregnant if they're really raped because of the trauma. Her not believing me made me more adamant about keeping Job. I felt like she was rejecting me and it made me more determined to not reject my child."

We were quiet for a long minute and then Jim asked, "Did the police ever have any suspects they were looking at?"

I shook my head. "If they did, I never heard about it. He was wearing a ski mask and I never saw his face."

I think Jim saw how difficult it was for me to even talk about it. He changed the subject, commenting, "It looks like you've done a great job of raising Job. He's a good kid."

I looked at him and smiled. "You know that scripture where Joseph told his brothers after their father died, that they'd intended to harm him when they sold him into slavery but God used it for good? I've felt like that about Job. How he happened was intentional harm but I got a really beautiful baby to raise, a precious soul that I know is a gift from God."

I felt the tears in the back of my eyes and reached for a tissue.

In the following silence, Mrs. Voden appeared in the kitchen doorway and said, "I'm going up to bed."

I answered, "I'm coming too," and got up and went with her.

As I went up the stairs, I thought about what else I now guessed but had no intention of ever telling anyone.

During the night, I had a terrible nightmare and woke up when I screamed. Then I heard Job in the hall. We had always all slept with our doors open and he stopped in my doorway and said, "Mom?"

When I answered, he asked, "Are you okay?"

I said, "Just a bad dream. Go on back to bed. I'll make myself some hot chocolate."

I got up, put on a caftan, and went downstairs to the kitchen. Jim appeared and said, "Nightmares are not nice. Would it help to talk?"

I asked, "Do you want some hot chocolate?" He came in and sat down at the kitchen table. He had showered before going to bed and his hair was a riot of curls. I liked the look but it did suggest his black ancestry.

When I put the hot chocolate on the table, he was still waiting quietly. It's something I like about Jim. He doesn't push but just waits until you're ready.

"It happened the summer after I finished ninth grade. I was 14. Mother and Dad had gone to someone's anniversary party and I was home alone. I heard someone in the house. When I went to look, it was a man wearing a ski mask. He wasn't all in black but wearing jeans and a hoodie that were pretty generic. Also gloves. I ran out the back door of our house but he was right behind me. I tripped and fell and he got me. He had something like chloroform on a cloth which he held to my face until I passed out."

I stopped talking. I needed time to pull myself together before going on. "I woke up naked in a cabin in the woods chained to a bed. He kept me for four days. He came and went and every time he came, he raped me."

I stopped again, remembering how terrible it was. "On the fourth day in the afternoon, I heard a vehicle and thought it was him again but it wasn't. It was a woman real estate agent and she found me because she'd taken a wrong turn."

I paused, searching for words to frame the painful memories.

"After it happened, I had a lot of nightmares but after Job was born, they mostly stopped. I don't watch TV shows or movies about rape. When Mother came and tried to get me to give Job up, I had a reoccurring nightmare where my rapist came back and was trying to steal Job. But since that man in black chased me, I'm having ones about rape again. In them he's the same man as my rapist."

"Do you think that's possible?"

"He's about the same size but my rapist was young and I think that intruder was older, but then if he was the same man, he would be older. But it's been 16 years so I think it can't possibly be the same man. It wouldn't make sense."

"Maybe when you came here to your grandparents, he couldn't find you."

I shook my head. "I'd come here every summer for years. It wouldn't have been hard to find me."

"Do you think talking about the details of the rape would help you?"

It took me a minute to say anything but talking about it was making me feel better, not so scared and alone. So I started, "He handcuffed me to one of those old iron beds. He'd taken all my clothes but the bed had a ratty old blanket. He left me water and food and a bucket to pee in. I tried and tried to break the handcuffs but I couldn't." I stopped, remembering how it had been. "It was horrible and what he said and his snickering made it worse."

"What did he say?" Jim asked gently.

"The first time he raped me, when he saw the blood, he snickered and said, 'Ooo, blood. How sweet.' After that, every time he raped me, he would snicker and whisper, 'Sweet,' when he went off."

Jim's face showed his distaste and he said, "That was sick – really, really sick."

I found myself going on, "He liked hurting me and he liked for me to fight. I figured that out but I couldn't stop myself from trying."

When I was quiet, Jim said, "Rape is not about sex. It's about forcing someone to do something they don't want to do. It's about humiliating someone. It's really all about violence and torturing someone."

I found myself sighing and said, "Yes. I think that's why I

couldn't see my baby as part of that. Babies are about love."

I was quiet and eventually Jim said, "Rape is diabolical. Among some of the American Indian tribes, the penalty for rape was castration. That might be a good idea. At least it would put a stop to repeat offenders."

I looked at Jim and felt the corners of my mouth turning up.

I told him, "Dad arranged for me to see a therapist for a while. It was helpful. I realized I wanted to give my baby the love I'd wanted, and hadn't gotten, from my mother.

"I also saw my father thought my rapist was a total perversion of what a real man was supposed to be. My therapist told me to hang on to that understanding because I would need it if I ever wanted to form a normal relationship with a man in the future."

Jim said, "Many rape victims never really recover. It was wise of your father to get therapy for you. Do you think it would help to see your therapist again now?"

I shook my head and said, "I expect I'd have to find a new one. She was already past 60 then."

"Grandmother types are easy to talk to."

I looked at Jim and then asked, "Why are you so easy to talk to?"

"Fellow soldier in battle," he said. "We survived that perp together. Comrades in battle always become allies."

"The military," I said.

He nodded. "I think all of us come home traumatized. I joined a therapy group for a while. It helped a lot and I'm still in regular contact with other veterans."

I nodded and then he asked, "Do you mind if I pray for you?"

"Please do," I told him.

His hands were on the table and when he reached across, I took his hands without hesitation. "Father," he prayed, "you know all about fear and terror. You sent us the Comforter to be with us in times of trouble. We ask now for his presence, and for your protection. I pray that you give Faith peace. In Jesus name. Amen."

I looked up and tried to smile. "Thanks."

We went back to our separate beds and I fell asleep thinking about Jim. Mrs. Voden had asked and he wasn't married. Even with his homely face, he was an attractive man and a true believer. I wondered why he was still single. Maybe it was his mixed ancestry. If he passed as white sometimes but black at other times, then he might feel stranded between two worlds, not really belonging in either.

I slept well the rest of the night and in the morning, I made pancakes and bacon which Job loves. At his age, he'd stopped hugging me goodbye in the mornings but today he did. He said, "Hang in there." After he was gone, it occurred to me that it was also what he was telling himself.

Job had turned the sign and on the heels of his departure, a woman drove in and pushed the buzzer for the greenhouse. I was still in the kitchen and when I went out, I was astonished to see it was Patty Springer, Roger's ex-wife. Their son and daughter both lived with her but the son spent time with his father and his father attended all of his football games. When I saw who it was, I stopped and looked back at the house. The living room curtains twitched so I went on to meet the woman.

She took off her sunglasses and said, "Can we talk?" I took her into the greenhouse which is warm but has fans and chairs. She said, "It's like a jungle, isn't it?"

I smiled and said, "The plants love it."

She said, "I tried to get Junior to tell me what happened and he said Job hit him and started the fight. When I heard the stories going around, I figured it all out. Junior probably called you a whore and Job came to your defense. I been asking around and that's about how it was. I also found out that Junior and some of his friends have been calling Job a bastard for months. I told Junior he either apologized to Job or moved in with his dad. He packed his stuff and went to his dad.

"Roger called me. He only has a one bedroom apartment and he don't want the boy living with him. I laughed and told him the choice I gave Junior. He tried to tell me you were a slut and I told him that when it came down to believing his story or yours, I'd take yours."

I said, "Patty, I'm glad to hear that. I hope other people decide the same."

"The school called me yesterday afternoon and said Junior has a one day suspension for bad language and provoking a fight. I told Roger and he said he was taking the boy to school himself this morning and talking to the principal. That's really why I came out here. I wanted to warn you in case they call you in again."

I told her, "They originally told Job he was suspended for three days but they called yesterday afternoon and said it was reduced to one day so Job went to school today."

Patty looked off in the distance and then back to me. She said, "You've done okay out here without a man. I've decided I'm going to try it for a while, at least until Gina's grown. I was dating a guy and then I saw him eyeing Gina. By sending Junior to Roger, I'll lose the child support from him but it's worth it to get him out of my life. You're not a slut or even a flirt and a couple of people told me Roger has tried to get you to go out with him but you said no. Is that true?"

I said, "Yes, I won't go out with Roger. He doesn't appeal to me at all. As to looking for a man, if a really good one came by, I'd take him, but it's something I've put in the hands of God and left it there."

She nodded. "Can I tell you a secret?" she asked but before I could give a response, she went on. "I been seeing someone for marriage advice and so on, and she's been talking about boundaries. She says there's a lot of difference between sex being a little rough and marital rape, between playing out a fantasy and actual abuse." She stopped and then said, "Is there any way Roger could've been your home invader?"

"No," I told her. "He was about Roger's size but no belly."

She looked relieved. She said, "You won't tell anyone I asked that, will you?" I hesitated. "Please," she begged. "If it got back to Roger, he'd kill me."

"We already considered Roger but it's true that the man was thinner."

Patty closed her eyes, took a deep breath, exhaled and opened them. "I broke up with Roger when I caught him with Sue Wilkins. Everyone knows she's really a prostitute. I found out he paid her to act out a rape scene with him. After we split up, he came twice and basically raped me. He's tried several times since."

"Do you have family anywhere else?"

"I've got an aunt down near West Plains."

"Get her to help you look for work and move."

Patty nodded. "That's what you did when you were pregnant, isn't it? Were you really only 15 when you had your son?"

I didn't want to talk about it but she had told me secrets so I said, "Yes, I knew my mother would insist on an abortion so I came here to Grandma."

"Was it rape?" she asked.

I was unprepared for the blunt question and I knew she saw the answer in my face. "Don't tell anyone," I begged. "Job doesn't know. He does know the story I told about his father dying in the middle-east isn't true but he doesn't know it was rape. If you tell anyone, it'll be all over town by tomorrow night."

She nodded. "I understand. Everybody always knew when Roger beat me. Did they catch the guy?'

"No," I said, "He held me for four days and raped me repeatedly. Someone found me by accident."

Patty used a crude expletive and then apologized, "Sorry, but no wonder you don't want a man."

I shrugged. "It was all a long time ago. I try to forget it. I have Job and he's a good kid."

As I said this, we heard a car pull up outside. Patty stood up and said, "I been looking at this basket of flowers the whole time we been talking. They're going home with me."

When Patty and the old man who was one of my regulars were gone, Jim came out of the barn. "Sorry, but I heard most of that conversation with Roger Springer's ex. I wasn't being nosy but I did want to protect you. Mrs. Voden recognized her and she might have come out here to avenge her son."

"She's sent her son to Roger who wants the fun parts like football games but doesn't want the boring parts like seeing that the kid gets fed, gets to school, and does his homework."

Jim smiled. "Being a parent is rather like tending all these plants. They need a lot of attention but the rewards are worth it."

"Do you have any children?" I asked.

"No," he said. "No wife, no children. Back when I was in college I lived with a woman I wanted to marry but she had other ideas."

"Why?" As soon as I said it, I knew it was an intrusive question. "I'm sorry," I said. "It's none of my business. It's just you seem like a good man and I was surprised."

He looked at me and said, "The woman was white and she was never serious about marrying me."

I looked at him and then said, "She knew about your father."

"At college I was wearing my hair in an Afro so everyone knew I was black."

I said, "You were just something different, like a new toy."

Jim gave me a wry look and said, "That about sums it up. But I was raised in a Christian family and I knew what I was doing was sin. God does try to keep us from doing stupid things but some of us have to learn the hard way."

He was silent for a minute and then said, "Last night I told Job about my father. I do understand how kids get teased at school about who their parents are."

"Oh," I said, "That's how you got Job to talk."

"What was it Paul said about hardships developing character? At least it gives you some understanding when you see others going through a hard time."

Mrs. Voden joined us and said, "I was surprised when I recognized Patty Springer. What did she want?"

"She was sort of apologizing for her son. She's sent him to live with his dad."

Mrs. Voden said, "Will his dad straighten him out?"

"No, but it does relieve her of dealing with a disobedient child who's too big to spank."

Customers arrived and Jim disappeared back into the barn. Later I heard our mower start up and he started mowing. Mrs. Voden had been here often with Grandma and she knew a lot about the plants and how we operated. She said, "You can go work on your computer job if you like and I'll take care of the greenhouse. I rather like talking to all the people. If I need you, I know how to use the phone to get you."

We usually just did sandwiches for lunch, everyone going when they had a chance. I plopped a roast, potatoes, and carrots in a crock pot for dinner this evening and went to work on my computer. When Jim showed up for sandwiches, he asked me about the cave. I told him, "Grandpa's family bought this land before the Civil War and he and Grandma both always said they were part Indian. He would never let anyone in the cave. He said when his family settled here, some Indians used to come and camp here during a certain season every year and his family let them. He said they considered the cave to be a sacred site and he was not going to have it desecrated. Job and I go in to explore but we're careful to never disturb anything. When we found that exit to the creek, those hand and foot holds were already there."

"Have you ever thought about having an archaeologist look at it?"

"No," I told him. "We didn't know anyone and Grandpa said often they were about as bad as treasure hunters only they carry everything off to a museum instead of selling it." I paused and then said, "I did wonder if my intruder might have been someone just trying to scare me into selling the place and moving into town."

Jim understood immediately. "You've had offers."

"Yes, and one was from a corporation which owns caves in other places that they've developed as tourist attractions. Grandma sometimes got inquiries by phone but she'd never discuss selling with the callers. Sometimes local people asked to explore the cave and she always said no. Some kind of spelunker club called her once and she said no but two men came out here and tried to talk her into letting them look but she still said no. Then Lassie caught a couple of men sneaking in.

"We ran the men off but then someone from that corporation came out here and we recognized one of the men. They came back again and Grandma finally talked to the sheriff. He said to call the next time they came so we did and he came himself. He told them we were getting a court order and if they came on the place again, he was arresting them for trespassing."

Jim took the name of the corporation and then asked who owned the land now. I told him, "I do. When Job was 7, Grandma fell and broke her hip. Somebody told her about inheritance laws and probate court. She called Dad and wanted to transfer everything to him. Dad has a sister but her husband's military and right now they're in Germany. Dad told her to transfer everything to me. He said if he got it, my mother would want to sell it. So I have legally owned it for a number of years now."

I thought and then added, "Once someone tried to file some kind of papers at the courthouse about Grandma getting a loan on the place and we think it was that corporation. The clerk at the courthouse knows us and she thought it was odd and checked. Surely a corporation wouldn't go as far as having me murdered but they might think a good scare would help them."

Jim smiled. "It's not likely but it is something to keep in mind. Has anyone local ever tried to buy it?"

"Yes," I told him. "Roger Springer's father has a tourist place – a motel, cabins, an RV park, and canoe rentals. He talked to Grandma once. He thought the cave would be a drawing point and he wanted to develop an RV park for horse owners. But his talks with Grandma were friendly. Over the years, several other people have asked, farmers, and a local saw mill who wanted the timber, but no one was aggressive."

"You said you knew who your trespassers were who've been partying on your place behind the north field. Could it be any of them?"

I sighed. "Jerry Sutter might have put someone up to it. It wasn't him. He's smaller but he might have suggested it to a friend. His grandparents are Cleve and Connie Dunbar. They're good people but when we discovered that Jerry and his friends were partying back by the spring, we also found a marijuana patch. I didn't know what it was but Grandma did. She said marijuana is really hemp and people used to grow it to make rope. Jerry was nasty about it all and said the marijuana patch wasn't his but his grandmother was really upset with him. She asked us not to call in the sheriff, that the family would deal with Jerry. The Dunbar's are neighbors and have been friends forever so we didn't. Jerry himself is smaller than that intruder but it could've been someone he knows."

Jim said, "Marijuana growers are people who know they're breaking the law and often they don't mind breaking a few more. I think we need to keep an eye on things."

"I considered whether that intruder could've had something to do with the marijuana but it happened all the way back last year in July and we never heard any more about it."

Jim agreed it was unlikely and went back to his mowing.

I was working on my computer when Jim came back in and told me, "I asked a State Trooper I know to check the file on your incident sixteen years ago. I thought it wouldn't hurt to have a look at the suspect list. Sometimes a perp gets incarcerated for some other crime and when he gets out, he looks up an old victim. My friend tells me the only thing in the file is your statement to the police. Nothing else. It's very odd."

I couldn't breathe. Was it possible my nightmares were right?

Jim said, "Do you remember the names of any of the officers working the case?"

I shook my head. I had to work at saying anything. "Wa – wa – Juanita S – Sn – Snider was the real estate agent who found me." I was so shook up I was stuttering. "Her cell phone was dead which is why she took the wrong turn and got lost. Sh – sh – she had some tools in the trunk of her car and she broke the handcuffs. She also had some clothes and I put them on and she took me to the hospital emergency room." I paused to pull myself together. "I wanted a bath but she said not to even wash, that the hospital would do a rape kit and we could catch that animal."

I stopped and Jim asked quietly, "So they did do a rape kit?"

I nodded. "I – I asked for a lady doctor. I don't remember her name but she was a foreigner. I remember that. Then a police officer came. I don't remember his name either but he was young and I asked for someone to stay with me while I talked to him."

"Was he the only officer you talked to?"

"Yes," I told him. "My father came and took me home. I remember I spent most of the next few days soaking in the bathtub. I – I couldn't face going out. Dad was teaching summer school but he got a sub for a few days and then he called Mrs. Spelling in to stay when he and Mother were both gone."

"Who's Mrs. Spelling?"

I smiled. "She took care of me when I was small and after I started school, I would go to her house until Dad came after me."

"Who did you talk to about the rape besides the police officer?"

I shook my head and when I answered, I was stuttering again. "N – n – no one then. Later I talked to my therapist and my grandmother."

There was something else I debated on telling Jim but then as I considered it, Mrs. Voden came into the kitchen. Her nose took her straight to the crock pot and the roast.

She said, "I think I'll make an apple pie."

Jim changed the subject back to the cave. He said, "Besides John, I also have two sisters. They're really my half siblings," Jim paused and looked at me before going on. "My mother married their father before I was born and he put his name on my birth certificate." Jim smiled. "One of my sisters teaches at a university in Oklahoma. She's trained in archaeology and she's been on digs at Indian sites. I haven't mentioned the cave to her but I could ask her to come have a look next time she's home on a visit. You could stipulate that she not disturb anything but she probably could tell you who your Indians were and when they were here."

I said, "I'll think about it."

Job came home from school and we gathered to hear about his day. He said, "Mom, it's like stitches get you some kind of special treatment. One guy called me Bastard today in PE and several other guys shut him up. That was great but what I couldn't believe was all the girls who were talking to me. You'd have thought that I won that fight with Springer, the way the girls were hanging around."

I didn't know what to say. I had talked to Job about girls but I knew how important image could be to a 15-year-old. Jim smiled at him and said, "Job, maybe we should have a talk about girls."

Job looked at him and said, "Mom and Grandpa have both talked to me but you might think of something they didn't."

I looked at Jim and realized I trusted him to give my son a talk on sex. I was astonished. Jim looked at me and said, "Sorry, I should have asked you first."

"It's okay," I said. "It probably would be helpful."

Jim and Job left together and Mrs. Voden said, "Faith, he's not even dating anyone right now. He's 29. He's not what you'd call handsome but he says he's a Christian and he acts like one."

I had to laugh. I said, "Mrs. Voden, I expect you scared the man half to death. He told me why he's not married. He probably thinks I put you up to asking all those questions. What I suggest is for you to pray about it and let God handle it."

Mrs. Voden said, "Your Grandma always hoped you'd find a good man someday."

I smiled at her. "I know. And I know you're just trying to be helpful but don't scare the man away."

"Apple pie," she said. "You can always hook a man with good food."

I had to laugh.

Jim

In the middle of a war, women are often raped. The American military tried to make sure it was not our soldiers doing it and I think mostly succeeded. One of our officers told us that in World War II, the penalty was execution. He implied that he might be willing to carry on with that tradition.

After Faith told me about being raped, I called Vern and asked him to look up the incident. It had happened at Pine Bluff and Vern was actually based there so it would be easy for him to check. I told him there was a remote possibility our current perp was the same man.

When Vern called me back, he told me the only thing in the police file was a copy of the statement Faith gave to the police. It contained no medical report, no report on a rape kit, and no statement from the woman who found her.

Vern said, "There's something off about this case. I phoned first and was told I would have to come myself. When I asked where was the rest of the file, they said that was all there was and they didn't know anything about anything else. I asked who worked the case and they didn't know. I asked to talk to someone who'd been around when it happened and they said someone would call me but no one has yet.

"They also wanted to know what case I was working on now. I just said I was responding to a request out of Shannon County."

Vern was right. It was weird.

I told Vern what had happened to the marijuana patch he had been told about. He laughed and said, "It figures." I also told him it had happened last year in July and the Johnsons had never heard another word about it.

Why he'd wanted someone not official to check it out was his source of information was one of his nieces. She was terrified if anyone discovered who told, something awful would happen to her. Vern himself thought she might be right and he didn't want to be seen investigating.

I also told him about the outfit which had tried to buy Indian Cave Farm in the past. I said, "They tried very hard, even tried to sneak in for a look at the cave. The Johnsons had to get the sheriff to warn them off. Maybe now that Faith's grandmother's dead, they thought a good scare might get her to sell."

Vern took the name of the corporation and said he'd see what he could find out.

After talking to Vern, I thought about what he'd told me. As a law enforcement officer himself, he was reluctant to accuse other law officers of a cover-up but it was the most likely explanation for what Vern had encountered. It was not just the lack of paperwork. Papers get lost, are often kept in an officer's desk, left in his car or home, misfiled by mistake, even taken out to be copied and accidentally thrown away. But being given a run-around when he asked to talk to an officer who had been in the department when it happened was not normal. True, sixteen years was a long time but not that long, especially when the crime was serious and the victim was the 14-year-old daughter of a school teacher.

༃ Chapter 4: Another Fight ༄

Faith

Friday morning it was raining again but as Job went off to school in his rain gear, he looked happy. I realized he had not been happy about school for some time. Yesterday had been busier than usual but not like the day before. Today, because of the heavy rain, we were getting few customers. I watered and then Mrs. Voden told me to work on my editing while she run the greenhouse. She had her crocheting and could sit comfortably in the greenhouse.

I finished the supposedly historical romance and prepared to make a start on a new children's book. My children's books are called the Joey Johnson Series. The first one I wrote was "Joey Meets a Snake" and had been prompted by Job's encounter with the copperhead snake that Lassie killed. It was basically an educational book about snakes aimed at lessening fear, giving advice on avoiding unwanted confrontations, and promoting the positive environmental role of snakes. Job, age 5, had supplied the illustrations with very little help from me.

"Joey Meets a Snake" had been followed by books on spiders, skunks, bears, raccoons, coyotes, and alligators. Then Job suggested doing stories on other things that scare kids. We did "Joey Starts School," "Joey Gets Lost," and "Joey Goes to the Hospital." This morning Job had suggested a new book called "Joey Meets a Bully."

Jim came in and noticed what I was working on and I showed him the Joey Johnson Series, neatly shelved together. He took the first one on snakes and read it through. He commented, "This is great." He looked through them and told me, "I told Job you were a smart lady but I can see he knew that already. Is he going to do the illustrations for this new one?"

"I don't know," I told him. "Probably. I need to write it first and I'm already wondering if I should turn that over to Job too."

"He really is a great kid. How did you do it?"

I shook my head. "Help from Grandma and Dad. And God." I paused and then said, "Grandma said his temperament was a lot like Dad, an easy child. She and I once discussed the role of heredity. She said all of us are born with both good and bad impulses and our job as parents is to teach the child to choose good. However, she said in the end, each person will do their own choosing. She said some kids learn more easily than others and some are more stubborn and harder to teach. She said Dad's sister, Lois, was impulsive and prone to do things without asking and without thinking it through. Dad is about six years older and she said he was a big help in keeping an eye on her."

Jim nodded. "The four us were all spaced about two years apart and each of us is different. My youngest sister, Joan, would cry if anyone just looked upset with her. Jenny was totally different and needed a smack just to get her attention. She's turned out well, long on perseverance and getting things done, but needed a lot more input as a child. My brother, John, is a charmer. If anyone gets upset with him, he'll talk them around."

"And you?" I couldn't resist asking.

He was so slow answering I wondered if I shouldn't have asked but he finally said, "I understand about you not wanting Job to know certain things." He sighed. "I've always known Bill Willis was not really my father. He treated me exactly like the rest of the kids and I called him *Dad* but I always knew. I was insecure and afraid to make anyone mad at me so I always tried to do what I was supposed to do."

"So you were never rebellious?"

"No. Maybe because I knew Bill Willis really did treat me like I was his." He paused and then said, "Mom says when I was born and they asked for my father's name, he insisted on giving his. She said someone in the hospital actually had the gall to tell him I couldn't possibly be his and he told the woman, 'I'm married to his mother and that makes him mine.' "

I asked, "If people in Ellington find out about your ancestry, will it really be a problem?"

"My brother's kids would get razzed at school but otherwise, I don't think it would make much difference. I am sure everyone knew Bill Willis was not my biological father. He and Mom are both blonde and blue-eyed. But people with the nerve to ask questions, did it a long time ago." He grinned. "They always joked about finding me in the cabbage patch."

He was quiet for a moment and then said, "I think it's possible a few people suspected. I played basketball in high school and I think my coach may have wondered. Sometimes we played teams with black players and black people always know instantly that I'm black."

I was puzzled. "How do they know?"

"I think it's my bone structure. And then they know when hair is being controlled and maybe even notice I look tanned but have no tan lines."

"So you always passed for white when you were growing up."

"No," he told me. "There was a reason why I started doing it. When I was younger, we lived in St. Louis and I attended an integrated school. I wore my hair in an Afro and was considered black. Then just before I started high school, my father was offered a good deal on a fixer-upper out in a much more upper class neighborhood and we moved. None of us thought about the high school being all white. I was harassed. Then when basketball got underway, I played. I was the tallest kid on the team and the coach thought I was great. After our first away game, three other players on my team attacked me in the locker room and dislocated my shoulder. They told our coach I slipped in the shower and they told me if I said otherwise, something worse would happen to me."

"So you didn't tell?"

"Not to the coach but later at the hospital when my parents arrived, I told them. They called in the police but nothing was ever really done. I thought the other kids on the team not involved in the attack would talk but my attackers scared them into keeping quiet. Mom and Dad took me out of that school and were able to arrange for me to go back to the school district where we lived before. Dad drove me to school every morning on his way to work. Every day after school, I went home with my best friend and Dad picked me up on his way home."

Jim was smiling and I asked what about.

He said, "My best friend was black and his mother called me *Whitey* but she always fed me good and I knew she liked me."

"So when did you move to Ellington?"

"The next summer and I did my last three years of high school in Ellington passing as white. My best friend's mother and her friends showed me how to make myself look white. Black women all know about these lotions for lightening your skin. They're mostly strong sunscreens but there's other stuff in them too. And taking the curl out of your hair is just the reverse of putting it in. Hair straighteners work well but it can be done with heat, gel, and hair spray. In Springfield, I just let it curl. Most white people don't think about me being black but black people always notice."

"So you see the world from both a black and white perspective."

Jim nodded and I told him, "You should write a book. Call it 'Black or White?'"

He smiled and said, "I read 'Black Like Me' and it was a bombshell when it originally came out but things are a lot different now. Maybe we do need a new book."

Jim suggested since it was a slow day in the greenhouse, it might be a good time to go sign those statements for the sheriff. We didn't want to leave Mrs. Voden here alone and she wanted to get some things from her house so we dropped her on our way into town.

In the sheriff's office, I introduced Jim to Janice Dunbar and said he worked for a security company in Springfield. She looked at him and said, "You look like you'd make a good security guard." Jim smiled at her.

Janice had typed a report up on a computer and I read through it and made a few adjustments. Then Jim read it and made one suggestion. Janice printed out several copies and had us sign them.

Then Sheriff Conners wanted to talk to me. Jim said, "I don't mind waiting."

The sheriff asked to read the statement first. Then he said to me, "Janice says you've asked that Roger Springer not be sent out to your place again."

He waited and I said, "He keeps asking me out and I don't like him. Frankly, last Monday he was a nuisance. He treated Jim Willis like he was a suspect. If Jim hadn't turned up, I am sure that masked man would've got me or I would've drown trying to get away from him. Then Roger told everyone the incident was two men fighting over me. His son was saying things about me at school and my son got in a fight with him. It's the only time Job's ever got into a fight at school."

"How many times has Roger asked you out?"

I shook my head. "So many it's hard to remember, a dozen maybe. The first time, I was shocked because I didn't know he and Patty had split up and when I asked around, I was told it wasn't even definitely a split yet."

"He asked you out last Monday?"

"Yes."

"How many other times has he asked you out when he was on duty?"

"Several. Once he even pulled me over and asked me out."

"Why did he pull you over?"

"Just to ask me out, I guess. He never gave any other reason."

Sheriff Conners regarded me thoughtfully and then said, "When did that happen?"

"Last year at the beginning of June." I was wondering if Roger had violated some rule. "It was two days after Cleve Dunbar had his stroke. You know the road out by our place has no shoulder. When Roger put his lights on, I pulled into the Dunbar's driveway. It's wide and I pulled over to the side. Roger parked in the middle and then Connie Dunbar came along and needed out so he had to move his vehicle. I asked her how Cleve was doing."

The sheriff did not comment but did say, "I'll have a talk with Roger."

I said, "Good."

When the sheriff showed me out, he asked Jim into his office. I wondered why but couldn't very well ask.

On the way home, I asked Jim what the sheriff wanted. He said, "He wanted my story on your home invader."

I said, "He asked me about Roger Springer and I gave him an earful. He said he'd talk to him. I hope he stops bothering me."

Dad was arriving about 8:30. The weather forecast for tomorrow was good and Jim and his brother were going canoeing with John's oldest son. I suggested that Jim stay over and his brother come here Saturday morning.

Jim asked, "Will it bother your dad?"

"No," I told him. "In fact, I think it will help if he meets you."

Next week was the last week of school for both Job and Dad. Then they would be out for the summer. Jim asked if my father could arrange to stay next week. I shook my head. "He teaches school. It's right at the end of the school year. He can't be gone."

I tried not to show my anxiety but Jim saw it. He said, "We'll think of something."

Mrs. Voden fried chicken and made yeast rolls. I'd told Dad dinner would be waiting. He arrived just after 8 and we immediately sat down to eat.

Dad and Job are close and I saw Dad was gauging how Job interacted with Jim. We had agreed we would not discuss anything serious until after dinner so the talk naturally gravitated to Job's farming project. The trespassers got mentioned and Jim said, "It's Friday and I was thinking we might take a quiet look later tonight."

At the end of the meal, Jim sent me and Dad off to talk while he and Job handled the dishes. Over in the greenhouse, Dad said, "So are those partiers really giving you trouble?"

I took a deep breath and told Dad, "It's a lot more than that."

When I finished telling it all, Dad said, "Why didn't you tell me? I'd have been right down here!"

I answered, "I know, Dad, but Jim and Mrs. Voden were both here so it was okay." I had told Dad about Jim working for a security company in Springfield.

Dad said, "This is bad. We need to do something."

I said, "Yes, I know. I'll go in and send Jim out to talk to you."

I went in and Mrs. Voden said, "Your Dad's always come about once a month and came and stayed some in the summer but your mother seldom came before you moved here and after your grandfather died, I never heard she came again."

I looked at the nosy old lady and knew she actually did care about me and Job but I also knew how she talked. I said, "I'm sorry, but it's really private family business. Talk would just make it worse."

She nodded and said, "I understand. I had an aunt who had funny spells. Once't she thought my mother was trying to kill her and she got a hatchet and was after Mom with it. We had to send her off to an institution. Mom used to go once a month to visit her. She said sometimes she's in her right mind and sometimes she weren't."

The story had me trying to picture Mother with a hatchet. The absurdity was humorous. Mother would never dream of doing anything so unladylike. I thought to myself, *It could have been worse.*

Dad and Jim come back in and said they were going to go check at the spring behind the north field where our trespassers had been making a mess. Job wanted to go but Jim said, "Someone needs to stay here on guard and if we need to call the sheriff, your grandpa will carry more weight."

They called the sheriff.

The sheriff and my dad had grown up together. They rounded up the culprits. Dad knew some of their parents and the sheriff knew them all. Jim looked them over but told the sheriff quietly, "None of these boys are our perp. When you question them, ask about any older guys ever being out here."

Dad said the sheriff made them pick up every bit of the trash before they left. The kids all had cell phones and the sheriff let them call their parents. One girl begged and pleaded to be let go. She said her Dad would beat her. Dad said the sheriff talked to her father. He told him the girl better be in school on Monday with no bruises.

The sheriff questioned every one of them. One of the boys was 18 and two were 19. All of them were being charged with minor in possession of alcohol as well as trespassing. Dad said only one parent tried to get the sheriff to forget about it. The sheriff passed two names to Jim besides Jerry Sutter who were not there tonight.

Dad told Job who had been out there and Job said, "I'm not surprised about any of the boys but two of those girls are not normally part of that crowd." Jim asked Job if Jerry Sutter had some older friends. He gave Jim a few names and among them were the two the sheriff had mentioned.

It was late before we got to bed but Jim's brother, John, arrived the next morning before 7 o'clock with little Johnny who was 6. Job went out to turn the sign while I cooked breakfast. John teased Jim with, "And here I pictured you sweating it out on guard duty while you were lazing around with two woman to cook for you."

John said part of my surveillance equipment had arrived and the rest should be here on Monday. They discussed installation and Dad asked Mrs. Voden if she minded staying on next week. She said, "I'm enjoying this. My family doesn't really need me any more and I was bored. This is a lot more interesting."

We cautioned Mrs. Voden strongly about talking about the surveillance system. I told her to not even tell pastor's wife. Dad would be back again on Friday.

Jim and John launched their canoe and Dad and Job got the tractor going. Customers were coming in a steady stream and Mrs. Voden and I were busy. I had my phone handy and I was carrying the shotgun across my back. Jim had said, "There's nothing like a visible firearm to put a stop to nonsense."

We quickly discovered people were coming this time to find out about the kids being arrested last night. They were trying to link it with my intruder incident but I told them, "I wish it was that simple. The reason I'm carrying this shotgun around is that intruder. If he comes back, I'm ready."

Most of my inquirers were women and they usually nodded and said, "Good idea."

More than one also said, "I heard you had a man staying out here too." I knew they were fishing for information and mostly I let Mrs. Voden answer them. She was good at it and made it clear she was here to protect my reputation.

Job and Dad came in for lunch. They said they had fixed the gates and the plowing was going well. Dad talked to a couple of customers before they left again. Dad had grown up here and he still knew a lot of people. I suspected he would have liked to move back but I knew Mother was not willing. She did her best to conceal Dad's unsophisticated roots. Her family was even more unsophisticated and I had finally figured out it was her insecurity about her own background which made her so concerned about social status.

Saturday afternoon Jim went home with John to Ellington but Dad had arranged for him to come back Sunday evening and stay until he could return on Friday evening.

Sunday after church we invited Pastor and his wife for Sunday dinner and Mrs. Voden filled them in on all the events. I told Sister Carson I felt like I was living in a soap opera. They stayed a while and I sent a basket of hot pink petunias home with them. Our church is too small to support a pastor but Brother Carson worked in a sawmill during the week part of the year and Sister Carson ran a small daycare at the church with the help of a couple of other ladies. They were great people.

Sunday afternoon Dad asked for another talk. He told me, "I

have to finish up next week but we're through at noon on Friday. I'll be down here before 5. I have some gear I'm bringing down and I plan to stay until this is over."

Dad shifted uneasily and then said, "Jim asked me about the incident years ago. He asked if the police ever had any suspects and I told him not as far as I knew. In fact, at the time I was frustrated with how little they would tell me. Jim said there really isn't much in the police file and he asked if I knew anyone in the police force. Do your remember Chuck Sells? He was another teacher at the High School. His son was a young officer back then. I thought I might talk to him."

I said, "I can't image how it could run back to that."

"Jim said it was highly unlikely but still he wonders why the file is so thin."

I debated on what to say. I had a guess and it might explain why no one was ever caught. Should I tell Dad what I guessed?

As I hesitated, Dad said, "There's something else I wanted to mention." He paused and I waited. "Your mother and I have been discussing divorce."

I was shocked. And then I thought, *Why am I shocked?* They were the most incompatible couple I've ever seen living peacefully together.

Dad said, "I'm sorry, Faith. Your mother wants it and I've decided I'm not going to fight it."

I said, "Dad, Mother divorced me years ago. When she came down here and tried to get me to put Job up for adoption, she said she didn't believe I was raped. I remember how I decided I wanted Job to have the love I wished I'd gotten from my mother."

"Faith, I'm sorry" I could hear the distress in Dad's voice. "Your mother and I almost split up when you were a baby. She was so cold and unloving with you I hired Mrs. Spelling and your mother went to work. She didn't want any more babies. She talked about a divorce then but I thought you were better off with two parents."

I hugged Dad. I said, "Dad, you and Mrs. Spelling made up for it. Then when I started school, I spent all my summers here with Grandma and Grandpa."

Dad sighed. "Your mother may change her mind. I'm not really sure why she wants a divorce now after all these years but when she insisted she was going to file, I went along and it's in process as an uncontested divorce."

"Dad," I said, "move here with us. Job would love it and I would too." When Job was small, he had followed Dad around like a duckling following its mother and I had encouraged the relationship. Dad had filled Job's psychological need for a father just as Mrs. Spelling and Grandma had filled my need for a mother.

He hugged me and said, "We'll see. She may change her mind. But I didn't want it to come as a total surprise."

Jim arrived and he and Dad talked briefly before Dad left. Jim had come in a pickup truck this time. I told him, "I feel guilty depriving you of your vacation."

He said, "I had a worse one once. Someone I thought was a friend talked me into going with him on a cruise. Turned out it was a singles cruise. I spent the entire time fending off women, most of them half drunk and the rest of them more than half. And that guy I thought was my friend monopolized our cabin. Some nights I slept in a chair on the deck."

"Weren't you flattered?" I was teasing him.

He looked at me doubtfully and then saw my grin. He shook his head. "Half drunk older women will go after anything in pants. I tried to get rid of one woman by telling her I was gay and she wanted to show me how much fun it was to do it with an experienced woman." He was laughing.

We went in and organized a game of Scrabble which was a favorite of Mrs. Voden's. She won but Jim gave her a good run and Job and I learned some new words.

That night after I went to bed, I thought about how comfortable it had become to have Jim and Mrs. Voden here. Somehow we were like a family and that was amazing considering how short a time it had been. I thought about it and decided it was the emotional intensity of those few days. That would explain why I felt so close to Jim when I had only known him a few days. I fell asleep praying.

Monday morning, Job left for school and turned the sign on his way out. Jim reminded me to keep my cell phone on me and said he was going to do some hoeing in the kitchen garden. I started sorting laundry but then I heard voices. I looked out and Roger Springer was talking to Jim. I decided not to go out.

Mrs. Voden appeared with bed sheets and she went to see what I was watching. She said, "I'm on my way. He needs to know I'm here too." I smiled. Mrs. Voden understood her job.

Then Roger started for the front door with Mrs. Voden tailing him, talking. I quickly went out the front door and down the steps to meet them. I did not want the man in my house. He stopped and said, "I came out here to talk to you."

"Why?" I said. I heard the challenge in my voice and I didn't care. Jim was still within earshot and it gave me courage.

He looked at Mrs. Voden and said, "I'd like a private conversation."

I said, "Anything you have to say to me, you can say in front of Mrs. Voden."

He shifted, adjusting his belt with its holstered gun. "Well, it's private."

I said, "Roger, the only thing I really want to hear from you is an apology and Mrs. Voden would make a nice witness."

"Apology! For what?" he demanded.

"For telling people what happened out here last week was a domestic disturbance. That's why Mrs. Voden is here. She's my witness that nothing is going on out here with me and any man. That includes you."

He looked at me and then said, "I heard a rumor you was butch but I didn't believe it."

I looked at him and knew what I wanted to do was slap his mouth. I said, "Roger, you have a filthy mind. All you think about is sexual innuendo. I'm busy trying to make a living for myself and my son. If God sends me a good man, I'll take him, but you aren't the one."

He glared at me, red in the face, and clearly very angry. Jim had quietly moved closer but Roger was so angry he hadn't noticed.

He came out with, "You fucking whore, you don't know a good man from a pile of shit. That man in black was probably your bastard's father come back to remind you what a man's like."

It was so outrageous, I wanted to explode. I said, "That is enough! Leave! Leave right now!"

Roger started saying, "I'm an officer of . . . .'

But Jim interrupted him saying, "You heard her. Leave!"

Roger turned and swung his fist at Jim's face, only Jim moved and it hit his shoulder. The fight lasted about a minute and a half. Jim did know some good moves. He had Roger penned down and he said to me, "Call the sheriff."

We used Roger's own handcuffs. He cussed and ranted and threatened.

Mrs. Voden scolded, "Roger, you need your mouth washed out with soap. You ought to be ashamed of yourself, using that kind of language."

Jim pulled out his phone and told Roger, "I am now recording everything you say."

Roger said, "I'm an officer of the law and you can't do this."

Jim said, "You were not here in a professional capacity. You were using foul language to a lady and you were asked to leave. Instead, you hit me and started a fight."

When the sheriff arrived, he had one deputy in his car and two more in another car following him. I hoped no one else needed a law officer right now because we probably had everyone currently on duty here.

I was shaking and I excused myself to go make coffee. I had to laugh at myself. Mrs. Voden looked and sounded like a sweet old lady but she was tougher than me.

When I took the coffee out, Roger was in the back of the sheriff's car, clearly still handcuffed. The second sheriff's car was gone. The female officer from the second car had stayed and was taking notes while the sheriff talked to Mrs Voden who was saying, "I never heard such language in my life!"

Jim was trying to deal with two avidly interested ladies who had come for the greenhouse. I set the coffee tray down on the small table on the porch where the sheriff was conducting his interviews and went to deal with the customers. I didn't take Roger any coffee.

I didn't know the women's names but they knew mine, and they knew Roger Springer. Jim drifted away but stayed where he could see what was happening. One of the women asked me, "What happened? That man called it a tempest in a teacup. What's a tempest?"

I tried not to smile. "A storm. It's a quote from Shakespeare. It means a storm over something not really serious."

"But the sheriff has got Roger Springer handcuffed in the

back of his car and Roger is one of his own deputies!"

I sighed. "Roger got mad at me and was cussing and I asked him to leave. He didn't go so Mr. Willis asked him to leave and he hit Mr. Willis and they got in a fight."

"Who won?"

I found myself wanting to laugh. "Mr. Willis," I told her. "He works for a security company. Since that incident last week, I've had someone here all the time."

"We heard about that. Some people was saying it was two men fighting over you but then we heard that was a lie. We heard some rapist tried to get you and you ran down to the creek and somebody going by in a canoe put a stop to it all but the rapist got away. Is that true?"

I wished that Mrs. Voden was free to deal with these women. I said, "I don't know if he was a rapist but my front door was locked and he broke in. I heard it and I just run out the back and toward the creek. I thought maybe I could use our boat to get away. But he was right behind me and when I saw a man going by in a canoe, I jumped in the creek. My home invader was all in black, even a black ski mask and gloves. He had a gun and he shot at us. Fortunately he missed. Then he used my own boat to chase us but we had time to hide. He shot the man's canoe full of holes and sank it."

The two woman both looked shocked. "Mercy!" one of them said. "He even shot at you! No wonder you've hired a guard!"

I added, "Mrs. Voden has been staying with me, as well."

The other woman asked, "What's Roger Springer got to do with all this?"

"Nothing really," I told her. "He was the officer who came out here when that incident happened and I heard he's the source of the rumor saying it was two men fighting over me. He keeps asking me out and I keep saying no. Today he wanted a private conversation with me and I told him anything he had to say to me, he could say in front of Mrs. Voden. He got mad."

The women were both nodding. One said, "Everyone knew he used to beat his wife."

Into this scene came a Fed-Ex truck. I signed for his delivery and he looked around in bewilderment and asked, "What's going on? Who would rob a greenhouse?"

I smiled and said, "It was a fight. I have an admirer who is having trouble taking no for an answer. I asked him to leave and he didn't, so another man here asked him to leave. Instead of leaving, he started a fight."

The driver grinned and said, "Ma'am, you're a fine looking woman but no is no and there's lots of fish in the sea."

The sheriff finished with Mrs. Voden and wanted me next. The Fed-Ex truck left but I saw Simone Oliver's van arriving. I decided Mrs. Voden was able to deal with him and sat down in the chair on the porch she had vacated.

I told Sheriff Conners what happened and he wanted Roger's exact words. He said, "So he said you were butch and called you a fucking whore and said your home invader last week was probably your bastard's father."

I said, "On the part about being butch, he said he had heard a rumor but didn't believe it. I told him if God sent me a good man, I'd take him, but he wasn't the one. That's when he come out with all that other stuff. I admit I provoked him but he keeps asking me out and I've tried to tell him no nicely but he doesn't seem to get it. So I thought I'd try being rude."

"All those times Springer asked you out, how many of them were while he was on duty?"

I thought. "Last Monday, of course. And the time I told you about when he pulled me over. Twice was at basketball games. His son doesn't play basketball and he was in uniform including his gun so I thought he was on duty. Once I was putting gas in my car and he drove up in a sheriff's car so I think he was on duty. And once I was unloading plants at the Bestway grocery store and that time also he was driving a sheriff's car."

The sheriff nodded. "And today he was on duty too. Can you give me dates?"

I tried. "The first time he asked me out was at the Bestway grocery. It was only four days after Patty caught him with Sue Wilkens and I hadn't heard about it yet. On the basketball games, one was the last game before Christmas vacation. That time he pulled me over last summer the was two days after Cleve Dunbar had his stroke."

"And Roger never gave any reason for stopping you?"

"He never said anything about why other than that he wanted to take me out."

The sheriff shook his head and said, "I'll have all this typed up and you can drop by the office later to sign it." He turned to his deputy and said, "Sally Ann, I'm going to have a word with Mr. Willis before we take his statement."

Mrs. Voden, Simone, and the two other customers were laughing about something so I went back to my interrupted laundry. Jim come in later and called me out for a conference. It was Jim, the sheriff, and his deputy, Sally Ann Smith. The sheriff said, "I'm going to fire Roger Springer so I really need for you to carry through on signing that affidavit and be prepared to testify if he fights it. Are you willing to do that?"

"Yes," I said. "Today was totally over the line. A woman ought to be able to tell a man no without getting cussed out or having him start a fight with another man."

The sheriff left with his deputy and Roger still handcuffed but more customers arrived. One of the first women had sent something out on her smart phone and our new arrivals were curiosity seekers. Mrs. Voden dealt with them while I went back to my laundry.

Jim brought in the coffee things I had forgotten and started washing the cups. I asked him, "Jim, do I somehow attract men who like to bully women?"

I was wondering if I was doing something that was inviting attention from the wrong kind of man.

Jim said, "Faith, you're a beautiful woman and some men are just first class jerks. Any man would find you attractive but you aren't inviting attention so they're not knocking down the door trying to get you to go out with them."

"How can I tell if a nice guy is interested?" I asked him.

He grinned. "They're probably sending signals but you're not seeing them. When a lady doesn't respond, a gentleman will look somewhere else."

I thought about it. "I live in such an out-of-the-way place, I almost never meet a man that's available. The only unmarried man near my age around here is slow minded. I did get asked out by a widower who's old enough to be my father."

"Maybe you need to get out more, mix around, ask your father and Job to help you. They both are pretty sensible."

"Maybe I will," I told him but I knew I probably wouldn't. I was afraid that even if I found a man I liked, when it came down to the physical side of things, I might find I couldn't do it. And I might not know that until my wedding night. It was better to just let the sleeping dog lie.

Jim said, "I put out a query on finding you a dog and I've had an answer from someone. She's a police dog being retired. She's only four and had just started service. She's lost a front leg but has recovered enough for doing what you need here. What's sad is it was friendly fire that got her. Do you think you're interested?"

I would have to pay some expenses but not too much. Her handler was willing to come work with us and the dog. Jim set it up for Friday and Saturday so Dad could be here for part of the training time.

When all the customers, including Simone, had left, Mrs. Voden came in and said, "That Simone is outrageous, of course, but so funny. He had us all in stitches. He said when he first moved here, Roger approached him in the Bestway and told him we didn't want his kind here. Simone said he looked Roger up and down with his best leering look and said, 'Ooo-eee, you're such a fine specimen of a man. If you ever decide to find out what it's like, look me up.' He said he thought Roger was going to have a stroke but there were too many people around for him to do anything. After we all laughed, Simone said, 'But actually he scared me and I went and talked to the sheriff about him. I'm glad I came out here today so I could see him get arrested.'" Mrs. Voden was still smiling. She added, "I don't think homosexuality is right but I can't help liking Simone. Maybe it's because he is so completely honest about it."

When Job came home from school, he said, "It was all over school before lunch and I wanted to skip out but I knew Jim was here. Did they really arrest Roger Springer?"

Job listened to what happened and said, "I'm not surprised." He looked at Jim and said, "I'm glad you're here."

Job wanted to go work on the north field. I was uneasy about him working alone. I wasn't afraid anyone would do anything to him but I worried about him getting hurt. Farm equipment is dangerous and inexperienced operators are high-risk. I looked at my son and said, "I know I have to let you grow up but please, please be careful."

He nodded. "Grandpa talked a lot Saturday about safety." I gave him my Track phone. He wolfed down a sandwich, hugged me and left.

To keep my mind off Job, Jim suggested a game of Monopoly. He was making jokes and it was contagious. Monopoly is supposed to be a cutthroat business game but we happily traded property and laughed about landing in jail. We were still playing when Job came in after dark.

In bed, I thought about Jim. Organizing a Monopoly game had helped me gain some distance from the incident with Roger Springer and take my mind off worrying about Job. He would be leaving on Friday when Dad came back. I realized I would miss him.

Jim

Friday when Faith and I went into the sheriff's office, I ended up telling the sheriff about the marijuana patch I'd found. I did not tell him Vern put me up to looking. I just said I was checking the boundaries of Indian Cave Farm and since I knew Vernon Chilton personally, I'd called him and asked what to do. Sheriff Conners said he was happy to let the State Troopers deal with it. Sheriffs are elected officials and if the marijuana growers turned out to be someone with local influence, it could get difficult for him.

Friday night after the break up of the party behind the north field, I called Vern again and told him about it. I told him no one had said anything about the burned over marijuana patch.

I said, "Also, Nathan Johnson has hired me to stay next week until he comes back on Friday. I didn't tell him about you and if I had said no, it would have looked odd. Also he knows someone who was on the police force in Pine Bluff sixteen years ago. He's planning to talk to him."

I told Vern tomorrow I was going to change the card on my spy camera at the marijuana patch I had found. When I picked up the card, I checked and my camera had caught good, clear pictures of two men. I called Vern and arranged for my brother, John, to inconspicuously pass the tiny card to someone in the parking lot at the Dollar General in Ellington.

Vern called me Sunday afternoon and said, "We've ID'ed your marijuana growers." He was laughing about it but refused to tell me who they were. He did say, "I'm sure neither of them is your perp." I asked if they could have arranged it and he said, "Highly unlikely but we'll check."

When I told Vern about the fight with Roger Springer and its outcome, Vern said, "Abe, you're getting in deep." Abe had been my nickname when I was in the military. In Afghanistan, the local men wore beards and one of my officers had suggested I grow one. With my darker coloring, it had make me look like a local which was sometimes quite useful. Then someone in the unit said I looked like Abe Lincoln and the nickname had stuck. Vern went on, "When you start getting in fights over a woman, it's serious."

"I don't think so. That Roger Springer is such a bozo, it just happened. I told Faith Johnson about my father so I don't think she's giving me a second thought."

Vern said, "You're too faint-hearted. Nobody in Ellington ever figured it out so why are you worried about it?"

I still remembered my dismay when I met Vernon Chilton in the military. He was from Eminence and that was too close to home but when I asked him to keep quiet about my ancestry, he did. Shared secrets, if they are kept, make friends but it was more than that. Vern was a Christian and willing to say so.

On his way back to Fredericktown Sunday night, Nathan had arranged to meet a Pine Bluff officer named Sonny Sells. I expected him to call me but he didn't. I assumed he had not found out anything useful but was surprised he didn't call me anyway.

ೞ Chapter 5: Disappearance ೞ

Faith

Tuesday morning Job went off to school and I went out to the greenhouse. I had told Job to leave the sign on Closed. Jim's brother, John, had called and he was coming with the equipment for my new surveillance system.

I watered in the greenhouse and then started re-potting a bunch of tiny Pin Oak trees which we had started from acorns. We had only started doing trees two years ago. Trees are slow and not good money makers but no one in the area was selling them so there was some demand. We had plenty of space for them and trees are lovely. Also they have no expiration date. They just keep getting bigger from year to year and you can charge more for them. Or you can plant them somewhere.

Bundles of small trees can be ordered from the Missouri Conservation Department. The first year, we had ordered Dogwood and last year we added Tulip Poplar and White Pine. We had gotten Redbud earlier this year but we had also planted 50 acorns last fall just to see what happened. Now we had 43 Pin Oak seedlings needing bigger pots. Jim turned up and started helping me. He told me, "There's something so satisfying about growing things."

It wasn't long before John showed up and they started installing my surveillance system. I decided that while they were here was a good time to go into town. I loaded plants in the back of my truck. In Eminence, the Bestway grocery store sold them. I dropped Mrs. Voden to her house and would pick her up on my way home. In town, I unloaded my plants and looked over what was still remaining from before. We had a special rack to hold them where I could put the ones which liked sun on top and the ones which liked shade on the bottom. Every day after school Job stopped by and watered. I had brought them four Dogwood trees earlier and they had called and asked for half a dozen more. I had asked about putting up a sign saying what trees could be ordered and giving prices. People could buy them cheaper directly from us but if they only wanted one or two, it wasn't worth the drive out to our greenhouse. We really were a long way out.

When I picked up Mrs. Voden, I reminded her again that the surveillance system was a secret. She said, "It's like being spies. We'll see who we catch."

When we got back, we both spent some time learning how to use the system. It was great. It had eight cameras and I could see everywhere near the house, greenhouse, and barn. One of them was even out at the gate. Jim also had a trail camera which he was going to put up where my invader had been watching my house. Jim said, "It records and I'll have to go check it but if we can get a good look at him or his bike, we might can identify him."

As John was leaving, Jim went back into the house for a forgotten tool. I was thanking John and his eyes followed his brother into the back door. "He said he'd told you. That's Jim, always a square shooter. He's a great guy." He looked at me and said, "He likes you."

My mind went flapping around. I wanted to know exactly what John meant but Jim was on his way back and I just said, "I like him too."

We told John to change the sign on his way out and Jim and I went back to our baby trees. Jim said, "I can't believe these little twigs will make Oak trees."

I laughed. "That's life," I told him. "If you're paying attention, you can never deny the reality of God. Life is a miracle."

Jim nodded. "You're a mother. You nurture. You embraced Job and loved him in spite of how he came about. I admire you for that."

"Do you? At the time I cried and cried. I ranted and raved at God. Then it was like God said, to me, 'Quiet. You're scaring your baby.' As I thought about the baby, everything changed. Maybe God gave me Job so I had something to live for, someone to love, a reason to forget what happened to me and move on with life."

Jim said, "You're a good mother."

I felt uncomfortable with the complement. I said, "I'm not perfect. Sometimes I blow it. Yesterday I very nearly told Job he couldn't go work on the north field alone. I have to let him grow up. It's my job to teach him how to be an independent, competent, happy adult. I have to back off enough to let him grow but it's not what I want to do. I want to keep him a child, dependent on me. That's selfish. It's meeting my emotional needs at the expense of his growth."

Jim looked at me in silence.

"Do I sound crazy?" I asked,

"No," he said. "You just said the sanest thing I've ever heard a parent say."

"Oh," I said. "I'm glad I didn't sound crazy."

We finished the trees and Job came home. Jim took him with him to set the trail camera up where the masked man had been watching our house. Then Job grabbed a sandwich and left for the north field. Mrs. Voden was doing dinner and I went to work on my computer. Jim was mowing again. He said he liked doing it. We had dinner and he helped me do dishes.

Job came home after dark and ate. He talked enthusiastically about the farming. I thought, *It'll keep him busy all summer.* He had set up bookkeeping on his computer and he was logging hours worked. He said, "When I was talking to guys at school whose families farm, some of them were enthusiastic and some of them said it was a terrible way to make a living. I'll find out."

I thought to myself that Job was intelligent. How many boys his age would think of logging hours as well as keeping track of expenses to see if farming paid off or if he'd be better off doing something else? He even said, "One of my teachers farms part-time. He said it works out well. He says he makes enough off the farming to be worth his time and it provides a relaxing change from teaching."

We had sort of settled into a routine and Dad called me every evening just checking. Then Thursday morning, Jim thought he saw movement up on the hill where someone had been watching before and he went to check. He didn't find anyone but the trail camera he had put in place was gone. Jim was worried and stuck close to the house.

Then Thursday afternoon Job did not come home from school. When he was half an hour overdue, we gave Mrs. Voden the shotgun and left her to answer the phone while Jim and I started for town, driving slowly, checking the roadsides, and stopping to look over bluffs. We found his scooter in the school parking lot. Two teachers were still in the building, marking exams, figuring end of the year grades, etc. The first thing we did was call the sheriff's office. Then we started calling his friends. With the second call I made, I learned that Job had been seen talking to a man in a white pickup truck after school. The man had a small motorcycle, described as a trail bike type, in the back of his truck. We tried to get a description but the man had never gotten out of the truck and all we got was dark hair with a burr type haircut and a tan or khaki shirt. The conversation had been described as brief and Job had gotten into the truck.

I sat in the school office, so distraught and terrified, I could hardly organize my mind enough to pray.

Jim

Each evening that week Nathan called Faith checking if everything was okay but he never asked to talk to me or called my cell phone. I wondered why but didn't call him and ask. Maybe his meeting didn't happen. Maybe this Sonny Sells was doing some investigating.

Tuesday John came and we installed Faith's surveillance system. Job and I installed a trail camera up where our perp had been watching the house. Thursday morning, I caught a quick flash of light and quietly told Faith and Mrs. Voden. While some customers were picking out plants, I got in my truck and drove slowly out to the county road but instead of turning left toward Eminence, I turned right. I pulled off the road where our watcher had been hiding his vehicle behind the trees. The space was empty.

Back at the house, I hid and scanned his watching point with binoculars. Nothing. Was what I saw a bird or the wind in a tree? I entered the woods behind the barn where I could not be seen and worked my way around to his perch. All I found were tracks proving he had been there. He was gone and so was the camera I had installed.

I didn't like it and I kept a good lookout. He now knew that we knew that he had been watching. Would it scare him off or provoke him to make a much more daring move?

When Job didn't show up at his normal time, I was immediately deeply worried. So was Faith and I tried not to show my own concern but by half an hour after his usual arrival time, we were headed for the school. We checked the roadsides all the way in so it took us an hour to get there. By then, school had been out for two hours and only the cleaning staff and two teachers were left – and Job's scooter, setting in the student parking lot, all alone.

Faith started making phone calls to other students while I called the sheriff. Then I sat praying until he arrived, followed by Mr. Fields who had been called by one of the teachers. When the sheriff said Job had probably run off, I said, "No. His scooter's here and Faith has already talked to another student who saw him leave with a man in a pickup truck." Then I added, "Tuesday I put a trail camera up where that perp had been watching Faith's house and this morning it was gone."

Part 2

A Father

℘ Chapter 6: Father ℘

Job

I came out of school Thursday thinking about how school was basically over for the year. We had to come tomorrow but it was a minimum day which would consist of cleaning out desks and parties so we'd be out at 1 o'clock. I had been working on the north field every evening after school until dark and only studying for my exams afterwards but I had been diligent all year about my studies. If I wanted to go to college, I needed a scholarship. Besides, school is mostly interesting and not hard if you pay attention. Most of the kids don't.

I started for my scooter and a white pickup truck pulled into my path. The window was down and the man inside said, "Job." I looked at him and he said, "Come get in. I want to talk to you."

I backed away. Did he think I was stupid?

Then he said, "Job, I'm your father."

I looked at him. I could see it immediately. I looked like him. There was no doubt. He repeated, "Get in. We can talk about it."

I got in. He drove south out of Eminence and our house is east. I buckled my seat belt and he said, "Let's go someplace quiet and talk. Have you got a cell phone?"

"No, sir," I answered and asked, "Where are we going?"

"Where we can talk without being interrupted."

"I need to call Mom. She'll be worried."

"I already called her and told her I was picking you up. She knows."

I didn't know what to say. I felt uneasy and wasn't sure why except why would my mom not say a word about my father for years and then him just show up without her telling me anything. I wasn't sure what to think.

It wasn't long before I saw he was not a careful driver. He was speeding where the highway was straight enough, which isn't all that often between Eminence and Winona, and worse, he was rounding the curves in the middle of the highway. I said, "This road is really bad and there's a lot accidents on it."

He said, "Yeah, kids trying to text and drive and women on their cell phones."

"I think it's mostly the curves. People run off the road all the time," I said.

"I'm police. We get special training for driving," he said.

I wanted to say something else but I couldn't think of anything tactful. His tone of voice reminded me of Coach whose typical response to any suggestion was an accusation of being a smart-ass. *Ass* was on the forbidden list at our house unless you were talking about a donkey. We made jokes at school about a donkey's hind end.

He told me, "I didn't know you existed until a few months ago. I tried to get your mom to let me see you but she refused. Why the Hell did she name you Job?"

"It's a book out of the Bible," I said. "It's about a man named Job."

He laughed. "It's a shitty name," he said. "We'll have to change it." Then he met a car on a curve and barely avoided a wreck. He cussed at the other driver even though he had been the one in the middle of the road. He sped up and said, "We'll find a place to talk."

I thought about what he'd said about my name. Did he think he had the authority to change it? I didn't like the idea at all. Job was a man who had all kinds of bad things happen but hadn't lost his faith in God.

Mom had never told me my father's name and Mom is not stupid. I should never have gotten in the truck with him.

He stopped at a bar on the north edge of Winona. As we got out of the truck, I saw he had a handgun which he placed under the seat. It rattled me. I realized that had I refused to get in his truck, he might have been planning to use the gun to make me. I was even more uneasy.

Mom didn't go to bars and neither did Grandpa so I'd never been in one. It smelled foul, cigarette smoke and other things I didn't recognize.

It was just opening and he asked someone, "Can we get some food?"

As we sat down, I took off my jacket and he saw the stitches in my arm and asked what happened. I didn't want to tell him but I said, "I got in a fight at school."

I expected him to ask me over what but instead, he asked, "Who won?"

Wanting as little discussion as possible, I said, "The teachers broke it up right away."

He said, "Police training includes a lot about fighting. I'll teach you." I didn't tell him Jim Willis had been teaching me. I knew he wouldn't like it.

He had ordered hamburgers and two beers. The beers arrived and I pointed out that I was underage, he laughed and said, "You're old enough."

I said, "Well, someone might ask and you don't want any trouble, do you?" So I ordered Root Beer. It came in a mug just like the beer.

He said, "I got something to show you." He pulled out a paper and said, "When your mom wouldn't let me see you, I took it to court. They sent her papers but she never showed up so they gave me full custody."

I looked at the paper with my mind spinning. How could Mom not have told me this?

To give me time to think, I read the paper over slowly. It was a court order giving full custody of a child known as Job Joseph Johnson to his father, Dylan Robert Robinson. It had my birth date right. To give me time, I read it all again. Then I saw it was a photo copy. I asked and the man said, "I put the original in a lock box. I didn't want to lose it."

I said cautiously, "This is quite surprising."

"She never told you, did she?" he grinned. "Why I didn't know about you was because she had slept with half the boys in the senior class. Then her family moved. Her father was a teacher in the high school so I figured he heard about what she was doing and decided to move somewhere else. Half the town knew about her."

I said, "She came to her grandmother. I was born here."

He said, "I've always wanted a son. I've been married twice and no kids. I've always wanted a son who looked like me. When I found you, I couldn't believe it. You look just like I did when I was your age."

"Well, I knew I didn't look anything like Mom or Grandpa.

I've looked at family pictures and I never could see that I looked like any of them."

He grinned. "No, you're my son and you look like me." I heard the satisfaction in his voice. He sounded like he owned me and I didn't like it at all. Then he asked, "Who the hell was Caleb Smith?" It was the name Mom had put on my birth certificate.

"Someone my mother made up. She told me they were planning to get married as soon as she graduated from school. She said he graduated and joined the military and got sent to the middle-east. She said I happened right as he was shipping out and when she told him, he was trying to get leave to come home so they could get married, but he got killed."

"Son of a military hero. That's a good story."

I nodded. "I found out last fall that Caleb Smith didn't exist. She said she didn't want me to feel like I was unwanted."

"She always was a good liar," the man said.

My mind was in turmoil. The only lie Mom had ever told me was about my father. She had always avoided talking about him. I had thought it was because it made her sad but after I discovered he didn't exist, I knew it was because she didn't like lying.

I didn't want to hear what this man was saying. I had always wanted a father but I wanted someone like Grandpa, or maybe Jim Willis. I didn't want a beer drinking sloppy driver who called my mother a liar.

But we don't always get what we want.

"Who's that long, tall bastard your mother's with now? I was watching the other day when he took out that deputy. How come he didn't get arrested?"

I thought. What should I say? My instinct was to not give out information but I had to say something. "Mom's not with him," I explained. "He's just there for protection. That deputy has been pestering Mom for a date and she finally told him off. He started cussing her out and Mr. Willis told him to leave. He hit Mr. Willis and started the fight."

"Yeah, I saw that. It's those big boobs of hers. Every man wants 'em. Back when she was a freshman, all us senior boys were drooling."

I looked at the man who was my father and I knew I didn't like him. "You were that man in black who broke into our house."

He answered, "I just wanted to talk to your mom about you. I had tried calling her on the phone and she just hung up on me. I had to try something else."

"With this paper from the court, you could have just picked me up."

He shrugged. "I figured she probably knows all the local law enforcement officers. Women who give out can always get men to do things for them. She'd have made a fuss. This way is better. You and me just drive off into the sunset."

I wanted to protest over what he was saying about Mom but I already knew I was in trouble. I needed to be careful what I said. I sidestepped and said, "Mom will be terribly worried about me."

He grinned. "I phoned and told your mom I had a court order and was picking you up. I've got a place in Colorado that's great. That's where we're going."

"I need to say good-bye to Mom and pack some clothes," I protested.

"No way," he said. "And you're not calling her. Like I said, she'll get the local law involved and it'll all turn into a fuss but in the end, you have to come with me so there's no point in starting it."

I said I had to go to the restroom which was true, but I was hoping for a chance to call Mom. However, he stuck right with me and I saw he was not going to let me out of his sight. Some small voice inside said, *Act like you're going along with this and sooner or later he'll relax.*

Before we left the bar in Winona, he'd had three beers. I wasn't sure what kind of blood alcohol level that would produce but his driving had been none too good before that. I suggested that I drive. "You're too young to have a driver's license," was his response.

But I knew he'd been watching the house. I said, "I've got a license to drive my scooter and also a driver's permit. I drive the tractor and our farm truck." But he didn't let me drive.

We took Highway 60 west and I was glad it was four-lane. He was speeding a lot of the time and I hoped we'd get stopped but we didn't. I worried about having a wreck and we had several close calls but no wreck.

In Springfield, he got off the main highway. The first thing he did was find a haircut place still open. He said, "You're getting a decent haircut, son." My hair was due a cut but he told the man to give me a buzz like his which I had never had before. I didn't like it but I didn't say anything. My hair is thick, grows fast, and curls like a girl's if I let it get too long. I always just wore a traditional haircut, like Grandpa.

Next he found a used car dealer still open this late. He traded his white almost new truck for a red four-wheel drive older model. The dealer helped us move the tool box and trail bike from his old truck to the new one. The dealer took the plates off his old truck and was going to put them on the new one but he said, "I've got another truck at home I'm going to put those on. It has a special vanity plate and I'm going to transfer that to this truck. Can you put some kind of paper on this one until I can get them all changed?"

Back on the road, he said to me, "I'll have to get Colorado plates for this truck so there was no use putting those on it." I considered why he didn't just tell the man that instead of lying about it and then I wondered if he was afraid someone in the parking lot at school had gotten his plate number. *Was he hiding? Why?*

He found a motel in Joplin. We had stopped at a convenience store where he'd bought a twelve-pack of beer. At the motel, he started on the beer and wanted me to have some. I said I was tired and went to bed. I was glad the room had two beds.

I pretended to sleep but really I was praying. I knew some of the things he'd said about my mother weren't true but even if they were, I still wanted to go home. I did not want to go to Colorado with this man.

The next morning, he still had beer and he drank one before we went to eat and another before we left. I decided he was an alcoholic. Who else drinks beer with their breakfast?

At breakfast he said, "I'm changing your name. You're Dylan Robert Robinson, the Second. I'll file the papers as soon as I get a chance but right now I'm calling you Rob. It's only one letter different from that stupid Job."

I didn't say anything but I didn't like it. I had read the book of Job in the Bible and I admired the man. I liked my name. It was unique. Even our small school had several Roberts, Robs, Bobs, Bobbys, and even two Dylans but I was the only Job.

We got on a turnpike headed for Tulsa, Oklahoma and he

started asking me about my life. I told him I liked school and he asked about sports. I told him I played basketball and he wanted to know why I didn't play football. I told him my school's team was dominated by several bullies I didn't like. I told him they were always razzing me because I didn't have a father and I had not wanted to join them.

He said, "Well, now you've got a father and I'll teach you how to play football." He started talking about how he played football in high school. It was mostly bragging which Mom always said was bad manners but maybe talking to your son is different.

I asked him if he played football in college and he said he hadn't gone to college but to a police academy. I got him talking about working on the police force. Again he was mostly bragging but I listened. I decided it might help if I knew more about him.

He had worked for several years in the town where Mom had lived and then had gone to work in St. Louis. I asked him why he moved and he muttered, "Damn bitch!" His talk had been laced with cuss words but this had exploded out of him with force.

"What?" I said before I had time to think.

"Some damn bitch claimed I raped her. She was a fucking liar. She offered sex and I took it. Then she ran to the damned hospital claiming fucking rape. The case was thrown out of court but she started all kinds of damned gossip and I quit and moved to St. Louis."

By that point, I had adjusted to his language enough to mostly tune out his cussing but the phrase "fucking rape" struck me as ironically humorous. I could hear my English teacher, Mrs. Pierce, calling it "a most unfortunate choice of adjectives."

Then I wondered how I could find anything amusing about a rape accusation. *Was this man's character rubbing off on me?* The thought horrified me. *Had I inherited his crudeness?*

Then I remembered our pastor once saying, "In the end, everyone chooses who they become, good or bad, honest or dishonest, stingy or generous, hardworking or lazy. Everyone chooses."

I said to myself, *I choose. I choose to be good.* Then I added a silent prayer, *Father God, help me!* I thought about how I used the phrase "Father God." Because I hadn't had a father, I had paid attention to the teaching about God being the ideal good father, loving me and helping me, teaching me and looking after me. Now I silently prayed for God, my Heavenly Father, to give me his help, his guidance, his protection.

Eventually the man, I had no desire to think of him as Father, asked me what I wanted to be when I finished school. I said I planned to go to college but I wasn't totally sure yet what I was going to choose. I said, "I like history and there's lots of options. I can teach or become an anthropologist or even an archaeologist."

He was derisive, calling those *sissy* jobs. He said, "You want real man's work, police or business. Build houses. There's good money in that."

Just for something to say, I remarked, "I been doing a little farming on our place but I don't think people usually get rich farming."

He laughed. "You got some fucking brains after all."

His lack of vocabulary was getting old. I decided I must have gotten my brains from Mom. Either that or he had fried his on alcohol.

As the day progressed, I could see clearly that he was not going to let me out of his sight. We stopped at truck stops with large restrooms so I couldn't even pee in private. His crude language was boring and so was his conversation. He liked to brag about his police work and I think I heard in detail about every criminal he ever took down. He used terms like *queers* and *niggers*. He was fond of using his gun and he bragged about killing several of them. The more I listened, the more strongly I disliked the man.

That day we drove all the way to Gallup, New Mexico. He bought more beer and drank steadily all day. He also bought some kind of no-sleep tablets and a couple of energy drinks. I started worrying about him going to sleep or passing out. His driving was bad but we were on Interstate 40 and the lanes were wide and the traffic light. Also other drivers are mostly alert. What I don't understand is how come we never got stopped for speeding.

It had gotten hot and he was wearing a long-sleeved knit shirt. Several times he started to push the sleeves up and then didn't. When he upped the air-conditioning to the point that I dug my light jacket out of my backpack, I started wondering. He had just slept in his clothes so maybe he didn't have a short sleeved shirt but why not push up his sleeves?

It was late when we got to Gallup. The motel room stank of cigarette smoke. He inhaled deeply and said, "It makes me want a smoke. I quit but sometimes I have a few." Then he asked me, "Have you ever smoked pot?"

"No, sir," I said.

He ripped out with, "Stop with that damned *sir* business. You call me *Dad*. Is that clear?"

"Okay, Dad," I responded but I was thinking, *What kind of man has to order his son to call him Dad?*

I didn't have any clean clothes but I took a shower anyway. Then I lay in bed again pretending I was asleep long before I really was. I prayed. He might have a court order but if I ran off, could I take care of myself? Maybe I could go to Mom's dad and he could think of something. He might be willing to hide me. They had school on the internet. But what about Mom's mother? I had never seen her and they never talked about her. I asked Mom once and she said, "You don't really want to know." She had looked real sad and I wondered if her mother was an alcoholic or something.

I'm pretty big for my age. Maybe I could just say I was 18 and get a job somewhere. But I wanted my life back. I liked living on Indian Cave Farm. I wanted my mother. I tried to tell myself I was too old for that but I knew it wasn't true. And I also knew my mother would be devastated by my father taking me away.

I loved Mom and Grandpa. I didn't love my father. At my age, didn't I get some say about which parent I lived with?

The next morning, we went to Walmart and he bought me some underwear and a couple of changes of clothes. He was still wearing the clothes he had on when he picked me up at school and was beginning to smell. I asked for him to buy some deodorant, hoping he would take the hint.

When we left Gallup, we were going north on a two-lane road. He was talking about his cabin up in the mountains where we were going. It was in Colorado but now we were were passing through the Navajo Indian Reservation. I was interested in what I was seeing but he was driving on the second rate road like it was the Interstate. Again he was drinking beer and energy drinks and I saw him taking pills. I suggested I drive while he napped but he said no. He was stopping to pee on the side of the road and not even trying to hide while he did it. It was embarrassing and I never watched the traffic going by to see if they were staring.

We stopped once at some place on the reservation. He asked for beer and they said they didn't sell alcohol on the Rez. He said, "Yeah, I heard these fucking Indians can't handle their liquor." I wanted to crawl in a hole and hide but there wasn't one. I tried to move away and he said, "Where you going, boy? You stay here with me."

I said, "I'm sorry," but I was looking at an Indian woman who was standing near him on his other side. As I intended, he thought I meant it for him. He snapped at me, "I told you to call me *Dad*."

"Yes, Dad," I answered. Inside I was mad enough to spit but I told myself, *Take it easy. Get him to relax.*

We eventually left the the Indian reservations behind and came to a small town called Cortez. We ate and went shopping. You can legally buy marijuana in Colorado and he bought some. He obviously expected me to be excited over the stuff but I just shrugged and said I'd seen it before. I wasn't going to tell him about the patch we found. Instead I said, "Grandma told me that in the past they used to grow it to make rope." Grandma told me about a couple of other things which also would produce a high if you were into that sort of thing.

I tried to pay attention to the roads we took to get to his cabin. They were mostly gravel and dirt and he was using the four-wheel drive. Once we almost rolled and he slowed down some. The cabin had clearly been built as a hunting cabin. It only had one room. There was a small wood-burning stove for heat which could also be used for cooking but I didn't see any wood anywhere. It had a two-burner table top affair for cooking which was attached to a small gas bottle with a spare bottle sitting beside it. There was a generator which he could not get to run. Water came from a stream and he said it wasn't safe to drink unless it was boiled or treated with some tablets he had which also made it taste terrible. It had no fridge. The beds were two sets of bunks.

I unloaded the supplies from the truck and put them away, checking inventory. He had a cooler and had bought bacon, eggs, and steaks. I wondered where he thought he would get ice out here. He had bought canned stuff, coffee, and sugar. I found a metal can with dried beans. Other cans had flour, sugar, salt, and cornmeal. I found baking powder. I saw signs of mice so I added the sugar we had brought to what was already in a can.

When I went out to the stream to get water, I discovered it was icy cold. I put a large pot to boil for drinking water and thought about using the creek to keep things cool.

Out some distance from the cabin was an outhouse. He complained about it not being closer and peed off the porch of the cabin. I was reminded of hillbilly jokes I had heard only I had never seen anyone actually do it. He said, "Why didn't they just build the shit-house over the creek?" I thought about telling him but decided he probably didn't want to know.

He started smoking pot while I was organizing supplies. I opened the doors and when I started on the windows, he yelled at me. I said, "I've had trouble with my ears and the doctor told me not to breath smoke." It actually was true but it was back when I was about 5.

He drifted off to sleep and I thought about trying to leave but he had the truck keys in his pocket and I didn't think I could walk all the way to town before morning. He also had his phone in a pocket but with no reception, it didn't matter. The cabin was cold but I slept in a reasonably clean sleeping bag. The next morning I heated water and took a bucket bath in a stall which had been build at one end of the back porch. It was great to put on clean clothes. I made coffee and cooked.

I spent all day cleaning the cabin. He grumbled about the generator not working but I found kerosene lamps and I knew how to use them. I asked if I could ride the trail bike but he said no. He smoked pot again and dozed off but when I tried to get into his pocket for the keys, he woke up. I had thought ahead and said, "Food's ready," like I had been trying to wake him up.

He razzed me about knowing how to cook but he ate what I fixed. At home, I normally didn't cook but Mom had said I needed to know how and it isn't that hard. People have been doing it since the Garden of Eden.

He was half drunk or high all the time and I looked for a chance at the keys. I had made up my mind. At my first opportunity, I was out of here.

On the second day we took the generator into Cortez and left it at a shop for repairs. He wanted more pot. After shopping, we went to a bar that did steaks. I could tell he had been here before. Again he tried to get me to drink beer but I evaded it. I said, "I read on the internet how research has shown that alcohol can cause problems when you're still growing. I'd like to get as tall as you." My guess that he would be flattered by my remark was right. He started talking again about playing football.

He said he was six foot two and he was a handsome man in spite of the signs of age around his eyes and month. I counted up and if he was a senior when Mom was a freshman, then he was only 33 or 34. I decided it was his lifestyle. He had mahogany colored hair, just like mine, and matching eyes, just like mine. Mom was blonde and blue-eyed. His build was stocky, like mine, and he was muscular but not really carrying much extra weight. He told me he worked out at a gym all the time and talked about it being a good place to pick up women. His face was my face twenty years down a rough road. I didn't like it and I didn't want to be named after him.

Two women were eyeing us and at first he didn't notice. Then they walked by our table and one of them brushed against him and giggled as she apologized. He watched them and asked me if I'd ever had a woman.

I knew I'd better be careful how I handled this or he'd have me in bed with one of them. I said, "Dad, I'm too young. And those two look a bit worn around the edges. I might get the pox."

I expected him to laugh but he said seriously, "That's true."

I kept looking for a chance to get away but he kept me right with him. I thought about making a scene and insisting someone call in the law but the paper stopped me. If he had legal custody, it would do no good.

We didn't leave the bar until they closed at 2 o'clock in the morning. I wanted to drive but he said no and we did make it back to the cabin. The next morning he didn't wake up when I got up. I checked but he still had all the keys in his pocket and he was sleeping in his clothes zipped up in a sleeping bag.

I had gotten a can of baking powder with a recipe on it for biscuits. The cabin had a Dutch oven and Grandpa had used one when we went camping so I got busy trying it.

When the food was ready, I tried again to get the keys but he woke up.

I sat down to eat and silently prayed before I started.

Jim

Job's disappearance had me frightened and Faith was totally devastated. After talking to Vernon Chilton and to the FBI, I took Faith home. She needed to be available in case of phone calls and Mrs. Voden should not be left alone. I put a recorder on her phone. The FBI was supposed to arrange a tracer.

At the sheriff's office, I saw the sheriff had believed us about Job not running off. I had asked Vern again if it was possible that our perp was connected to the marijuana growers. He told me, "Abe, I'll tell you so you quit worrying but don't tell anyone else this. Your two growers are women dressed as men. And they don't have anyone close to them who could be your perp. I am pretty sure they didn't hire anyone to do it either." No wonder Vern had laughed about ID'ing the growers.

Finally about 11 o'clock, Mrs. Voden had gone to bed and the house got quiet. Faith wanted to wait up for her dad to arrive. She decided to make hot chocolate. I sat down on the sofa to watch the late news and Cheshire appeared and climbed into my lap. The last of her spring litter of kittens had just been given away and she wanted cuddling. She was a good hunting cat and apparently in cats, it tends to be hereditary. Her kittens were carried away by greenhouse customers and neighbors. They had more than half a dozen other cats on the place, mostly Cheshire's off-spring, and their job was to keep the area free of mice, rats, squirrels, and snakes. Faith said all the other cats had been fixed so only Cheshire produced kittens. She was also the only one who came in the house.

Faith brought in the hot chocolate and some cookies and sat them on a TV tray in front of me and I turned off the TV. She sat down beside me and reached over and stroked Cheshire.

"I can't believe Job got into a truck with someone he didn't know. I was so sure someone would know who it was and I can't think of any reason why Job would go with anyone he didn't know well."

I knew she needed to talk. I said, "He's too old for the lost dog trick but what if someone said you had been hurt in an accident and taken to hospital and he had been sent to pick him up."

"But it would have had to be someone he knew and no one recognized the man or the truck."

"People do change vehicles and if they intended to abduct him, they would make sure the vehicle wasn't recognized. You can't think of any reason for anyone to abduct him?"

"No," she said. "Only if they thought I had the money for ransom. Maybe that's it. I could borrow money on this land. The last offer from that corporation was a million dollars."

"Who locally knows about that offer?"

"No one that I know of but it wasn't really a secret either. Dad did say he was not going to mention it to Mother or his sister."

I said, "Faith, can we pray together?" We held hands and she prayed and then I prayed. Somehow she ended up with her head on my shoulder. Then I realized she had fallen asleep. I put my arm around her and shifted a little to get more comfortable and she snuggled up to me.

I looked down at her blonde head and knew I'd do anything in the world for her. If I had any idea at all who had taken Job, I'd go after him with no hesitation. If it meant risking my own life to get her son back for her, I'd do it. And after Afghanistan, I did know what that meant.

The true nature of my feelings for Faith hit me like the light that blinded Saul on the road to Damascus. My heart almost stopped. *I loved Faith!*

I had carefully blocked my mind from even considering loving Faith but my heart had done its own thing. I knew there was no doubt about what I felt. In the days I had spent here at Indian Cave Farm, I had come to know Faith, not just her fears and anxieties, but her courage, her determination, her resiliency. It was not her physical beauty I saw but the splendid nature of her character. I saw the woman who as a teenager with her life in shreds, had looked to God in her distress and accepted an unwanted baby, loving him, nurturing him, letting her life revolve around the child who needed her. I saw her as a hero more brave than any I had ever known.

What I felt for her went down to the deepest core of my being. I had strongly resisted acknowledging, even in my most private thoughts, the feelings which had been growing in my heart for Faith. Only in this moment, when she slept in my arms, demonstrating the trust she had in me, could I allow myself to see myself clearly. She was a woman who had been been abused in the worst possible way a man could abuse a woman and she did not trust men easily. But she trusted me. The wonder of that filled my mind and soul.

She was exhausted and now she took rest in my arms.

I would give Faith, not only my heart, but my life. I thought about her son, Job, and knew I would do anything to find him.

Not wanting to disturb Faith, I was still and in that quiet, I also dozed off and that's how Nathan found us when he arrived. He had keys and slipped in quietly, thinking everyone might be asleep.

I woke up when he said, "Faith?" When he saw I was awake, he said, "Sorry. Am I interrupting something?"

"No," I told him. "We were praying and she fell asleep. I decided to let her sleep and then I fell asleep too. It isn't what it looks like."

"Yeah," he said. "I see Cheshire curled up in the middle of it."

The talking had awakened Faith and she exclaimed, "Dad!" and sprang up and into his arms. She said, "It's so awful. Who would take Job?"

She was crying again and we went back over all the same ground again with Nathan. He said he had not told anyone about the million dollar offer for the place but he said, "It wouldn't be too hard to figure it out. Unimproved land in this area is often a thousand dollars an acre or more. Part of the main place was never logged over so the timber is worth a lot. Then there's the house and barn and greenhouse plus the cave."

"Yes," I told him. "It's a real possibility but with kidnappings for ransom, the parents are normally contacted immediately and told not to call in the police. There have been no calls. We have put a tracer on the line hoping there would be. The fact there hasn't been makes the kidnapping for ransom unlikely."

Faith eventually went up to bed, taking Cheshire with her which I had never seen her do before. I wanted to talk to Nathan and I had the idea he also wanted to talk.

As soon as Faith was up the stairs, he headed for the kitchen and said, "Let's keep our voices down."

Sonny Sells had been a rookie cop when Faith was kidnapped. He had not worked the case but had heard all the talk. He told Nathan that immediately after Faith was found, rumors were going around saying she had faked the kidnapping. The story was that with her parents gone to a party, she also went to one. The rumors said she had been sleeping around for months, mostly with the football team members but also with others. That night she got so drunk, she stayed out all night and was afraid to go home. She supposedly hid in that cabin and had boys coming and going, bringing her food, alcohol, maybe drugs, and having sex with her. Then she arranged to be found handcuffed to the bed naked and told the rape story.

Nathan said to me, "It isn't true. I know it isn't true." Then after long pause, he repeated, "I know it isn't true." I thought he was protesting too much and had not called me all week because of his own doubts.

"It isn't true," I assured him.

Nathan said, "You're sure?"

"Yes," I told him. "When she told me what happened this time, I knew she'd had a similar experience before. When she heard someone in the house, she ran immediately without going to look. Only people who have been victimized in the past do that. And her reaction to the incident showed serious prior trauma."

"Damnation!" Nathan said. "Whoever it was who kidnapped and raped her then was someone in the community. He started that story so the police would not do a thorough investigation."

I nodded. "Someone in her social circle and someone with a conduit to get that rumor heard by the police quickly."

Nathan said, "I always thought it was just a random stranger, maybe a burglar who thought the house was empty and then when he found her there, he took her."

"No," I told him. "She told me he had a cloth with something like chloroform and he held her down until she passed out. It was planned. Her kidnapper knew she would be there alone and he planned ahead."

Nathan shook his head. "I never knew about the chloroform. It was someone who knew us!"

"Yes," I said.

I had other thoughts I did not share with Nathan. He was already under enough stress. The kidnapper had waited until Faith woke up before he raped her. He was someone who enjoyed subduing and humiliating his victims. He was not a drunk wanting sex. He was an out-and-out sadistic pervert.

He also had been someone who knew Faith but he had gotten

away with it. Why would he come back years later and kidnap her son? Was he someone so obsessed with her that he wanted her and her son? If he was obsessed enough to come after her this many years later, why had he waited so long?

Or was my gut-level conclusion wrong? Was it all totally unconnected?

But if it was the marijuana growers, they too would have called right away and made their threats. Why would anyone take the boy if they didn't want ransom or compliance on their marijuana growing?

The only answer I could think of was a mental case who kidnapped, tortured, and killed teenage boys. That type of murderer usually went for younger boys but with mental cases, anything was possible.

~ Chapter 7: The Girl ~

Job

If you use a Dutch oven on a campfire, you pile live coals on top too but you can't do that with a gas stove so I just heated the lid. My biscuits didn't get brown on top but they were okay to eat. I fried bacon and made gravy. I decided he was less unpleasant when he was well fed. I cleaned up and wondered what to do. He was smoking pot again and griping about the cabin being cold because of the open doors and windows. I was bored.

I started to go outside and he yelled at me to get back in the cabin. I asked him what I was supposed to do with my time. He decided we'd go hunting. I asked about a hunting license and he said it didn't matter. I decided that getting the attention of the authorities of any kind might work to my advantage.

He asked me about going hunting in the past and I told him Grandpa had always come during deer season and we'd hunt. He asked what was the biggest buck I ever got and I said big bucks were tough and not good eating. Young ones were tastier. He clearly thought hunting was for bragging, not eating.

In the tool box in the back of his truck he had two rifles. If he let me have a rifle, could I use it to get away? But I figured that if he let me have a gun, he'd have one handy too.

We went into the San Juan National Forest. We never saw anything to hunt and he got lost. He refused to stop and ask directions from anyone and it was midnight when we got back to our cabin. He put the rifles behind the seat in the pickup and locked the doors.

The next morning when I woke up, he was still asleep. Again, he was in the sleeping bag and I knew I could not get to the keys in his pocket without waking him up. I considered just starting to walk but not only was it miles to town, but when I had gotten into that truck with him, I had exactly one dollar and seventy-seven cents on me. I could call my mother and she'd come but with that court order, she could not take me home.

Then he woke up because he had to pee. He was in a foul mood. I had made biscuits again and did steaks hoping food would improve his mood but he cussed at me for getting the steaks too done. His was pink in the middle but he wanted it bloody.

Finally he said, "I know what we need." He never said what but we got into the truck and headed to town and I thought we were going after the generator and more pot. He was drinking beer and tossing the cans out the window. Maybe he'd keep doing it when we got close to town and we'd get stopped.

He started talking about women, bragging about how many he'd had and how they all were always coming on to him. I just let him ramble on and said as little as possible.

In town, he gassed up. It was like he could sense my desire to run and he kept me right with him. It was too early for his bar and we took off south, toward the Indian reservations and New Mexico. He said, "There's a casino down on the Ute Rez. There's always plenty of action at a casino."

I thought maybe if he got busy gambling, I'd get a chance to get away. But when we got to the casino, they wouldn't let him in because he had caused trouble in the past. He was really mad but they had armed guards. He said, "We'll go to Gallup. Always something going on there."

He was talking about woman again and I was only half listening when he said, "Virgins are the best. No chance of getting the pox and if they're really a virgin, they bleed." I was disgusted.

Then he said, "Your mother was the sweetest fuck I ever had, those big boobs and the blood – and she always tried to fight. She was really sweet."

I froze. *He had raped my mother!*

My mind raced, sorting out what he had just said. All that he told me earlier about Mom sleeping around was a lie. He had raped her and she had been a virgin and he had raped her more than once.

My stomach rolled over like I was going to vomit. I thought, *He's a sick, perverted puddle of puke who needs to be sent to the deepest level of Hell!*

I decided right then that at my first chance, I was running. Even if I had to walk three days to get to town, I was leaving.

Maybe I could sabotage the truck and the trail bike so he couldn't follow me. Maybe I could figure out how to hotwire the bike. I could even legally drive it.

Traffic was light which was good, considering his driving. Then we saw an Indian girl leading a horse along beside the road. The horse was lame. We passed her and then he did a U-turn.

I couldn't figure out why he was stopping. We couldn't help her with a lame horse. He got out and reached under the seat for the handgun. He also pulled out a pair of handcuffs. I watched in horrified disbelief as he handcuffed the girl, then tied her feet together with the rope she had been using to lead the horse, and put her in the tool box in the back of his truck.

While he was doing this, I thought about trying to run but I couldn't leave that girl alone with him. *She was just a kid, maybe 12 or 13. Surely he didn't plan to rape her!*

Somewhere down in my tortured guts, I knew he did.

The horse had moved off to the side of the road to graze. Three vehicles went by while all this was going on. I watched, planning to signal for help, but the people paid no attention to us.

When he got back into the truck, I was too scared to say anything at first. We headed back toward Cortez. I finally forced myself ask, "What are you going to do with her?"

"She's for you, son. Your first woman."

He said it like she was some kind of fancy present that I was sure to be avidly pleased over.

"She's too young," I protested. "She's just a kid."

"No she's not. She's got boobs," he said. "I checked."

My mind scrambled around trying to think of something but I was so appalled and sickened, it was hard to think. He had put the rifles behind the seat but he had the handgun in the waistband of his pants. I couldn't think of any way to get it.

We traveled all the way back to the cabin in total silence. When we arrived, he unlocked the toolbox and put the keys back in his pocket. I wanted those keys.

He made me help him get her out and he cut the rope on her feet. When she tried to get up, she fell and he jerked her roughly to her feet. I reached out and said, "I'll help her. You said she was mine. I'll hold her."

He leered. "Can't wait to get your hands on her, can you?"

I put my arm around the girl, turning my face away because I was afraid he would see the utter contempt and distaste I felt. She said, "Please, I need to use the bathroom."

I walked her to the outhouse and hoped for a chance to talk to her but he trailed along. He said, "She's pretty. When you've had your fun with her, I think I'll have her."

I said, "Dad, she'll tell everyone."

He said, "No she won't. If they've seen your face, then don't leave them where they can be found."

I thought about what he had just said and a chill ran through me. *He did not intend for the girl to leave here alive!*

The girl stayed in the outhouse until he dragged her out. He was marching her to the cabin and I ended up behind him. I saw he had stuck his handgun in the back of his waistband and with the idea that I might not get another chance, I grabbed the gun. It had a safety but it was like the one Jim Willis had and he had taught me how it worked. I undid the safety while he shoved the girl so that she fell and he started to turn. Jim Willis had told me the best way to take out a perp without killing him was to shoot him in the leg. The lower leg was best, debilitating but fatal only if you hit the artery – in which case, you made a tourniquet. As he turned, I aimed and fired.

He fell and was screaming at me, mostly cussing, and I moved around him, still holding the gun. The girl had gotten up and took off running toward the cabin. I backed up slowly watching him. He was screaming that he was going to bleed to death. I could see he was bleeding but it was not squirting. I said, "Put pressure on the wound. Use your T-shirt for a bandage."

He was calling for me to come help him but I turned away. He was not that bad and I knew better than to get near him again. To my surprise the girl was waiting for me by the cabin. "You shot him," she said.

I said, "Yes, he wanted me to rape you and he planned to rape you himself. Eventually he would have killed you."

She muttered something which wasn't in English and I said, "What?"

She was looking as scared and shocked as I felt. She said, "He's an evil man."

I nodded and said, "We need to leave. He isn't hurt all that bad and he has all the keys in his pocket. If I try to get them, he'll get me. We're going to have to walk. We'll find a phone somewhere and you can call your family to come get you."

The cabin had some tools and I broke the handcuffs he had put on the girl. I emptied my backpack of the school supplies and gym clothes which I had been carrying home last Thursday. This was Wednesday. I had been with him six days; it felt like at least a month.

I made a pile of nuts, trail mix, other snacks, and got a gallon of water. I told the girl, "It's miles into town, a long walk, and I didn't really see any houses."

She said, "I can carry food and water too." She took a pillow case and got another gallon of water and was looking at our food stores.

I said, "I'll carry the water in my backpack. It's heavy. You carry the food." We packed quickly and she also took a blanket and folded it over her shoulder.

We were ready in just a few minutes. I looked out to check on him and he was dragging himself along and was almost to the cabin. I said to the girl, "Run!"

She said, "The gun!"

I had left it on the table. I grabbed it and we took off. But as we ran, I thought about what I had just seen. Dylan Robinson had used his shirt for a bandage and I had seen a lot of stitches on his right arm. Lassie had gotten him good.

Once we were out of sight of the cabin, I said, "We need to listen. He can still drive and he'll take himself to a doctor. We need to make sure he doesn't see us. He has two rifles."

I didn't know the time but I knew it was now the middle of the afternoon. I started watching the side of the road for potential hiding places.

When the girl asked me who that man was, I realized we had not even traded names. I told her, "His name is Dylan Robert Robinson. Can you remember that and tell the police?"

She said, "You can tell them."

I said, "I don't want to talk to the police. That man is my father. He went to court and got custody of me. I don't want to live with him. I want to go back to my mother. But he has a paper saying I have to live with him. If you tell the police about him kidnapping you, then maybe my mother can get custody of me again."

She said, "Tell me his name again." I did and she repeated it several times. Then she asked, "What is your name?"

"Job," I told her, then said, "Job Johnson."

"Job Johnson," she said. "That's a good name. I am called Kai."

I said, "Kye. That's easy to remember."

She giggled. "It's not Kye. It's Kah-ee but you say it fast. We spell it k-a-i."

"Oh," I said. I worked on it until she said I had it right. I asked, "Kai, how old are you?"

"14," she said. "How old are you?"

"15," I told her.

She said, "How can you be only 15? You are big."

I said, "Yeah. I'll probably get as tall as him." I was not going to call him *Dad*. I didn't even want to say *my father*. But she knew who I meant.

She said, "I'm Navajo. Among the Navajo, children belong to the clan of their mother. Traditionally when a man and woman married, they lived with her family. So in the Navajo system, you belong to your mother and her family."

I smiled. "I like that idea. My mother and I lived with her father's mother but she died this spring. My mother's father comes and takes me camping and fishing and hunting."

She nodded. "He's a good grandfather. Why did the court give your father a paper saying you had to live with him?"

"He says they sent papers to my mother telling her he was asking for custody but she never gave an answer and she didn't go talk to the judge so the judge said I had to go live with him. But now I'm wondering. I have only been with him since last Thursday but I know he's a liar and he kidnapped you so we could rape you. From something he said I am sure he also meant to kill you. Like you said, he's an evil man."

We heard the truck coming and we found a place to hide. When it got dark, we kept walking but eventually I told Kai, "It's so dark, I'm afraid I'm going to get lost. I think we are going to have to wait for morning."

We found a sheltered place out of the wind. With no sun, the night had gotten quite cold. She said, "I will share the blanket with you but you must never tell anyone."

I said, "At home we have a cat who comes and sleeps with me

sometimes. Her name is Cheshire. I'll pretend you're Cheshire."

She laughed. I was so tired, I was asleep almost immediately. It was dawn when she woke me up and I went off to do necessary business. When I came back, she was singing. Somehow I felt like it was some kind of prayer but it wasn't in English.

I decided praying was a good idea and so while she sang, I prayed. When she was finished, she asked, "Why do you sit with your eyes closed?"

I said, "I was praying."

She nodded and said, "That's good." Then she said, "You will remember not to say we shared a blanket?"

"Yes," I told her.

She said, "Among my people *sharing a blanket* means something else."

I said, "Yeah, I understand. Our phrase is *sleeping together* and if I said we shared a blanket, they would ask what else happened."

We ate and started walking. Then we heard a vehicle coming from the town direction. We hid and watched it go by. It was a sheriff's vehicle with two deputies in it, one female.

Kai said, "Why did you not ask for help?"

I said, "Kai, when we find a phone, I'll leave you. I'm going to try to get back to my mother's house."

She said, "Won't the police help you go home?"

"I'm afraid not. That man is a good liar and he actually works as a policeman. If I were you, I would wait until your family got there to tell the police about him kidnapping you and intending to rape you. He will have already told the police some big lie. They may not believe you or me. We're kids and he works as a policeman."

She nodded. "Not all policemen are good."

We walked on for some minutes and then she said, "We will go to my family. They will help us. They will know what to do."

Then I found out we could not phone her family. They had no phone. She said, "If we are walking and any of my people see us, they will stop and help us."

Every time we heard a vehicle, we hid and watched but only a few vehicles went by and none of the drivers looked Indian. It took us all day to reach Cortez. It was getting dark which I thought was good. We skirted around the town and found the road south. We walked a while but then we were both tired and hiding every time a car passed was a pain. In the dark, we couldn't see the vehicles so we didn't dare try to hitchhike. We shared the blanket again although it was not as cold as last night.

The next morning, Kai said, "If anyone asks, you can say you're my cousin. You have dark hair and dark eyes. Other Indians will know you're lying but white people wouldn't know. Maybe we can get a ride."

I said, "We can try. I'll only signal pickup trucks and we'll only agree to ride in the back. I still have the handgun."

We were lucky right away when an old man stopped and we rode in the back of his pickup for a while but he came to a gate and turned and stopped. We got out and thanked him. He said to Kai, "Girl, you ain't running off with this boy, are you?"

"No," she told him. "He's my cousin." The old man nodded so he must have believed her.

Then we walked for nearly an hour with me putting out my thumb when it was a pickup truck. But when one finally stopped, the man looked Indian and Kai immediately started talking to him in their language. She said, "This is good. He will take us to the casino and my uncle works there. It's where I was going when . . . when it happened."

We got in the cab and on the way, Kai told me everyone was looking for her. Her horse had been found but not her and her picture was all over the news and the information had been put out on the Navajo radio.

When we got to the casino, Kai's uncle was not working that day and the young man said he would take us to Kai's family. A guard at the casino let us use the restrooms and Kai told me, "I didn't tell Jessie that the kidnapper was your father, only that he was a policeman, so we wanted to be safe with my family before we talked about what happened. I told him you rescued me and you also were afraid of that policeman and you thought he would tell lies and everyone would believe him because he was a policeman."

I found out why Kai had been unfazed by the long hike from the cabin to Cortez. The road back to where her family lived was worse but Jessie also seemed untroubled by it. Once there, we were given food right away, beans cooked with some meat, along with what they called fry-bread and it was delicious. I saw two men and five woman. The kids kept ducking in and out so I never got a count but I saw a baby and a toddler plus at least four more.

Kai had gotten a small notebook and a pen. She had me write my father's name. I added "age about 33 or 34, policeman, St. Louis, Missouri" and I also told her, "He's raped other women before. I know from some things he said."

I was leaving with Jessie, riding with him back out to the main road. I was going to try to hitchhike home. I asked Kai for her address and told her I would write and tell her what happened.

Jim

All week we checked everything with the vaguest resemblance to a lead and got nothing. Faith looked haunted and I felt her pain. With her father here to protect her, I had suggested going back to my family at Ellington but it was Thursday before she and Nathan agreed to my going. She was so distraught that twice she clung to me just like she did her father with nothing sexual about it. She was simply so absorbed in her fears for Job that she didn't realize what she was doing. These were bittersweet moments for me. I felt her distress and anxieties over Job but savored knowing that she trusted me enough to let me hold her. I was someone she had confidence in, just as she did her father. I knew I loved her fiercely. I was like one of the knights in the King Arthur tales. I was hers to command.

Our marijuana growers were being checked out thoroughly. They were from the next county and it was a small, local operation. Law enforcement wanted to watch them long enough to locate any other patches they might have and identify their buyers. But it seemed they had gotten into the business because of a family member who was using marijuana for medical purposes and so far, it seemed that their business was more in the nature of supplying a herbal remedy than a dope operation.

By Friday, Faith was keeping the greenhouse closed. She wasn't sleeping properly at night and was reading on the internet about kidnappings.

On Saturday morning, a week and two days after Job's disappearance, we had a conference. It was Sheriff Conners, myself, Faith's father, the State Trooper Vernon Chilton, a West

Plains FBI agent named Jason Elfrink, and Sonny Sells from the Pine Bluff police department. He had rang yesterday evening and I had him call the FBI agent. We met at the Twin Pines Conservation Center just east of Winona. It was convenient and the FBI agent had arranged a conference room.

It was a little hard getting started because all of us with experience knew this was no ordinary kidnapping. When a 15-year-old boy disappears and doesn't resurface in over a week, then he either ran off or is probably dead. I knew he hadn't run off. I also knew I did not want to accept the alternative. And I knew his grandfather, Nathan Johnson, couldn't even consider it.

Jason Elfrink took charge. He said, "I asked Officer Sells from the Pine Bluff police to come after I talked to him last night. He's on his own time so I really appreciate his participation. Sheriff Conners, I'm going to fill you in on some background we want kept confidential. You were not told earlier because we thought it had no connection but with the boy not resurfacing and the elimination of other leads, we're taking another look."

The sheriff looked surprised. Elfrink began, "Faith Johnson was kidnapped when she was 14 years old. The kidnapper held her for four days and raped her repeatedly. She was found by a Real Estate agent with a dead cell phone who had taken a wrong turn. Her kidnapper was never caught and her son, Job, is the result of that incident."

He paused. Nathan Johnson was looking down and I knew it was hard for him to even hear this talked about. The sheriff looked shocked. Vern Chilton had his professional face on but I knew he was feeling that kind of cold anger which law officers develop after a while when they hear about the depraved behavior of the criminals whom they hunt and the savage pain they inflict on their victims. The Pine Bluff officer looked both angry and surprised. He knew about the kidnapping and rape and Job's kidnapping but had not known Job was the result of the rape.

Elfrink went on, "All of you know about the masked man who broke into Faith Johnson's house and chased her down to the creek. What was noticed right at the beginning was the fact that the perp's mode of operation was the same as the kidnapper from the incident when she was 14. He broke in the house when he knew Faith was alone. He was wearing both a ski mask and gloves."

Elfrink paused and Sheriff Conners asked, "I assumed you've had a look at the original suspect list."

He nodded. "That's where Officer Sells comes into this. He was a rookie when the incident occurred and was not one of the officers who worked the case but he heard all about it. When the incident happened, immediately after Faith's rescue rumors were all over town saying she had faked the kidnapping. The story went that she had been sleeping around and with her parents gone to a party, she had gone out and gotten so drunk, she stayed out all night. She was afraid to go home and had faked the whole kidnapping story. Because of this rumor, the police never did a thorough investigation of the incident. The rape kit was never processed and now cannot be found. The file on the case contains almost nothing. Even the doctor's report is missing."

Sheriff Conners said, "Somebody covered up!"

I nodded and said, "No one at Pine Bluff PD wanted to talk about it and Vern Chilton had to insist before he got a copy of the file. I was just looking for background and thought we might have another look at the suspect list. Vern had such a hard time getting the file and when it was so sparse, it stirred our interest. So I asked Nathan if he knew anyone in the Pine Bluff police department to ask. That's where Officer Sells came into the picture."

Sonny Sells said, "After I talked to Nathan, I decided I'd just do a little checking around. The woman who found Faith is now dead. I tried getting records from the hospital but they have moved to a new facility and said they'd look but I've gotten no answer. The lead investigator on the case is also dead. The girl was interviewed at the hospital by Clayton Smith who hadn't been on the force much longer than me at the time and he's still with us. He told me it was his first rape interview and he remembers it clearly. He says they had let the girl take a shower and get dressed before he talked to her. He says that during the interview, he had no doubts about her telling the truth. He said she was so scared, they had an older nurse sit with her while she talked to him.

"He says he also interviewed the woman who found her. He told me the woman was sure that what the girl said was true. She described the scene and was graphic about the state she found the girl in. Clayton told me that even now, he was sure the woman was sure that what the girl said was true.

"He said the very next day, the rumors were already going around and the case was turned over to an older cop. He says that as a young cop, he got some razzing for not realizing the girl was lying. I asked him what he thought now and he said he still had doubts and why was I asking about it?"

Sonny looked around at us and said, "Nathan gave me a list of Faith's friends from back then and I started making phone calls."

He paused and was already shaking his head. "Her best friend then was Betty Richardson. She lives in Arnold now so I phoned her. She immediately gave me an earful. She said all those rumors about Faith sleeping around were a lie and Faith did not fake the kidnapping. She asked me if I knew where Faith was now. She said Faith had told her she was going to stay with her grandmother because her grandfather was dying of cancer. She said when school started again, she found out Faith's parents had moved to Fredericktown and she's never heard from Faith since."

He looked around the group and I did too. They looked like a good bird dog with his nose pointing out the birds, all except Nathan who was nodding.

Sells went on, "So with that, I was off and running. Next I tracked down Mike Edwards who was the boy Faith had gone to her end-of-the-year freshman class party with. He's a truck driver now living over at Dexter. When I got him on the phone, he asked why I was asking questions all these years later. I said maybe we had another incident that tied in. He said nobody believed Faith back then and were they changing their minds? I said maybe and he asked to meet me and talk to me personally.

"We met at a restaurant yesterday evening and he said immediately that all those stories about Faith sleeping around and faking the kidnapping incident were hogwash. He then said that with her 'developing early' – that was his phrase – all the older boys at school were after her. He said she hated it. He said Faith and her mother were always arguing over her clothes. She wanted to wear things that covered up and her mother wanted her to wear things that showed off her 'assets,' as her mother put it."

I looked at Nathan. He looked pained. Sells had stopped talking and Nathan said, "It was true. Her mother even wanted her to enter some beauty pageant and Faith adamantly refused. What Faith wore became such a point of contention that she started buying clothes at thrift stores and leaving in the morning wearing something her mother insisted on and then changing as soon as she got to school. She rode to school with me and went home with me so I helped her out with it."

Sells looked at Nathan and said, "You and your daughter were close?" His inflection made it a question.

Nathan said, "Yes. Her mother is not an affectionate sort of person." He paused and then said, "Right now we are in the process of a divorce."

Sells said, "Mike Edwards said Faith was much closer to you than to her mother. He also said you were a good teacher." He paused and then said, "I asked him who he thought might have kidnapped Faith and then started all those stories. He immediately said the football team. I asked him why and he said the team that year were mostly seniors and they had a championship year. He said they had all been after Faith and only the fact that her father was teaching in the school had kept a damper on them harassing her. He said several of the boys beat him up after he took her to their class party.

"I asked him for names and he gave them." He paused again and then said, "Mike Edwards rated three guys as most likely and then five more whom he said if they didn't help do it, they might know about it. As soon as I left the restaurant yesterday evening, I called Jim. I think we need to talk to those football team members."

Sells looked at me and said, "I have also been asking people who were around at the time of the incident where they heard the 'she faked it' story. I got a lot of 'I don't remember. Everyone was talking about it.' I also got a lot people who said, 'I didn't really believe it.' The people who did remember named two main sources. One was the football team members or someone who said they heard from a football team member. The other was the police department, which I found very interesting. When I started trying to track that, I was immediately pointed to Bob Robinson who is now the head of our drug enforcement. I asked him about it and he told me that when the incident happened, his son had told him about the girl being at a party that night and having sex with at least one boy before she left with a couple of older guys whom his son didn't know. He said he'd heard them talking about a hunting cabin."

Sells again stopped and then said, "Bob Robinson's son was on the football team, the leading star that year. He went to the police academy and joined the police force. He got married and then he and his wife divorced. About that same time was an incident in which some black woman he stopped for a traffic violation claimed her raped her. The woman didn't have a good reputation and the case was thrown out of court but young Robinson got a job with the St. Louis police department and left town."

Sells looked around at the group and said, "I think we need to check on those football team members and I think we should especially take a look at Dylan Robinson."

After a pause while everyone was thinking, Jason Elfrink said, "It seems so unlikely that a perpetrator who got away with his crime would come back and victimize the same person years later by kidnapping her son but I think we should look into it. You said the rape kit disappeared? What if the perp is afraid someone will run DNA tests on the son and prove he was the rapist?"

Sheriff Conners nodded. "That makes sense." Then he added, shaking his head, "There's men out that ought to be castrated."

✤ Chapter 8: The Journey Home ✤

Job

Jessie was helpful. He took me to a trading post and waited until someone came along going to Gallup. It was a young Navajo woman in a white sedan. Jessie warned me, "Don't tell her what happened. She's a lawyer and she'll think she has to do something."

I normally don't tell lies but when the woman asked why I needed a ride, I said my truck had broke down and I lived in Gallup. I noticed she was breaking the speed limit most of the time but she was a good driver and slowed down when she needed to and passed other vehicles carefully. I relaxed and dosed off.

As we approached Gallup, she asked me where I wanted out and I asked if she could drop me at Walmart. I remembered it was right on Interstate 40. When she asked why Walmart, I said my uncle worked there. I felt uncomfortable. I don't like lying.

Kai had given me a smaller water bottle, a half gallon milk jug. She had also added food. She folded the blanket and tied it to my backpack. She gave me nine carefully folded one dollar bills, saying, "You're going on a long journey and you'll need food." I suspected it was all the money she had.

I went into Walmart and I knew the woman who had given me a ride was watching me. I asked the door greeter to hold my backpack for me and I went to the restroom and then drank water. When I was leaving, I checked to make sure the woman was gone before I went out. I think she thought I was lying and was suspicious.

As I started for Interstate 40, I was praying. Hitchhiking is dangerous. But before I got to the end of the on-ramp a pickup truck stopped. It was an Indian family. The cab was full with three people already in the back and I joined them. I found out they had stopped because they thought I was Indian. They thought I was Indian because of the way Kai had tied the blanket to my backpack. Also they told me white people all had cars and didn't walk anywhere.

They only took me down the road about 30 miles to the turn off for Fort Wingate but as I climbed out of their pickup, another one stopped. It was another Indian family with one teenage boy in the back. They also expected me to be Indian. They said they were from Laguna Pueblo and I could ride that far. I joined the teenager in the back. It was evening when we arrived. They asked me where I was going. I said, "Missouri."

The mother said, "That's a long way. Now it's almost night. You come sleep with our family and go on in the morning."

So I spent the night on a sofa in a small house but I saw the pueblo. They told me less people lived in it now than in the past but they maintained it. They said, "It's where we hold all our festivals."

They gave me food, beans again but with more spices, rather like chili. It was good. When they asked, I told them something closer to the truth than the broken down truck story. I said, "My parents are not married and I have always lived with my mother but my father wanted me to go to Colorado with him and I went. He spends most of his time drinking beer and smoking pot so I left."

They told me in their tribe also the children belong to their mother's clan. They said, "The mother's brothers are responsible for teaching boys." I told them my mother was an only child but her father had taught me a lot. They nodded. "Grandparents are important," they said.

The next morning, they insisted I eat before I left and they took me out to Interstate 40. Again I got a ride immediately. It was an older couple in a big car and I had not been signaling but they told me to get in the back. They had seen me dropped off and asked where I was going. I said, "Missouri," and found out they were on their way to Louisville, Kentucky.

Then I found out they thought I was Indian. I considered not telling them otherwise but decided it might get awkward if I didn't so I did. They asked how come I was staying with the Indians and I told them, "They picked me up yesterday. They thought I was Indian because they think all white people have cars and never walk anywhere."

When they asked why I was hitchhiking, I told them what I had told the Indians. They said, "Can't you call your mother and she can get you a bus ticket?"

I squirmed and said, "She doesn't have much money and the bus doesn't go where we live. I think West Plains is the closest and she would have to go down there to arrange it and then again to pick me up. It would cause her a lot of trouble. It's better if I just hitchhike."

They introduced themselves as Hank and Agnes Butterfield and asked me my name. I knew Dylan Robinson might have told some story about me shooting him which might have the police looking for me. I had settled on "Joe." Not only was it close enough to Job that I would hear it and my middle name is Joseph but also the children's books which Mom had published were called the Joey Johnson Series and her pen name was Joey Johnson. Mrs. Butterfield asked, "Joe what?" and I said, "Joe Willis." I had not thought it through but I thought to myself, *If I can't be Johnson, then I'd like to be Willis.*

Then she asked me where I was from and I said, "We live out in the country between Eminence and Ellington, Missouri."

They had an atlas and she looked it up. She said, "Hank, it's near Ozark National Scenic Riverways." She told me, "When we went out to our daughter's, we went via St. Louis but on the way home, I want to stop in Paducah, Kentucky to see their quilt museum. Since we will go right through the Riverways, we had decided we would see it too."

I said, "If I get to Winona, my mother can easily come get me."

So I traveled with the Butterfields for two days. When they stopped for gas in Albuquerque, I saw a store and asked if they minded if I took a minute to buy some underwear. I think they had noticed how dirty my clothes were because Mrs. Butterfield asked if I had any other clothes. I had to tell her no. The store had cheap clothes but I was afraid to spend more money. When they stopped for food, I told them I had food in my backpack and I did.

That night they stopped at Eric, Oklahoma. We talked and they were willing to let me ride all the way to Winona but I had no money for motel rooms. I suggested I sleep in their car. It was a big car with a comfortable back seat. I said, "If you have the keys, I can't run off with it."

Mrs. Butterfield laughed and said, "I think you're a nice boy who wouldn't run off with anything." But she talked to the motel people and they provided a cot. When I asked what it cost, Mrs. Butterfield said, "Very little. Apparently they often cater to families."

I took a shower and it was wonderful. After all the walking and sleeping outside for two nights, I was dirty. Mrs. Butterfield said, "I think you and Hank are close enough to the same size that you can wear a set of his pajamas. This motel has a laundry room." She insisted on taking my clothes and washing them. She asked me how they got so dirty and I told her my father's cabin had no washer and I had walked a lot.

I slept in Hank's pajamas and put my own clothes back on in the morning, clean, and we continued our journey. During the afternoon, Hank asked me if I had a driver's license. I said, "Not exactly. We live way out in the country. I have a permit. I ride a scooter to school and I drive our farm stuff locally."

Mrs. Butterfield asked, "How old are you?"

I had not thought things through. I had to confess, "15."

"You look older," she said.

I said, "Yeah, I know. Sometimes it's helpful but sometimes it's not. I shouldn't really be traveling on my own but I look old enough so no one has asked."

"But you told me the truth," she said. "I think basically you're a good kid."

Hank was sleepy but Mrs. Butterfield said she could drive for a while. He got in the back seat to sleep and I sat up front with Mrs. Butterfield. She never went over 60 miles per hour and mostly drove 55. I saw she was tense and I asked if she would like for me to read road signs for her. She said "Yes," and then she asked, "Am I driving too slow?"

We were on the turnpike between Oklahoma City and Tulsa. The posted speed limit was 75 and the traffic was whizzing past us like bullets in one of those war movies. Occasionally someone hit their horn and Mrs. Butterfield would speed up to 60. I said, "That's better than driving too fast. My father's driving scared me stiff. He not only drove too fast but he was drinking beer all day too."

"You ran away," she said. "That's why you have no clothes."

"Yes," I said. "When I got the chance, there was no time to grab clothes."

"Will he have reported you as a run-away?"

"Maybe," I told her, "but when I get home and tell them how it was, it'll be okay." I hoped so. Shooting someone was serious. I needed to talk to Jim Willis.

She said, "What's your family like?" She had made herself a coke and was sipping on it as she drove. Maybe she too was sleepy and wanted to talk to keep awake.

I said, "My mother and I lived with her grandmother but she died at the end of March this year. We have a greenhouse and my mother also edits manuscripts to earn money. She does that over the internet. She has also published some children's books. I help with the greenhouse and also this year I'm trying farming. We have a 30 acre field and Mom's father knows about farming. He teaches school somewhere else but he can come on the weekends and show me things."

"Why did you go with your father?"

I was stuck. I didn't know what to say. Finally I said, "He said I had to, but when I get back home and tell them about him, they won't make me go back."

"Didn't your mother object?"

"He didn't give her a chance to object. He just picked me up from school and said I had to go with him."

"You're 15. It may not be the same in Missouri as in Kentucky but at your age, you should be able to chose which parent you live with."

I nodded. "That's what I'm thinking."

Then she said, "We had a grandson named Joseph. We called him Joey. He died when he was 8 from leukemia."

I said, "That's very sad." And I knew why the couple had taken to me so quickly. I felt bad for lying about my name. I asked, "Do you have any other grandchildren?"

"Seven," she said. "The oldest is our Jenifer. She's 16. Then Amelia's 14 and Johnny's 12. They belong to our daughter who lives near us. Joey belonged to our son and he and his wife have Maddy now who's 4 and Emma who's just 1. They live near Lexington so we see them often. Our other daughter lives in California. She has Jason who's 12 and Jaylyn who's 10. We've been out to see them."

I started to ask if they had a good time but something in her voice made me suspect it might not have been. Instead I asked, "What's California like?"

"Hot," she said. "Our daughter lives in Bakersfield which is north of Los Angeles in the San Fernando Valley. Outside the town are farms and orange orchards. Our daughter works for a furniture store. It seems like a good job. We had planned to stay until school was out and bring the grandchildren home with us for the summer but they had their summer planned already, summer school and camp and things like that. We did go up to Sequoia National Park on a Saturday. It was lovely but the kids had been before and they were bored."

"Sequoia is where they have the big trees, isn't it?

"Yes," she said, "the redwoods. They're huge. I was amazed."

"We have a set of DVDs of the National Parks. I've watched them all. I'd love to go see them."

"Your father didn't take you to see anything?"

"No," I told her. "We drove through Indian reservations and I thought they were interesting but he was rude because they don't sell beer on the reservations. When I started home, I met some Navajo people and they got me to Gallup. Then I rode with two different Indian families. Where you picked me up, I had stayed the night with an Indian family. They all were really nice to me."

"Most people are nice," she said. "Does your family go to church?" she asked.

"Yes," I told her. "We go to a small country church. I've been praying this whole trip and I think God has been listening."

"Yes, Hank and I picked you up because we saw that Indian man drop you off. We thought you were Indian too. Was staying the night with them interesting?"

"Yes, the Navajo people I met said in their tribe, children belong to the clan of their mother and those Indians at Laguna told me in their tribe, it's the same. They said grandparents are important in teaching children."

She nodded. "Every child needs grandparents." she said.

I agreed and asked her about her other grandchildren. She prattled on happily until we reached Tulsa. I helped her navigate through town. When we reached the entrance to the turnpike to Joplin, she pulled over so Hank could take over driving.

Instead of getting out, he said, "Joe, why have you got a gun in your backpack?"

I had left my backpack on the floor in the back seat of the car. I looked over the seat and he was pointing the gun at me. I said, "Be careful. It's loaded. Is the safety still on?"

"Why are you carrying a gun?" he demanded and I knew he meant it.

I said, "I took it away from my father."

He said, "Why did you keep it?"

"Hitchhiking isn't all that safe," I said. "If you want me to get out here, I will."

Then Mrs. Butterfield asked, "Joe, why did you take the gun away from your father. What did he do?"

I sat there and knew I didn't want to tell any more lies. I said, "It was really bad and I need to get back to my mother. We know someone who will know what to do."

"What do you mean by *really bad*?" she asked and it was just like my grandmother asking me about sneaking cookies out of the cookie jar. I couldn't lie to her.

I said, "It was so bad, I don't think I should tell you because then you would become part of it and if I can just get home, Jim Willis will know what to do about it all."

She said, "Jim Willis. Your name is not really Joe Willis, is it?"

"No, ma'am," I said. "It's Job Johnson. Jim Willis works for a security company. Someone tried to hurt my mother and he was guarding us."

"Job Johnson," she was nodding. "It was on the news about you disappearing, kidnapped they said."

"Was it?" I said. "That's good."

Mrs. Butterfield said, "What happened?"

"I never had a father. My mother had told me he was killed in the war in the middle-east but I found out that wasn't true. She said she wanted me to feel like I was wanted. Then this man was in the parking lot of my school a week ago Thursday. He said he was my father and I could see I looked like him. He said he wanted to talk to me and I got in his truck. I know now I shouldn't have but I did. He showed me a paper that was a copy of a court order giving him custody of me. He took me to a hunting cabin in Colorado."

I stopped and thought about what else I should say. I looked at Mrs. Butterfield and said, "It was like I told you. He was driving too fast and drinking beer and when we got to Colorado, he started buying marijuana. All he wanted to do was smoke pot and lay around drinking beer."

I stopped again. I really didn't want to tell the rest. I said, "Then he did something really bad and I had to do something. I got his gun and ran off. If I get back home, I can tell Jim Willis what he did and he'll know what we should do about it."

"And just where is home?" Mr. Butterfield demanded.

"Where I said, out from Eminence. It's a farm really and we do have a greenhouse. Everything I told you about where I live is true."

Mr. Butterfield asked, "Honey, can you drive?"

She said, "I'd rather not. They're all driving so fast. I kept talking to Joe while you were asleep to keep my mind off the traffic."

I said again, "I can just get out here."

It was Mrs. Butterfield who objected. She said, "Hank, I think we need to take this boy home."

Mr. Butterfield asked, "Can you really drive?"

I said, "Yes, I drive our truck and I drive a scooter to school every day. Also I drive a tractor. If I can make straight rows with a tractor, I should be able to keep this car between the lines."

He said, "Show me your permit." So I dug it out and he inspected it. Then he said, "Job Joseph Johnson. Honey, you turn off the car and give me the keys." When she had done that, he said, "Now you get out." Then he told me to slide over behind the wheel. He got out and holding the gun pointed at me, he got into the front passenger seat. Then he told his wife to get into the back.

So I drove up the turnpike to Joplin. It was nerve racking. In the beginning, I was afraid to go over 60 but I slowly became more confident. The car was easier to drive than our truck and the road was good, smooth and wide with only the most gentle of curves.

At Joplin, Mrs. Butterfield needed a restroom so we bought gas. Mr. Butterfield made me put it in and then he accompanied me to the restroom. Like my father, he was not going to let me out of his sight but somehow it was different. I understood and made no attempt to get away.

Back in the car, we followed the signs to Interstate 44 and Springfield. I knew they had originally planned to stop for the night at Springfield but now nothing was said about stopping and I followed the signs to Highway 60 East.

Highway 60 runs all the way across Southern Missouri. It's four-lane but not limited access. Just before dark, we stopped again for gas at a station with a McDonalds. Mr. Butterfield had his wife buy us hamburgers and fries and cold drinks. She asked me. "Joe, I mean Job, are you okay to still drive?"

"Yes," I told her. "I want to get home."

It was past midnight when we turned off the county road at our sign saying "Indian Cave Greenhouse." The house was dark. Our truck was in the carport and Grandpa's truck sat near the house. No other vehicles were in sight so I knew Jim Willis was not there.

A dog started barking at us and I knew the new dog had arrived. I told the Butterfields, "This is a new dog and she doesn't know me. Someone killed our old dog and I think it was my father. If we wait, someone will wake up." The dog only had three legs but her barking and growling made up for it.

Sure enough, I saw curtains twitch. Then the porch light came on and the front door opened. I had put my window down and now I called out, "Grandpa, it's me, Job."

He got the dog quiet and came out to the car. I got out and he said, "Job," and hugged me. Then Mom came running out and grabbed me. She was crying.

Mr. Butterfield got out of the car with the gun still in his hand and said, "Is this your kid?"

Grandpa looked at the gun in shock but I said, "Grandpa, it's okay. This is Mr. Butterfield. He and his wife have brought me home."

But Grandpa asked politely, "Is there a reason why you're holding that gun?"

Mr. Butterfield said, "Your grandson had it in his backpack."

Grandpa looked at me and said, "I think we all should go inside and talk about this."

I asked about Jim Willis and Mom said he was at his family's house in Ellington. I said, "Call him and ask him to come. He needs to come now."

She said, "Now?"

I nodded. "Now. There's stuff I can only tell him."

Jim

Our Saturday conference had started at 9 o'clock and was over soon after 10. It was decided that Sonny Sells would try tracking down each of the names Mike Edwards had given him, starting with Dylan Robinson. He would ask each of them about the party the night Faith was kidnapped. He would ask names of the boys with whom Faith was supposed have been having sex. And if they denied first hand knowledge, he would ask from whom they heard the stories about her.

Jason Elfrink took the list of names and he was going to do criminal background checks on them. He said, "Criminals normally start out small and build up to major crimes. Let's see what I can find."

Sells reported in Saturday night. He said, "I been at this all day. I haven't found Dylan Robinson yet. His precinct in St. Louis says he's on personal leave and they don't give out information on their personnel, not even to someone claiming to be from another police department. Your FBI agent might can find out more.

"I found the two other guys on Mike Edwards' list of three. One of them denied ever having had sex with Faith. He also said he was not at this party Faith was supposed to have attended. He heard about it later after Faith was found. I asked who he heard it from and he said Dylan Robinson and his best friend, Riley Ellington. Riley Ellington was easy to find. He's buried in the City Cemetery here in town. He died less than a year after he graduated from high school. He was drunk and missed a curve. No seat belt.

"One guy on the list of five has moved to California. I got a phone number from a relative and left a message but he hasn't returned my call. Another one claims he never knew anything until all the rumors started flying around town. He was not at that party and he says he and Riley Ellington and most of the other guys on the list were at another party. He says Dylan Robinson was at the party early on but left, telling everyone he had a hot date.

"He also denied having sex with Faith and he says he thinks

the rumors about her sleeping around was mostly hot air from guys who wanted everyone to think they'd had her. He said he didn't hear any of these stories until after the kidnapping.

"He added that he understood why her parents took her and moved. He said the newspaper and news reports never gave her name but everyone in town knew about it. So I asked him what he thought about it all now and he said he thought she actually had been kidnapped."

Sells snorted and said, "He added that having the police asking about it all these years later confirmed that idea."

"He also told me about being with Dylan Robinson, Riley Ellington, and another boy one night when Dylan hit another car. Dylan had been drinking and tried to leave the scene but someone who saw the accident followed them. He says Dylan's dad paid off the people in the other car and got the charges dropped. He also says he gave Dylan a whipping with a belt which left welts all over his back. He saw them at school. But he says Dylan didn't quit drinking, just got more careful."

Sunday evening Sonny Sells called again. He said, "I went to church with my family this morning but this afternoon I spent on the phone. I got another one of the five on the secondary list. He said he'd never had sex with Faith but when everyone else on the football team started saying they had, then he'd said he had too. He called it stupid teenage stuff and wouldn't be at all surprised if the kidnap story was true.

"I tried the guy in California again and got him. He cussed me out and told me to go to hell, that he had nothing to do with it and he wasn't answering any questions. That means we hit a hot button somewhere and I suggest having your FBI agent take a good look at him."

Then Sunday night after midnight, my phone rang. It was Faith. Job had come home. She said, "He wants to talk to you. He says there's things he can only tell you."

❦ Chapter 9: Talking ❧

Job

Mom looked thin and I could see my disappearance had really torn her up. She kept touching me like she needed to confirm the fact that I was real. With Grandpa's help, she made hot chocolate and produced some cookies. She kept thanking Mr. and Mrs. Butterfield over and over for bringing me home.

Mrs. Butterfield told Mom, "I could tell he's a nice boy. He was polite and he never used bad language."

When we were settled around the kitchen table, Grandpa said, "What part of this can you tell us?"

I said, "On Thursday when I come out of school, a man in a pickup was waiting in the parking lot who said he was my father. I knew what he said was true because I look like him."

Mom looked at me and I saw tragedy in her eyes. She turned pale and then slumped. Grandpa caught her before she fell and gently lowed her to the floor.

Grandpa said, "She's fainted."

I said, "I shouldn't have told her."

Mrs. Butterfield got a wet cloth and in a few minutes, Mom started waking up. She started crying – sobbing and wailing.

I had never seen anyone cry like that before. It was awful. It was like Mom was broken apart. On the heels of my shock came anger and following the anger came the thought that I should have gone ahead and killed Dylan Robinson.

We helped her up and put her on the sofa in the living room. I sat down on the floor beside her and took her hand. "Mom, it's okay," I told her. "I got away and when I tell Jim Willis what all happened, I'm sure he'll be arrested."

After a while, she calmed down and said, "I never wanted you to know."

I said, "Yeah, I understand. From what he said, I know he raped you. Nobody likes hearing they were born because their father raped their mother. But we choose who we become. Just because he's a terrible man, doesn't mean I have to be one too."

Between hiccups, Mom said, "I had no idea who kidnapped me until last winter at one of your basketball games, I suddenly realized who you looked like. It was seeing you in a sports uniform. I thought I might be wrong but on the internet, I found pictures from when he was in high school and I could see you looked like him. I didn't want to tell anybody. I didn't want you to know what happened."

I said, "Mom, I understand. When Jim gets here, I'll tell him everything and he can decide how much we tell you."

I saw Cheshire sneaking around the furniture, dodging the strangers, going out the front screen door which she knew exactly how to open. To help Mom calm down, I asked, "What's the new dog's name?"

"Ginger," Mom said.

"No!" I said.

Mom added, "And she's too old to change her name now."

I looked at Grandpa and he was grinning. "We'll never tell her," he said. Then he said to the Butterfields, "Faith's mother is named Ginger." Then he sighed. "She and I are in the process of a divorce. She'll be mortified over the uproar this is going to cause."

Mrs. Butterfield looked puzzled, "But if the man raped her daughter, surely her mother wants him caught and punished."

Mom said wryly, "Not if it means everyone talking about it." I decided Mom was recovering.

Mrs. Butterfield started to say something but only got, "But that's . . ." before she quit.

I noticed Mr. Butterfield was no longer carrying the gun. He looked tired and I said, "Mom, where can the Butterfields sleep? They're tired."

We settled on the bedroom with twin beds which normally was never used. I told Mom, "You stay here. I know where the sheets are. I'll go get the room ready."

Mr. Butterfield and Grandpa went out to get their luggage. I went up the stairs and Mrs. Butterfield followed me. We made the beds and Mr. Butterfield and Grandpa came up with the luggage. I showed them the bathroom and left them to get settled.

Downstairs, Grandpa said, "Let's wait until Jim gets here

before we go into it all."

I asked, "Can I go take a shower?" I told Mom about Mr. Butterfield loaning me pajamas and Mrs. Butterfield washing my clothes for me.

When I came out after my shower, Mom looked at me and said, "I hate that haircut."

I grinned. "I do too but at the time I decided it was not worth arguing over. It'll grow out."

Grandpa was examining the gun. He said, "Where did this come from?"

I said, "He had it. He ordered me to call him *Dad* but I'm never going to again."

Grandpa looked at me and didn't say anything else.

I said, "So is the new dog working out okay?"

Grandpa shook his head but he was smiling. "We're still working on her letting customers wonder around. She thinks Faith is her special charge and she doesn't want anyone near her."

I said, "You'll have to introduce me. Maybe she'll like me."

Jim arrived and I knew I was extremely pleased to see him. He looked at me and commented, "I don't like that haircut," and I laughed.

We went out and sat in his truck to talk. I told him everything from the beginning to the end. When I was quiet, he said, "Dylan Robert Robinson. We were closing in on him. I suspect that by tomorrow night, we would have pinpointed him."

Jim got out a small notebook and took down names, places, everything. Jim said, "Job, you've done a good job. With all these details, it will be easy to prove you're telling the truth. He might have run, maybe even to Mexico or Canada, but we'll get him. Sooner or later, we'll get him."

I gave Jim the gun. He said, "We'll check and see if it was the same one used to kill the dog and sink my canoe."

"How much should I tell Mom?" I asked. I told Jim, "When I told her who had been waiting for me in the parking lot at school, she fainted and then she cried like I've never seen before. I'm afraid she'll have a nervous breakdown or something."

Jim said, "No, your mother is stronger than that. Tomorrow morning, I think you can tell it all. None of it is worse than what she went through when she was 14. It might help her to know you kept another 14-year-old from enduring the same fate."

I told Jim, "From something he said, I think Robinson has raped a lot of women."

He nodded and said. "That's likely."

I added, "I think he was even planning to murder Kai."

Then I asked him why men raped women. I could hear the anger in his voice as he explained. It made chills run up my spine. No wonder Mom fainted.

Jim prayed for me and I went into bed feeling a lot better.

Jim stayed out in his truck. He said, "I need to make phone calls." He added ironically, "Everyone's going to love this." By then it was 3 am.

Mom and Grandpa and I all went up to bed. I told them, "Tomorrow I'll tell you all about it but tonight, I'm exhausted. I drove all the way here from Tulsa, Oklahoma." I smiled at their surprised faces. "That's where Mr. Butterfield found the gun in my backpack and I drove and he held the gun."

Jim

When my phone rang, I surfaced and answered it. Faith said, "Jim, Job's come home. He wants to talk to you."

I said, "Is he okay?"

"I think so," she answered. "An older couple from Kentucky brought him home. Jim, they have a gun and they say Job had it in his backpack."

"Are they threatening you with it?"

"No, not at all. They seem like nice people. Can you come? Job says he wouldn't tell us what happened until he talks to you."

"I'm on my way."

When I arrived, Job and Faith and Nathan were all waiting. Job said, "Can we go somewhere and talk?" So we went out to my truck.

Job started talking. I recognized that his experience had been bad, scary, even traumatic, so I encouraged him to tell me every detail, not only what happened but how he felt about it.

He told me about Dylan Robinson waiting for him in the parking lot at school. He told me, "I figured out pretty quick I should never have gotten into his truck but I also think he had that handgun handy so he could use it to force me to go with him."

He paused, looking at me and I responded, "Probably." I added, "Not nice at all, was it?"

He told me about the truck trade and haircut in Springfield, adding, "They were both done to hide me. It was the kind of haircut he had and anybody looking at us would know we were kin."

He talked about the beer drinking. He said, "It was scary. He was a bad driver and I saw people dodge him several times to avoid an accident. On the way to Winona, I thought he was going to hit someone going around those curves in the middle of the road and he almost did once. So by the time we got to Winona, I already knew I had made a mistake."

He went on, "It was in the bar in Winona that he showed me the court paper giving him custody. I read it over carefully. He said the court had sent Mom papers and she hadn't come or responded in any way so the judge gave him full custody. The paper was a photocopy. He said he had the original in a lock-box. It was issued by a court in St. Louis. Do you think we can prove Mom was never contacted?"

I said, "Or it may be a total fake. At your age, you would have been called to court and asked what you wanted."

Job nodded and said, "He's an absolute lazy slob. All he wanted to do was drink beer and smoke pot. He was too lazy to walk to the outhouse and he peed off the porch. Using a bush is one thing but peeing right next to your house is another."

Then he said, "When I said I was bored, he took me on a hunting trip that turned into a total fiasco. He had two rifles and I was hoping he'd let me use one but he didn't."

He paused before starting the next part. He said, "The next day was Wednesday and that's when it got really bad. We took off in his truck and in Cortez, his favorite bar wasn't open. We drove down to a casino on the Ute Reservation but he'd made trouble there before and they wouldn't let him in. He said something about going to Gallup but we passed an Indian girl leading a lame horse and he stopped and kidnapped her."

Job stopped and looked at me. I was thinking, *Oh, no. This is why he wouldn't talk to his mother or grandfather.*

He told me, "He had a pair of handcuffs under his seat as well as that handgun. He put her in his tool box and drove back to the cabin. When I asked him what he intended to do with her, he said she was for me, my first woman."

Job was shaking his head, "He'd talked a lot about playing football in high school and working as a police officer. He also talked about women. He'd told me he hadn't known about me because my mother had been sleeping with a lot of guys. He said she faked the kidnapping and then her family moved.

"But that day in the truck he started talking about women again. He said virgins were best because you couldn't get the pox and if they were really virgins, they bled. It was so disgusting I didn't want to hear it but he kept talking. Then he said my mother was the sweetest fuck he ever had. Sorry about the language, but that's exactly what he said. He said she bled and she fought. That's went I realized that everything he'd told me about her before was a lie." Job paused and then said grimly, "He raped my mother."

I could see the cold anger in his face. I knew what I was seeing because I felt the same. He said, "Right then I wanted to jump on him and beat him senseless but I knew he'd win the fight and he might even kill me. I was trying to think what to do when he stopped and kidnapped that girl. While he was doing it, I could have run but I couldn't leave that girl alone with him. I knew what he'd do to her and she looked like she was just a kid.

"When he told me she was for me, I said she was too young and he said she wasn't, she had boobs. He said he'd checked. The man is a disgusting pervert.

"When we got to the cabin and got the girl out, she asked for a bathroom and I took her to the outhouse. I was hoping for a chance to run but he followed us. When she wouldn't come out, he broke the door open and dragged her out. She was fighting and he was taking her to the cabin when I saw he had stuck his handgun in his waistband at the back. I grabbed it and shot him in the leg."

He stopped and I said, "You remembered."

He nodded and said, "Yes."

He went on, "The girl had run but she stopped at the cabin and waited for me. He had all the keys in his pocket and I knew if I tried to get them, he'd fight and the only way I could get them would be to shoot him seriously and without help, he'd almost certainly die. I thought about killing him. It's what he deserves. But then I thought about possibly ending up in jail for it and

Mom needs me here."

He looked at me and I nodded. He'd made the right decision.

"That girl and I quickly packed some food and water and took off walking. He passed us in the truck on the way to town but we hid. It got dark and I was afraid of getting lost so we slept and then we walked all the next day to get to Cortez.

"By then I had found out that the girl was 14 and her name is Kai Begay. She's Navajo. Her family doesn't have a phone or we would have tried to call them. I knew Dylan Robinson would have probably told the people in Cortez a bunch of lies so I was afraid to go to the police. Kai and I decided we'd try to get to her family and that's what we did.

"Then the Navajo man who picked us up and took her home, took me back out to the main highway and got me a ride to Gallup. I started hitchhiking and rode that day with two Indian families. They picked me up because they think all white people have vehicles and only Indians hitchhike. The second family lived at Laguna, New Mexico and they asked me to stay the night and the next morning they took me back to the Interstate."

He stopped and then said, "This whole time I was praying and I know God heard me. When I got out at the Interstate, the Butterfields saw me being dropped off and thought I was Indian and picked me up. They're from Louisville, Kentucky and had been out to California to visit their daughter and grandkids."

He paused again and said, "They're really nice people. I didn't want to lie to them but I told them my name was Joe and they'd had a grandson named Joe who died of leukemia. I felt really bad about lying to them. I told them part of the truth about why I was hitchhiking. I said I'd gone with my father to Colorado but all he did was drink beer and smoke pot so I had decided to go back to my mother.

"Then the next day in the afternoon, Mr. Butterfield was sleepy and he had Mrs. Butterfield drive from Oklahoma City to Tulsa. She was nervous and only drove 55 miles an hour on the turnpike where the speed limit is 75. She and I talked the whole way. She's really a nice lady. Grandmothers a great people.

"But I had left my backpack on the floor in the back of the car and Mr. Butterfield used it for a pillow. When we stopped at Tulsa to change drivers, he felt the gun in my backpack. I told them I had taken it away from my father and kept it because hitchhiking is dangerous. They wanted details but I just said my father had done something really bad and if I could get back here, I knew someone who would know what I should do."

Job smiled at me and said, "When Mr. Butterfield found the gun, I told them they could just let me out but they decided to bring me home. Mr. Butterfield had me drive and he held the gun." Then he said again, "They're really nice people."

I thought to myself how God must have had angels hovering all around Job during this whole affair. I knew how often deals like this ended in tragedy. Nice people who are scared will shoot the wrong person.

I said, "Job, I think God was looking out for you."

He nodded. "I know," he agreed.

Job gave me all the details, names, locations, make and modal of vehicles, license numbers, even the label on the tool box in Robinson's truck. He had the girl's name and address.

He commented, "She gave me nine dollars to buy food on my way so I got her address."

I took notes and told him, "Dylan Robert Robinson. We were closing in on him. I suspect that by tomorrow night, we would have pinpointed him." I told Job he might run, maybe even to Mexico or Canada, but sooner or later, we'd get him.

Job told me that from Robinson's talk, he thought he had raped a lot of women, maybe even killed someone, and I said it was likely.

When I had the details all down, Job was quiet for a minute and then asked, "Jim, you talked to me some about sex and so has Grandpa. Why do men rape women?"

"Rape is not about sex; it's about power. It's about making someone do something they don't want to do. It's about being in control and forcing the woman. It's about torture. It's about humiliating her. It's even more than a violation of her body. It's a violation of her soul. It takes something which is supposed to be a bonding activity between a man and a woman and perverts it into violence and terror." I realized that as I talked, I had gotten passionate. I added, "In some ways, it's worse than murder. Many victims never fully recover."

Job nodded. He said, "The last couple of years, I've realized men think Mom is pretty but she's not interested. I wouldn't mind having a step-father if it was someone like you but I'm never calling Dylan Robinson *Dad*. He's a sick, perverted monster and I hope someone shoots him." He paused and then said, "That's bad, isn't it?"

So did I. I said, "Maybe, but understandable."

Then Job asked how much I thought he should tell his mother. He told me how she reacted when she heard who had taken him and he was afraid she'd have a nervous breakdown.

I told him, "No, your mother is stronger than that. Tomorrow morning, I think you can tell it all. None of it is worse than what your mother went through when she was 14. It might help her to know you kept another 14-year-old from enduring the same fate."

I asked Job if he would like for me to pray for him. I asked for justice and I asked for God's peace for Job.

He went in to bed and I started making phone calls.

Part 3
Into the Cave

❦ Chapter 10: Home ❧

Faith

The dog woke me up. I heard a car outside. I glanced at the clock. It was 12:47. I was scared. Who could be out there? I slipped on the caftan I used for a housecoat and went out into the hall. Dad was up and started down the stairs. He said, "Don't turn on any lights inside." He looked out the window and then turned on the porch light. He had the shotgun.

Then I heard Job's voice saying, "Grandpa, it's me, Job."

Dad put the shotgun down and went out the door. He got the dog quiet and Job got out of the car and hugged him. I ran out and grabbed him, so happy I was crying.

I didn't see the man who got out of the car with a gun until he asked if Job was our kid. I stared at the gun in shock but Job said, "Grandpa, it's okay. This is Mr. Butterfield. He and his wife have brought me home."

Dad asked the man why he had the gun and he said, "Your grandson had it in his backpack."

Dad suggested we all go inside and talk about this but Job asked me, "Where's Jim Willis?"

I said, "Ellington."

Job insisted that I call him to come over now, saying, "There's stuff I can only tell him."

My heart sank. As we made our way inside to the kitchen, I kept Job's hand in mine and he didn't seem to mind. What could have possibly happened that Job couldn't tell me or his grandpa?

I noticed Mr. Butterfield laid the gun down casually on the kitchen table and I started making hot chocolate. We all introduced ourselves and in the light, I saw them as a normal looking older couple, early to mid 60's. Their car was a cream colored Lincoln Town Car so I suspected they had money.

Mrs. Butterfield said about Job, "I could tell he's a nice boy. He was polite and he never used bad language."

When we were settled, Dad asked Job what he could tell us now.

Job said, "On Thursday when I came out of school a man was waiting in a pickup in the parking lot who said he was my father. I knew what he said was true because I look like him."

I looked at Job and everything faded. I felt Dad catch me. I knew I was falling but everything was gone.

When I woke up, I was sobbing. I knew I should have told Jim Willis what I had concluded but I had just not been able to do it. It was all my fault. Then Job said to me, "Mom, it's okay. I got away and when I tell Jim Willis what all happened, I'm sure he'll be arrested."

I told Job I had never wanted him to know.

He said, "Yeah, I understand. From what he said, I know he raped you. Nobody likes hearing they were born because their father raped their mother. But we choose who we become. Just because he's a terrible man, doesn't mean I have to be one too."

Between hiccups, I told Job, about realizing last winter at one of his games who it was that he looked like. I told him I had never wanted him to know.

Job was holding my hand. He said, "Mom, I understand." Then he said that when Jim got here, he'd talk to him about it all and let him decide how much the rest of us should be told. My heart was quivering. What could possibly have happened that my son wasn't sure his grandfather and I should be told?

Then Job started asking about the new dog. I knew he was just trying to distract me but I let him.

It was pretty funny. My mother is named Ginger and so is the new dog. My mother is an elegant woman who is always prim and proper, hyper-sensitive to social status and always determined to portray herself as the ultimate proper lady. A dog with the same name was so inappropriate, we had laughed about it. Dad told the Butterfields what was funny about the dog's name. Then he told them he and my mother were in the process of a divorce and she would be mortified over the talk about what had happened now.

Mrs. Butterfield said, "But if the man raped her daughter, surely her mother wants him caught and punished."

I said, "Not if it means everyone talking about it."

Mrs. Butterfield started to comment but didn't. She is a nice lady. I suspected she wouldn't like my mother much.

Then Job suggested we give the Butterfields beds and we got busy with that. Job asked to take a shower. He told us about Mr. Butterfield loaning him pajamas and Mrs. Butterfield washing his clothes for him. He said, "I suspect I stunk."

I looked at him and knew that whatever had happened, it had been serious. Job had never been a slob. He liked clean clothes. And why was his hair all cut off? He looked like a young soldier or – my heart stopped – a young policeman.

I said, "I hate that haircut."

He grinned at me. "I do too," he told me, "but at the time I decided it was not worth arguing over. It'll grow out."

Then Dad asked Job where he got the gun.

Job said, "He had it. He ordered me to call him *Dad* but I'm never going to again." Then he started talking about the new dog.

Inside, I was crying, crying for my son who had a monster for a father.

Jim Willis arrived and he and Job went out to his truck to talk.

Jim

After Job and I talked, I sent Job in to sleep and I started making phone calls. Law enforcement is a 24-hour-a-day operation. Phones get answered.

Job's guess about Dylan Robinson lying to people in Colorado was right. Law enforcement there wanted to talk to Job. Robinson had said Job had linked up with the girl and then he'd found out she was underage and was objecting when he and Job got in a struggle over a handgun and it went off and hit him in the leg.

I told them Job's story and said I was sure the girl would back it up. I said, "We'll fax you a warrant for Dylan Robinson's arrest for kidnapping as soon as it's processed. Job Johnson is back with his mother and grandfather and he's not about to go anywhere."

The Navajo Tribal Police had passed Kai's story on to the local FBI. She had been kidnapped on the Reservation so they had authority. I got Jason Elfrink to check on it and he called me back. He said. "They have not put out a warrant and had not made the connection to Job Johnson's kidnapping. I wanted to ream someone out for stupidity but I knew it would be counterproductive. I told them we had the statement of Job Johnson. He was with Dylan Robinson when he kidnapped the girl and he managed to get the man's gun and shoot him in the leg so they could get away."

Elfrink told me, "The dimwit on the other end of the line actually asked me if I was sure this all happened. By that time I was gritting my teeth and just said yes, I was sure it all happened. All he said was 'Huh.' I told him we were putting out a warrant for Dylan Robinson and we'd send him a copy."

Jason Elfrink sighed and said, "I was going to call you first thing in the morning anyway. I was trying to check on priors and I think Dylan Robinson's father got him out of trouble more than once but all I found in the records was a note of one DUI being dropped. However, I found the rape accusation which was dismissed. Your boy says Robinson said he quit and went to work in St. Louis but I think he was asked to resign. There's no record but you know how these things work.

"Now for the real kicker. Robinson was put on leave from his current job because of a rape accusation. When it was reported in the news, two other women came forward. They were all black and say they were pulled over for traffic violations late at night. They said he'd told them if they reported him, they wouldn't be believed. The woman who reported him first was a nurse and she went straight to the hospital. She had managed to get a washcloth he was using for a sweat rag and she knew how to get it processed. She said she wanted to scratch him but realized if she did, he'd kill her. She said he was already wearing a condom when he pulled her over so she knew he was a serial rapist."

I asked Elfrink to check on the custody order. "Job says it was issued in St. Louis. My personal thought is that it's a fake but check."

By that time, it was 5 am and I called Sonny Sells. I said, "Job Johnson is back home and our perp is Dylan Robinson."

Sells said, "That's what I was beginning to think. I got told more gossip but if you've definitely ID'ed him, we'll skip it. Have you got enough for a warrant?"

"Yes," I told him. "He kidnapped a 14-year-old girl. Job got his gun, shot him in the leg with it, and took the girl home. Then he got himself back here."

After a brief silence, Sells said, "Future law enforcement officer."

I said, "Maybe. Right now he's got three more years of high school and he's trying farming."

Sells said, "Some kids are amazing. And talk about poetic justice. The man rapes a woman and 16 years later, the son he fathered is responsible for bringing him to justice. God does work in mysterious ways."

I told Sells the FBI would fax the Pine Bluff Police Department a copy of the warrant when it was processed, just in case Dylan Robinson tried to appeal to his father for help.

I got off the phone and thought about it all. It would soon be over. I looked out at the house and the greenhouse and the barn. I didn't want to tell this family goodbye. Faith had gone through hell and then embraced the child who came out of that and raised a son which anyone would be proud to claim.

If Faith ever married, she would want more kids. With me, there was always the risk of having one darker than me, too dark to pass. I felt a deep sadness.

◈ Chapter 11: Telling It All ◈

Faith

We let Job sleep and it was almost noon before he woke up. We had sent the Butterfields on their way, after promising to let them know what happened. I made cinnamon rolls which I knew Job adored. He hugged me and said, "Mom, I really missed you."

After he ate, we were waiting. Job said, "Can Jim set in on this too?" I was more than agreeable. Somehow Jim made me feel safe.

As he started, Job told me, "Some of this is bad. If you feel faint again or it's too much, just say so." I nodded and he started.

As I listened, tears began seeping out of my eyes and running down my cheeks. When Job saw them he stopped talking but I told him to go on. When he told me about the girl, Kai, I felt faint but I managed to stay upright. When he told me about shooting his father and he and the girl getting away, I wanted to cheer.

When he finished his tale, I said, "Job, I'm proud of you."

He looked embarrassed and said, "I just did what any normal person would do."

Jim told us, "I've made phone calls and put things in process. A warrant has been issued for his arrest. Hopefully he'll soon be behind bars."

Job said, "I need to meet this new dog. I can't believe her name is Ginger and she only understands commands in Dutch. That's wild." After meeting the dog and working with her a while, learning the Dutch commands, he went to work on the north field. I had him take the shotgun as well as my Track phone.

Late afternoon, Jim got a phone call. Dylan Robinson had been arrested out in Cortez. He'd had a doctor's appointment and when he came out, they had picked him up.

Jim told us, "I'm hoping he'll just plead guilty to some reduced charges and it'll be over but if he doesn't, Job will have to go to court and you probably will too, Faith."

I shuttered and said, "I hope not."

Jim said, "I was waiting to hear about Robinson's arrest before I left. I'll go up to the north field and say goodbye to Job." Then Jim looked at me and said, "He's a fine boy."

I smiled and nodded. "I told you I decided God gave him to me. He may look like Dylan Robinson but his character is totally different."

After Jim left, Dad said, "I wouldn't mind at all if that man stayed around. I got the idea he likes you."

"I like him," I said. Then I considered what to say. Not telling things can be a problem. So I said, "Jim told me his ancestry is mixed. He said he uses sunscreen and straightens his hair a lot of the time because it makes his work easier but he considers himself black."

Dad grinned. "He told me. But a good man is a good man. I didn't know there were any black families in Ellington."

"The rest of his family isn't black," I told him. Dad said, "Oh," and I added, "I didn't ask so I don't know how it happened. And part of why he passes is because no one in Ellington knows he's black."

Dad said, "I doubt if he'll ask you to marry him. If you want him, you'll probably have to ask him."

I grinned and said, "Dad, are you trying to match-make?"

He grinned back at me and said, "You've proven to be such a successful parent, I'd like some more grandchildren."

Jim

I found Job hard at work. He saw me and stopped the tractor and came out to the edge of the field to talk to me. I told him, "The police in Cortez have arrested Dylan Robinson."

He said, "That's good." Then he said, "Does that mean you're leaving?"

"Yes," I told him.

He said, "I wish you didn't have to go." He paused and then looked at me intently. "Do you have a girlfriend?" he asked.

"What?" I said in surprise.

He said, "You've never mentioned a girlfriend. Mom likes you. I wouldn't mind at all if you married her."

I said, "What put that idea in your mind?"

He said, "I got the idea you liked her too."

I suddenly decided to be completely honest. I said, "Job, I do like her. I would like to marry her but I don't think she wants to marry me. And your mother would want more kids and with me, she might get one that was black."

"You're not very dark. No one notices. Could you have a baby that's darker than you?"

"Yes," I told him. "It normally doesn't happen but it's always possible."

Job said, "I don't think she'd care."

I said, "Maybe we should just let it set for a while," I said, hearing the uncertainty in my voice.

"Okay," he said, "but I really like you being around. If you come and give me more combat lessons, I'd like that."

I nodded. "So would I."

✤ Chapter 12: Match Making ✥

Faith

With Dylan Robinson in jail, we relaxed. I talked to Job about the "Joey Meets a Bully" book and he suggested, "Should we do one where Joey meets a kidnapper?" We laughed but then I thought, *Why not?*

Dad told me he needed to return to Fredericktown to meet with Mom and the lawyers about the divorce. I was busy with the greenhouse and my editing work and Job finished planting the north field.

Job also spent a lot of time with Ginger, the three legged dog. He learned all the Dutch commands and the proper way to issue them. I'd been told police dogs are often taught their commands in a foreign language so no one other than their handler could accidentally, or even intentionally, get the dog to obey them. It seems that German is the most common language used but Ginger had been taught Dutch.

Dad returned from Fredericktown in only two days with his truck loaded. Job looked at it all and said, "Grandpa, are you moving in with us?"

Dad nodded. "I think so, at least for the summer."

Job happily helped him unload. He asked Dad, "Do you want your old room back?" It was the one Job was in now.

Dad said, "No, I'll take the one I've been using."

I offered him the room downstairs which Grandma had used but he said he preferred to be upstairs with us. Then he added, "That's where Jim Willis was sleeping and we might need for him to come back."

When customers came for the greenhouse, Job went out to deal with them and Dad said, "Faith, I need to tell you some things but not with Job around."

So when Job was looking something up on the internet about soybeans, we slipped out to the greenhouse.

Dad said, "I found out why your mother suddenly wants a divorce. She's planning to marry J. Charleton Willingham."

I thought. "Isn't that the lawyer she works for? I thought he was married."

"He was," Dad said, "but his wife died last fall."

I considered it. Mom had gone to work for Willingham right after they moved up to Fredericktown. He was considered a high-powered successful lawyer but I knew Dad considered him a bit shady. Well, maybe not really shady but willing to work for whoever paid the most, even if he knew they were guilty.

Dad went on, "Willingham is handling her divorce and I overheard something. They don't know I know so keep it quiet. Also instead of the house, she wants this farm. She thought with my mother dead, that I was getting it. She was shocked to learn Mother had given it to you years ago. She had one of her fits in the meeting, told me to get it back from you because she wanted it."

"Why does she want the farm?" I asked.

"I expect it's money," Dad said. "She was going to let me have the house and her take the farm. The farm is worth a lot more but she acted like she didn't know that and was just trying to be helpful to me letting me keep the house because I was working in Fredericktown. My lawyer is saying we should sell the house and split the money and we both keep our own IRA's and 401K's. I didn't tell you before but when Ginger asked for a divorce, I discovered she had withdrawn the money in all of our joint bank accounts. Now she wants half of my IRA's and my pension as well. My lawyer says she's a Harpy. It was a highly charged meeting. You know how Ginger can throw one of her cold fits, and my lawyer is female and she threw a hot one so it was quite a scene. If I wasn't so involved, it would have been funny."

Dad went on, "When I started packing my personal belongings, I found a lot of things gone. Everything that could be easily sold was missing, even the gun Dad brought back from the war and the silver dollar Grandpa gave me on my tenth birthday."

Dad looked sad. He said, "I should have divorced her years ago when she drove you away but I'm not the kind of man who runs out on a commitment."

I gave him a hug and said, "I know, Dad. I understood how it was. But you have me and Job."

He said, "I talked to my superintendent in Fredericktown and he's willing to let me out of my contract without prejudiced if he can find someone to take my place. It's early enough in the summer he has a couple of good possibilities. I've called the school here and put my name in. James Hillis knows me so if they have anything come open, he'll call me. He said if I'm still available next year, I have a job for sure. Their Junior High Math teacher is retiring."

I knew Dad was grieved over the divorce. The marriage relationship had never been good but he had made the best of it and had intended to see it through to the end. That was my dad – reliable, dependable, a man of his word.

So Dad settled in and it was nice having him living with us. On Sunday we went to church together and Job was welcomed back with enthusiasm. When asked what happened, he said, "I was stupid and got in a truck with someone I shouldn't. Charges are being filed so I don't think I'm suppose to talk about it."

Later he told me, "Maybe I should have told them what happened. Somebody asked me if I got raped. What happened was bad enough but what some of these people think up is worse."

On Monday Job asked, "Mom, can I call Jim up and ask him if he would like to see the cave?"

I said, "Well, he saw part of it but didn't see the interesting parts. Call him and see if he's interested."

Jim had finally told me what he was working on when he rescued me but I had not told Job. He had told me the investigation was still going on but when Job called, he came. I let Job take him into the cave and he came back saying, "I have never heard of pictographs like these in this area. I think a lot of them were destroyed by early settlers. I took photos. Do you mind if I share them with my sister?"

I said, "No, but do explain why we won't let her go in there."

"I will," he said. "I do understand. I think you could get the cave declared some kind of historical site but then a lot of researchers would be given access. Most of them are people of integrity but all it takes is one stinker."

I had fried chicken and we ate. Jim helped us with clean up and then he and Job went to look at the north field.

When they were gone, Dad said, "I was watching Jim. I was

right. He's interested."

I said, "Oh, Dad. I can't say anything to him. I don't have the nerve."

"Job asked me about having Jim over. He says Jim admitted he would like to marry you but is afraid of having a black baby."

I said, "Job asked Jim if he wanted to marry me? You two are terrible! The poor man. He probably didn't want to be rude to Job and say he wasn't interested."

"That's why I was watching him today. He is interested."

"Dad, are you sure?"

"Sure enough that I'll talk to the man myself if you want me to."

I said, "Let me think about it a little." I went up to my room, got down on my knees and prayed about it. The incident which had produced Job had happened when I was so young that I had never fallen in love with anyone. Was I in love with Jim? I thought so. But was he really in love with me? He had never said anything to indicate he was. I told God, "I'm not sure at all what I should do about this, if anything. I really need your guidance."

I felt restless and went out to the greenhouse and started working. When Jim and Job come back, they went into the house and then Jim came out to the greenhouse.

He said, "There's something so satisfying about growing things. Job is really enthusiastic about his soybeans."

I said, "I know. I love growing things in this greenhouse." Then I looked at Jim and I said, "Jim, I can't thank you enough for the help you've given us. If you hadn't turned up that day in your canoe, I'd probably be dead. With me dead, Dylan could have gotten custody of Job. If you hadn't taught Job about using a handgun, he would never have been able to save that girl."

I looked into Jim's eyes and said, "I wish you didn't have to go."

Jim looked away and I thought, *He isn't interested*. But then he looked straight into my eyes and said, "I don't really want to go."

I looked away, gathered my courage, and asked, "Jim, what do you want out of life?"

I waited, knowing he needed time to frame his answer.

"Family, a wife and children." He paused and then said, "A wife who loves me and children to watch grow up, children to teach and love."

His answer was simple and direct and honest.

I looked into his eyes and saw longing. I said, "Jim, I . . . I really like you. I think I'm in love with you . . . but I've never been in love." I wasn't sure what to say. "I'm not really sure I could have a normal relationship with a man."

Jim was looking at me intently and I saw caution but behind that was hope. He said, "You're afraid of the physical side of things."

I nodded. He took my hand and said, "Come."

Without hesitation, I let him lead me out of the greenhouse and beyond the kitchen garden to an open grassy slope overlooking the creek and screened from the house and greenhouse by trees and shrubs. At this time of the year, it was decorated with yellow daisies. Jim sat down and I sat beside him. He asked, "Faith, do you want more children?"

"Yes," I said and a knew a smile came to my face.

Jim said, "With me, there is always the chance of having one darker than me, too dark to pass."

I said, "Jim, I wouldn't care. If I could accept and love Job, a black baby should be easy. Especially if it was yours."

"Why me?" Jim asked.

I wanted to laugh. *Did the man not see himself?* I thought a moment and began, "Jim, it's not just that you rescued me and were willing to protect me. Dad would have done that if he had been here. It's more than that. You're a good person. I know you will always want to do what's right. Also . . . do you remember what you said about fellow soldiers? I can talk to you about anything, even my fears and my nightmares. You understand."

Jim sighed. "Yes, I understand why you're afraid but normal sex is nothing like what you experienced. If you need it, we could find a therapist."

I reached out and put my hand on Jim's arm and asked, "Will you kiss me?"

Jim turned and put his hands on my shoulders, lightly, and I closed my eyes and turned my face to him. He placed a small kiss on my forehead. Then he kissed my eyelids, one by one. Then he lightly kissed the tip of my nose. By the time he got to my lips, I was ready. His kiss was gentle, sweet, and took a while.

When he finally pulled back, I looked at him and caught my

breath. He asked, "Are you okay?"

I said, "Yes," and I reached up and ran my fingertips lightly down the sides of his face. He closed his eyes and I did it again. I said, "You have such a solemn face but when you smile, it lights up." He smiled. "I've . . . I've never wanted to touch anyone before."

I slid my hands around his neck and tugged gently and he started kissing me again. He kissed my lips but he roamed around, showering gentle kisses on my cheeks, my forehead, my nose, my eyelids, my ears, and my neck. He was running his fingers lightly up and down the nape of my neck. It was more than pleasant. As I relaxed, I found it interesting.

Eventually we ended up with our arms wound around each other. I snuggled up to him. He leaned back, lying on the slope, and I found myself half on top of him. He had his arms around me but when I pushed myself back up, he made no attempt to stop me. He said, "It's okay. You won't squash me. I'm too big. I'll just lie here and if you panic, you can get up and run."

He was grinning at me and I leaned over and kissed him. Half an hour later, I was snuggled up to him. I said, "Jim, I like this but . . . ."

When I didn't go on, Jim said, "Faith, we can always find a therapist if we need one. I love you. As I've gotten to know you, I've admired your strength, your resiliency. What happened to you was terrible but you survived and healed. You didn't shut yourself off but recovered and went on with life."

I thought about it and then said, "I tried. When life hurts, it's easy to build a stone wall and refuse to participate any longer but I didn't want that and I didn't want it for Job. I want to live a normal life." I hesitated and then said, "Jim, I do love you."

Jim said, "Are you sure?"

"Yes," I answered. "I'm sure."

He said, "Will you marry me?"

"We'd better. All this we've told Job, we better set a good example."

Then he asked, "How long of an engagement do you want?"

I said, "I think we're both old enough to know our own minds. I don't see any reason to wait. Is next Sunday afternoon too soon for you?"

He grinned. "Not at all."

We went back to the house holding hands and told Dad and Job. They both grinned. I told them, "You two are a couple of sly foxes."

They laughed.

Jim

When Job called and offered to show me the cave, I went. I was interested but I was even more interested in seeing Faith again and I knew it. I loved her and my talk with Job had fanned the flames. I knew I should stay away but I couldn't. I went.

When I went out to the greenhouse to say goodbye, she threw out a line. She said, "I wish you didn't have to go."

I started to give a flippant answer and then I saw it in her eyes. She really did not want me to go. We talked about her fears and then we spent some time out on a sunny slope by the creek where we did some kissing and cuddling. She is basically a normal woman who had the stuffings scared out of her but it was a long time in the past.

We went in holding hands to tell Job and Nathan and I saw the two schemers had both been at work.

I took Faith over to meet my parents. They were delighted. Mom hugged her and said, "Welcome to the family." Later Faith would say, "Jim, you look a lot like your mother." It was true. I had her face but she was blonde and blue-eyed and so was Dad.

They called John and he came over bringing his wife, Esther, and their three kids. They've also got another one due soon. Esther hugged Faith and said, "Welcome to the family. John told me about you."

Faith asked, "What did he say?" and I wanted to groan.

Esther grinned. "He said you were a real good-looking woman with no attitude about it and a lot of common sense. He said he thought Jim was attracted but he didn't think he'd have the nerve to move on it."

Faith laughed and nodded, "I had to ask him to kiss me."

It was Esther who said, "Jim, you're blushing." But Faith was too.

Chapter 13: Wedding Preparations

Faith

With only five days to prepare, no written invitations were going out. I was blank on who to have for a bridesmaid until I thought of Patty Springer. Sometimes I have an ornery sense of humor. She had up and moved down to West Plains but I called her. She saw the funny side of it.

Mrs. Voden said, "I'll organize the reception," and Jim's family were all on board. His brother was going to be his best man and he talked to me about having Job as a groomsman. He said, "We'll draft my sister, the archaeologist, for another bridesmaid."

I said, "But what about dresses?"

He laughed. "My sister has a enough clothes to open a boutique."

When I talked to Patty, she said, "Let's do a Prairie Dress thing. I have a lovely one I got two years ago for that festival we had but the day before, Roger gave me a black eye and I never wore it. It's pale blue and I've lost enough weight to get back into it. I'll find a garden hat to wear with it. The wedding is in the afternoon so it'll be great, like a garden party."

When I talked to Jim's sister, Jenny, she said, "I have the perfect thing. It's lavender. I'll get a hat and we'll put flowers on it."

So that left me. I couldn't find anything in Eminence I even wanted to try on. I took Mrs. Voden with me and made the triangle across through Mountain View to Willow Springs, down to West Plains and then Thayer, back up through Alton to Winona and Eminence. Nothing would fit without being altered. I was too big in the bust and too small in the waist. And worse, almost everything was completely bare-shouldered leaving my bust bulging out, half uncovered. My last try-on had puffed sleeves but was so low necked, I told Mrs. Voden, "I look like a dance hall girl."

The sales girl said, "But you look alluring."

I said, "I'm marrying a man who's never seen me in anything except the sort of thing I wore in here. I don't need to look alluring. This dress would give the man such a shock, he might run."

As we headed home, discussing a trip all the way to Springfield, Mrs. Voden said, "I used to sew and my daughter and one of her daughter's still do. Maybe they can make you a dress."

We consulted and Mrs. Voden's daughter pulled out some patterns from back about 1970 when granny dresses were in vogue. We found some lovely very pale ivory fabric and matching lace and went to work. It had puffed sleeves with ruffles, a fitted waist with ties that made a big bow in the back, a high neck, a yoke in front with a strategically located ruffle that helped de-emphasize my over-sized bust, a deep ruffle around the full skirt, and the women gussied it up with lace trim everywhere. It was lovely.

On our travels, Mrs. Voden and I had found a hair piece to hold a veil and netting matching my dress was not hard to find. We sprinkled it with small pearl-like beads.

We called the Butterfields and they were coming. The FBI agent, Jason Elfrink, was coming as was Vernon Chilton and another friend of Jim's from when he was in the army. I called my mother and asked her if she wanted to come. She called back and said she was arriving Saturday and wanted to talk to me. I felt a cold chill in the pit of my stomach. But this was my territory and it was my wedding. I was not going to let her ruin it.

I coached Job on dealing with Mother. I said, "Call her Grandmother and stay very formal. She doesn't like casualness and she has no sense of humor. If possible, keep her from finding out our dog is named Ginger. She doesn't like animals so she won't ask the dog's name. Cheshire always avoids strangers so I don't think she'll be a problem. We'll put her in Grandma's room downstairs. She doesn't like sharing a bathroom. If she says something hurtful, just walk out."

Job asked, "Are you serious about walking out on her? That's rude."

I said, "Job, she can say very sharp and nasty things. You have permission to walk out but please try to avoid saying rude things back to her."

Job said, "I did wonder why you and Grandpa never talked about her. I thought she must be an alcoholic or something."

I said, "It's *or something.*"

When Mother arrived, the Butterfields were sitting on the front porch having iced tea and talking. I quickly told them, "It's my mother. I don't think she knows everything about recent events so it's better not to mention them."

Dad went out to greet Mother and Job trailed along to carry the luggage. He had shut Ginger up in the barn earlier. As Mom climbed out of the car, my heart sank in dismay. I had not seen her in fifteen years but she had not aged. We could pass for sisters. She was wearing a navy blue suit with a white blouse. Her purse and shoes were navy also and she was wearing nylons and gloves in this summer heat. I had just that day gone and got a professional hair cut. Her hair was cut just like mine.

I heard Dad say, "This is your grandson, Job."

She looked at him and said, "You're tall for you age."

Job said, "Yes, ma'am."

Job went in with her bags, three of them, for what I hoped was only a two night stay. I introduced Mother to the Butterfields. Mrs. Butterfield said, "Mrs. Johnson, how nice to meet you. Your daughter looks just like you. She's lovely."

My mother warmed up to the flattery and asked the Butterfields if they were neighbors. Mrs. Butterfield said, "No, we're friends. We live over near Louisville, Kentucky. We're retired now and we've been doing some traveling."

Mother said, "How did you meet my daughter?"

Mrs. Butterfield explained, "We met your grandson, Job. He brought us here to meet his family. He's such a fine young man. You should be very proud of him."

I held my breath, wondering what Mother would ask but she said, "Well, he is certainly becoming a very handsome young man."

I thought, *Appearances. Mother always focuses on appearances.*

"Yes," Mrs. Butterfield responded, "and a good moral character."

Before Mother could reply, Job appeared with iced tea and I said, "Mother, we will all go to church in the morning. You can go or stay here. The wedding is at the church at 3 o'clock. Immediately after the wedding, there will be an informal reception on the church grounds."

"Outside!" I could hear the disapproval in her voice.

"There won't be all that many people and the church grounds has all those lovely oak trees," I said.

"Could you not afford a proper reception hall?" she asked.

I said, "We didn't want a proper reception hall. We even discussed having the wedding here but Jim and I both liked the idea of having it in church."

Mrs. Butterfield said, "Job, dear. The last time we were here, it was a bit chaotic and Hank and I didn't get to see the greenhouse. Why don't you take us on a tour and then we'll be off to Eminence."

As soon as Job took the Butterfields off, Mother started giving me the third degree. "I had someone check on this man you're marrying. I could not believe what I was told. He is Negro!"

I looked at my mother and I knew nothing was ever going to make her accept Jim so I just said, "Why did you come for the wedding if you didn't approve?"

"I am hoping I can talk you out of this! Surely you are not going to do it!"

I said, "Yes, I am going to do it. A good man is a good man. I don't care what color he is. If you don't approve, then you don't have to come to the wedding."

"You should have married your son's father! He's white and he comes from an acceptable family!"

"Mother, I can't believe you just said that! He kidnapped me and held me prisoner for four days! He raped me repeatedly!"

Mother looked at me with her stubborn face on and said, "You know that isn't true."

I knew I was going to burst into tears so I got up and went into the house and out the back door. I saw the Butterfields were still over at the greenhouse. I refocused and joined them. I thanked them again for bringing Job home.

Mrs. Butterfield said, "Job says he'd never met your mother before."

I sighed, "She came after Job was born and tried to get me to put him up for adoption. She's never been back since."

"She's a bit difficult, isn't she? Too bad. She's a lovely woman.

Job said he shut the dog up and hopes she doesn't find out her name. I do see why you found it so funny."

When the Butterfields were gone, Job asked, "What have you got left to do?"

"Not much," I said. "After church tomorrow, Mrs. Voden will bring someone to take flowers to the church. That's why I put 'sold' on most of our big pots of ferns and flowers. Here are the urns we'll use."

Job asked, "How are we going to keep her entertained this evening?"

I knew who *her* was. "I don't know," I told him. "She used to have bridge parties. I haven't played in years. Dad never played. Maybe Dad will have ideas."

Job said, "I'll try. I don't think we should lie to her but I don't think we should talk to her about what happened either."

I said, "When you took the Butterfields out here, she immediately started in on me. She had someone check on Jim and found out he's black. She's horrified."

Job shook his head. "She doesn't know Jim."

I remembered and said, "Exactly. She actually said I should have married your father."

"How could she think that? Doesn't she know what he did?"

I said, "She doesn't believe I was raped."

Job looked at me with big eyes and finally said, "No. How could she not believe it? What did she think happened?"

I said, "She heard the rumors going around town saying I had faked it and believed them."

Job looked at me in disbelief and then said, "How could she?" and then he said, "That's awful."

"I'm sorry, Job. Maybe I shouldn't have told you but so much has happened, it seems like small potatoes now."

Job said, "No wonder you and Grandpa never talked about her. This is worse than being an alcoholic."

We worked quietly for a few minutes to finish the plant rearranging and then Job asked, "Do you think I could possibly do a snow job on her?"

I was puzzled. "A snow job?" I asked.

"You know," he said. "Swarmy-charmy. Flattery. Sweet talk. There's one teacher at school who eats it up."

I laughed. "I don't know. I never tried."

For dinner, I had put a casserole and an apple pie in the oven. Mother had been the casserole queen when I was growing up and it was one of her recipes. I'd done steamed broccoli with cheese sauce on the side. Mother had never served broccoli but we all loved it.

Mother was in her room and Job went upstairs to wash his hands. I heard his voice and Dad's. Eventually Job came down and began setting the table. When the food was ready, I called up the stairs and Job knocked on Mother's door.

Mother had not changed. She did not come out right away so we all had to wait. When she eventually appeared, Job jumped up to help her with her chair. I had known not to put the food on the table until she emerged from her room. When we were all seated, we bowed our heads and Dad did the blessing. I peeked and Mother did not bow her head. She was staring at Dad while he prayed. I suspected I was not the only one who peeked but everyone acted like things were normal.

Job moved the casserole dish to where Mother could easily serve herself and said, "Mom says this casserole is one of your recipes. You did a good job of teaching Mom to cook."

Mother had a stiff look on her face and I knew what she was thinking. She hated to cook. Mrs. Spelling cooked when I was little. After I started school, I went to her house until Dad picked me up. Mom always had a casserole in the oven. Saturdays were sandwiches and Sunday we went out to eat after church and ate left overs for supper unless Dad grilled, which he often did in the summer.

Job passed the casserole to me and set the broccoli where Mother could take some. "No, thank you," she said stiffly. Since I was busy with the casserole, Job dipped himself a good serving of broccoli and passed it to Dad before dipping the cheese sauce. I passed Job the casserole and Job said to Mother, "I really can't believe you're old enough to be Mom's mother. You look young."

It was said so guilelessly that if it weren't for our conversation out in the greenhouse, I would never have suspected.

Job went on. "Mom says you work for a lawyer. Lawyer stuff is complicated. You must be quite intelligent."

Mother unbent and said, "It's often complicated and requires strict confidentiality."

Job nodded. "Yes, but it must be really interesting. I mean

you would know all about what really happened and things that never got into the newspapers."

Job was looking at Mother like she was the Queen of England and I could tell she liked it. He said, "Are there any old cases, you know, ones that are finished, that you can talk about?"

She said primly, "We never talk about our clients or their business."

Job grinned. "Wow," he said, "imagine knowing all kind of things and never talking. You're great, Grandmother."

She said, "That's why I work in a lawyer's office."

Dad was looking a bit perplexed until Job gave him a wink. Dad put his face down and I knew he was having a hard time not laughing.

Job said, "I plan on going to college but I'm not sure what I should be. Is being a lawyer really a good job?"

Job kept things going the entire meal and Mother lapped it all up. Dad and I didn't dare look at each other because I knew we would both collapse in giggles.

At the end of the meal, Mother rose and said, "Nathan, I want to talk to you."

They went to the front porch and Job and I did the dishes. I said, "Job, I would never have suspected. Now I'm worried about you. You're a first class con artist."

Job said, "Don't worry, Mom. I never actually had a go at it before but one of the guys at school drips all over the teachers and Mrs. Wickersham thinks he's the most wonderful thing since the wheel was invented. I just started thinking about the things I've heard him say."

Then he said, "I did try it a little with you-know-who. He was wanting me to drink beer and I said I'd read that it wasn't good for you if you were still growing and I wanted to get as tall as him. It worked with him. Maybe that's what made me think of it today."

I looked at the son I'd raised and said, "Job, Dad said you've turned out so well that he wants some more grandkids."

Job grinned. "That'll be fun."

Entertaining Mother wasn't a problem. She and Dad talked for a long time and then she went in her room and shut the door.

Dad came back to the office where Job and I were both on computers and motioned us outside. We went all the way to the barn where Ginger greeted us happily. Our cats had all been used to Lassie and with a little coaching, Ginger had accepted them as part of her new home. She had been snoozing with three or four of them.

I could tell Dad was agitated. "She was carrying on about Jim being black and how could I have let you get involved with him? I told her I liked Jim and had encouraged the match." Dad sighed and I knew Mother had been appalled and had no hesitation in letting him know about it.

Dad then said, "Now she's trying to negotiate a deal for the divorce. She will give me a divorce if she gets this farm."

Job said, "She can't do that. It belongs to Mom, not you."

Dad said, "I know and I can't think why she wants it except money. She has never lived here and hates the country so she must plan to sell it. I wondered if that corporation who offered my mother a million dollars has contacted her."

"Maybe," I said.

Dad said, "She says she's not leaving until we get this settled. I've had enough. If she doesn't leave Monday morning, then I am. I can go camp at Alley Spring for two weeks and if she's still here then, I'll move to another campground."

I said, "Jim and I will be returning on Saturday. If you leave, then Job needs help. Let me call Mrs. Voden."

I phoned. Then I told Dad and Job, "Mrs. Voden's coming Monday. I told her she's going into the downstairs bedroom and she's to maintain she's too old and feeble to climb the stairs. I'll tell Mother tonight that we need the room on Monday. She won't like it at all. If she won't leave, what can we do?"

"Mom, you own the place," Job said. "If you don't want her here, then doesn't that make it trespassing?"

I sighed. "Maybe," I replied. "I'll tell her we have to have the room on Monday and see what she does. I need to tell her about the dog anyway."

At first, Mother would not open the door. When I said I needed to tell her about the guard dog, she unlocked the door and opened it about three inches. I said, "We have a guard dog who runs loose at night so don't go outside. She doesn't know you and she'll attack. Also I've assumed you're leaving on Monday. Mrs. Voden is arriving then and she will be using this room. If she comes before you leave, that's okay but she'll need it by mid-afternoon for her nap."

"What!" Mom said. "I'm not leaving Monday. I have business with your father and I'm not leaving until it's finished. Your Mrs. Whoever can sleep upstairs."

"Mrs. Voden is elderly and I don't want her climbing the stairs. But she knows all about running the greenhouse and Job will need her help because Dad is not going to be here."

"Why not? Where's he going?" she demanded.

"You can ask him," I said and walked away.

She opened the door and said, "Faith Marie, you get back here!" I kept walking. She followed me into the office room and said, "Faith, I'm your mother. You . . ."

I interrupted her. "Mother," I said firmly, "I'm not a child anymore."

"You're being disrespectful and rude," She said coldly.

I said, "And so are you."

"I will not listen to this!" she said.

"You don't have to!" I answered, and walked out the back door.

I was sitting in a backyard chair hugging Ginger and crying when Dad came and found me. He said, "Faith, I'm sorry."

I looked at him and said, "Dad, it isn't your fault." I took a big breath and said, "I should be over it by now but I guess everyone wants their mother to love them."

Dad nodded. He said, "I'm glad you decided you didn't need a wedding rehearsal. She would have probably attended and caused problems."

I said, "John said he didn't need a rehearsal; he'd had one when he got married. He told Job, 'You just follow me.' Jenny said she's been a bridesmaid in nine weddings. Can you believe that! Patty is the only one who said she wasn't sure what she was supposed to do and she and Jenny are going to discuss it while we're getting dressed. Can you believe Patty has never been in a wedding! She said she and Roger got married in a Justice of the Peace's office down in Thayer. She was six months pregnant with Roger, Junior and her father had told Roger if he didn't marry her, he had better not sleep, because he was going to get him."

Dad laughed. I had known he would.

Jim

I was ecstatic, floating on a cloud I was so happy. Faith was willing to marry me. Five days. There was a lot to do. We got the marriage license in Eminence. My brother, John, would be my best man and I asked Faith for Job as a groomsman. John and I both had navy suits and I checked Job's size and called Vern Chilton. My guess that they were near the same size was right and he did have a navy suit. In fact, he could no longer wear the one he got married in and it fit Job perfectly. Vern laughed. "What is he, 15? If you buy him a suit, he'll grow out of it in about three months."

Vern went on, "Since we're not on official phones, I'll pass something on to you. When I knew there were gaps in Robinson's records, I asked a cousin to have a look. She's not hampered by all our rules for evidence and sometimes she looks around and tells me where to look, if you know what I mean. Anyway, she got into Dylan Robinson's medical records. He's been married twice with no kids and his second wife finally got him to a doctor. He's sterile."

I protested, "But he's clearly Job Johnson's father. Everyone who's seen them knew it."

"Yeah, but sometime between the episode with Job's mother and his first marriage, something happened. The doctor had made a note saying STD with a question mark. I was thinking it might explain why he kidnapped Job Johnson. He wants a son and Job's the only one he's ever going to have.

"It's not clear why the doctor had scans done on Robinson's brain, but he did and they showed clear signs of brain damage. The doctor wrote football and car accident as causes."

I thought about it. Brain damage might explain a few things. Vern was also informing Jason Elfrink.

John and Job and I went shopping together for new shirts and ties. I asked Job about shoes and he said his grandpa was loaning him some black dress shoes. He said, "Right now I can wear his but Grandpa says I'm still growing so there's no point in buying me a pair of dress shoes I would wear only once."

Faith lamented the lack of choice of wedding dresses and went into a marathon sewing session with Mrs. Voden and some of her family. Mrs. Voden also was organizing the rather casual reception that would follow the wedding. I got the idea their church saw it as an excuse for a potluck picnic. It was to be held under the large oak trees on the church grounds and I hoped it wouldn't rain. Faith just smiled and said, "If it does, we'll manage."

Then Thursday evening, Jason Elfrink called me. After some discussion, it had been decided to send Dylan Robinson to Missouri to face charges for kidnapping Job first. Kai's kidnapping was going to be harder to prove than Job's. His kidnapping had other witnesses and evidence like the faked court custody paper. Also the rape case was still pending in St. Louis so that is where he was sent. He had escaped. Elfrink thought we needed to know.

I phoned and talked to Nathan but we decided it would just worry Faith needlessly. If the guy had any sense, he would run. But I did tell Sheriff Conners.

Jenny arrived from Oklahoma on Saturday afternoon with an old-fashioned lavender dress and matching garden hat. As a surprise, she had also brought our other sister, Joan, who lives with her husband and two children in Idaho. Joan had flown down to Tulsa and Jenny had picked her up. Joan said, "I'm not going to miss this."

Joan hugged me and said, "Mom says she's perfect for you. Does she really have a 15-year-old son? How old is she?"

I said, "30 and it's a long story. He's a fine boy."

She said, "Jim, you never have done things the usual way."

Jenny asked, "Do you think I can talk her into letting me have a look at that cave? The pics were fantastic."

"That you'll have to take up with her but her family has been protecting that cave since before the Civil War so don't ask me to sneak you in for a peek."

Mom and Esther arrived back from Pine Bluff. Mom was giving Mrs. Voden some help with the reception and she had gone after some items where she said the selection, and the prices, were better. She was also borrowing platters from friends.

John had asked me if I wanted a bachelor party and I said, "No, I want a last evening with my family. Let's do a barbecue."

ॐ Chapter 14: Disaster ॐ

Faith

I was sleeping with my door open which we all usually did. I'm not sure why but it had started back when Job was small and we had never changed. Old houses have creaky floors and I woke up as someone walked across my room to my bed. I think I knew even before I saw anything that something was wrong. Job or Dad would have stopped at the doorway and called my name.

I turned over and looked up into the face of a nightmare. He said, "If you don't do what I say, I'll tase you."

I'd attended that self-defense camp and done lots of reading on how to avoid a kidnapping. Your best chance is right at the beginning. I rolled out of the bed onto the floor screaming for help and tried to knock him off his feet but didn't succeed. He tased me.

I collapsed but was not completely out. I heard him laughing. He grabbed my hands and started dragging me. Out in the hallway, Dad was lying prone and Job was exiting his room with an older man behind him.

Job exclaimed, "Mom!" and started toward me. Dylan Robinson turned me loose and tased Job. He was still laughing.

I closed my eyes and pretended I was out. Bob Robinson told his son, "Quit laughing like a hyena and start cuffing them."

Dylan jerked my arms around and cuffed my hands in front. Then he put his hand on one of my breasts and squeezed. He was kneeling and I swung my cuffed hands and hit him. It was a weak blow but he was caught off guard and landed on his rear.

I yelled, "You slimy pervert, keep your hands off me!"

As Dylan stood up, his father asked, "What did you do?" but Dylan was not listening. He kicked me.

His father came out with, "Stop that! What are you doing?"

"She hit me," Dylan complained.

His father moved to put cuffs on Job. "So what? You're a

man. Control yourself."

I wondered how often Dylan's father had repeated that injunction. Maybe I could appeal to him somehow. I said, "Mr. Robinson, why are you doing this?"

He had stood and now he looked at me and said, "You are not marrying that damned nigger. You are going to marry my son like you should have done years ago when you were pregnant with his son."

"Mr. Robinson, Dylan has told you a bunch of lies."

"Dylan said you would say that."

I came back with, "It's true. That's why he knew I would say it."

But Robinson just got all three of us to our feet and told us to go down the stairs. We were all still in our night clothes and I was glad mine were so modest. Not only was I wearing sweat pants and a t-shirt, I even slept in a sports bra because as big as I am, it's more comfortable. Dad was in pajamas but Dylan was only wearing a pair of loose sleeping shorts.

Downstairs my mother was waiting. I don't know why I was surprised. As Dad and Job were told to set on the sofa in the living room, it was clear Mother was a partner in this.

Now Dylan was left to watch Dad and Job while Robinson and my mother took me into my office. Mother said, "Faith, you will call that negro and tell him you have changed your mind. You are not going to marry him. You are going to marry your son's father instead."

I just looked at her and said, "No."

Robinson said, "Don't sass your mother."

I said, "So shoot me. You might was well get it over with. I'll die before I marry that sadistic rapist you call your son."

I though he might hit me but instead he said, "I see we are going to need to use a little persuasion."

He took me back into the living room and sent Mother to her bedroom. They made Job lie flat on the floor and then Dylan hit him across the back three times with a leather belt, leaving red welts. Job did not make a sound. Dylan was obviously enjoying it.

Robinson was watching Job, not his son. He said, "That's for disrespecting your father." Then he said to me, "If you don't make that call, we'll keep on until you do. The boy needs discipline which you clearly have not been giving him."

I had been thinking furiously. I agreed to make the call and moved toward the living room extension but Robinson insisted on going back to the office. I think he was afraid Job or Dad would start yelling while I was on the phone.

My cell phone was upstairs in my room under my pillow and I was glad. It's normally what I used to call Jim. Now I used the landline and called the number for Jim's parents, instead of his cell phone. I knew that alone would make him wonder what was going on. It was starting to get daylight but it was really early for phone calls. When someone answered, they sounded sleepy. I said, "This is Faith. May I speak to Jim, please?"

I could hear them calling him and then he said, "Faith?"

My heart leaped at the sound of his voice. I did love him. I had planned carefully what to say. "Jimbo," I began, "I'm really sorry but I've decided that I can't marry you. I have to think about what's best for Job and I've decided I should marry his father. Jimbo, I'm really sorry." I hung up.

Robinson nodded. "That was good, real good," he said with approval in his voice.

I turned away knowing Jim now knew we were in trouble. When he told me about being called Abe in the military, he had said, "I just laughed about it. At that school where the boys dislocated my shoulder, they'd kept talking about Little Black Sambo and calling me Jimbo."

Robinson said to Mother, "You call her preacher."

He took me back to the living room but I heard Mother behind me saying, "Reverend Carson, this is Faith's mother. She asked . . . ." Her voice had that pleasant professional tone of the really good receptionist.

I joined Dad and Job on the sofa knowing Mother was canceling my wedding. It was only a couple of minutes before she came back to the living room saying, "That was easy. I just told him Faith had found out that Jim Willis was half negro and the wedding was being canceled."

I was looking down and not at mother. Jim and I had told Pastor Carson about his mixed ancestry when we asked him to do the wedding so now I knew Pastor also would be suspicious. The phone rang and Robinson said, "Let it ring."

Pastor's voice came on the answering machine saying, "Faith, this is Pastor Carson. Give me a call back."

Robinson said, "In case someone comes looking, I think we need to do what we discussed."

They were going to take us all into the cave and leave Mother here alone. She would tell anyone who came that we had all gone with Dylan Robinson and his father to Branson and that Dylan and I were getting married."

Dad said we needed shoes and I said I needed the restroom. They sent Mother in with me and she did not completely close the door. I gathered up both shoes and socks for all of us with Robinson almost on top of me with his taser. Because of the cuffs, I got a shawl but he would not let me get anything for Dad or Job. I protested about the cave being cold and he said they'd just have to tough it out.

As we went through the woods, across the small brook which was only a thread of water, and up the steep hillside to the cave entrance, I tried to leave as much of a trail as possible without being obvious. I touched the leaves of plants and shrubs and the trunks of trees. As we climbed, I managed to kick loose two fair sized rocks and one of them thumped Job who was behind me. I don't think even Job or Dad suspected what I was doing. I wondered what they had done with the dog but didn't want to ask. If she was not already dead, they might go kill her.

Inside the cave, they lit two lanterns. The path was clearly single file and when Robinson told Dylan to bring up the rear, I made sure I moved out right behind Robinson. Dad put Job next so he was the one just in front of Dylan.

When we entered the first large room, Robinson took the path going almost straight ahead but slightly to the left and never even glanced at the route which went sharply to the right and led to the pictographs and Indian remains. We followed the left wall until we came to a smaller tunnel going off to the left. Robinson asked no questions but turned in and it was not far before it ended. He looked it all over carefully and then said, "We'll park right here."

Both Dylan and Robinson were carrying tasers but Robinson also had a handgun in a holster. We sat down against the wall and I tried to give my shawl to Job but he wouldn't take it. Because of his back, he was sitting cross legged. Robinson was going to leave Dylan to guard us while he went to watch the house. I saw Dylan ogling me and I knew it was going to be trouble. I thought about saying something but then wondered how much of a charge his taser had left. He had already used it twice. Could he incapacitate all three of us with it?

Then Robinson changed his mind. I don't think it was Dylan's leering. Maybe he also wondered if Dylan could handle three of us. He could have left his gun with Dylan but instead, he sent Dylan to spy.

After a long silence, during which I was praying silently, Job said, "Mr. Robinson, I suppose you're actually my grandfather."

Robinson said, "Yes."

"Can I call you Granddad?" Job asked. I thought about the snow job he did on my mother and I kept praying.

Job said, "That day Dylan showed up at my school and said he was my father, I got in the truck with him. By the time we got to Winona, I knew I shouldn't have. Then he showed me that fake court order saying he had custody. That's why I didn't run off immediately."

Job paused and the said, "Granddad, do you have any idea how much your son is drinking and how much pot he smokes?"

"A few beers never hurt nobody and the stuff is legal in Colorado."

Job said, "What did he tell you happened with that Indian girl?"

"He said you all picked her up to give her a ride because her horse was lame. Then she was all over you and you all went back to his cabin. He said at first he thought it might be good for you to have your first woman but then he found out the girl was underage. He said you two got into a fight and you tried to get his gun and while you were fighting over it, it went off and hit him in the leg."

Job said, "If that's what happened, why did I take the girl back to her family?"

"Dylan says the two of you were laughing and went into the cabin and had sex before you left. He says he had the keys and he was surprised you didn't come and get them. He thought it was because you're too young to drive."

Job said, "I'm not too young to drive. I have a permit. I drive our pickup truck and the tractor. I ride a scooter to school all the time. He had been watching our house so he knew all that. He was drinking beer the whole time and his driving scared me. I tried to get him to let me drive. He knew I had a permit and could drive."

"So why did you not take his keys and drive off in his truck?"

"He had the keys in his pocket. I could have pointed the gun at him and demanded the keys but if he refused, I would have had to shoot him again to get them. I didn't want to kill him. Also he was hurt and needed to get to a doctor. So Kai and I packed some food and water and we walked all the way to Cortez."

"Dylan says you left him to die."

Job said, "I didn't leave him to die. If I wanted him dead, I'd have shot him again. I knew he wasn't bad hurt and frankly I was tempted to kill him. He had told me about raping Mom. But if I killed him and ended up in jail, Mom would be even more hurt. She loves me and she needs me to run this place. She can't do it on her own."

"But she was marrying that Jim Willis."

"No, she wasn't. All that happened after I got home. Grandpa and I played matchmaker. We like Jim."

"You want your mom to marry that nigger!" It exploded out of Robinson so violently that I found my heart pounding.

Job let it set for half a minute and then said, "Granddad, a good man is a good man."

Robinson shot back, "And your father is not a good man."

"No." Job said it quietly but firmly, with no hesitation.

"You've been brainwashed," Robinson stated.

Job said quietly, but again positively, "No, Granddad. You think about everything everyone else has said. Dylan is your son and you love him but that doesn't make him what you want him to be."

The silence sat and no one said anything for a long while.

Robinson's phone rang. In the stillness of the cave, I heard Dylan say something about a truck arriving. Then I caught the word "couple" and I figured it was Pastor Carson and his wife. Robinson told Dylan to stay on the phone and tell him what happened. It was a while before I could hear Dylan say something about leaving. Pastor and his wife left.

Robinson told Dylan to keep watching and Dylan started to complain about being hungry and why couldn't he go down to the house and get some food.

Robinson said, "Dylan, grow up. You aren't going to starve." But when he got off the phone, he called Mother and asked her to fix some sandwiches and call him when they were ready.

I knew what Mother would think about him expecting her to prepare food but she made nice and agreed to do it. I wondered if she was a little afraid of the Robinsons or maybe she just wanted to keep them happy.

Then Robinson addressed me. "Why did you not marry Dylan back then? Marriage and a kid would have settled him down."

I found myself unable to breathe, feeling faint, and Job spoke for me. "Mom did not know who raped her until last winter. I was playing basketball and at a game, she realized who I looked like." Job paused and glanced at me. I was staring at him and he probably saw the look on my face. He said, "She still never told anyone because she did not want me to know I was the result of rape."

"You believe that bullshit?" Robinson demanded.

Job said, "When I got back home and told Mom who had taken me, she fainted. That is what happened. If you refuse to believe the truth, I can't do anything about it. But the rape story is true. Out in Colorado when your son was drunk and high on pot, he told me he raped Mom."

Sitting against the rock wall, I put my head down and tried not to faint.

I heard Robinson say, "Her mother even says the rape story is not true."

Job said, "Grandmother is the most out of touch with reality person I ever met. All she cares about is social status and money. She objects to Jim Willis because of social status and she has some way she thinks she's going to get money out of this deal."

Robinson said, "She says your grandpa is divorcing her and she's agreed to take this farm so he can keep the house in Fredericktown where he works."

Job said, "She can't get this farm because it belongs to my mother. And she wants it because it's worth a million dollars. How much of that has she offered you?"

Even in the poor light, I saw Robinson's body language. He had not known. Job had found a weak spot and he wasn't slow to move on it. "Grandmother hadn't told you, had she? She has a plan somehow."

After another long period of silence, I recovered and I decided to say something. "Mr. Robinson, this whole scheme is totally impractical. How are you going to get a marriage license and force me to marry your son? You can threaten to beat Job, and Dylan would enjoy doing it, but I don't think you are going to kill your grandson."

Robinson said, "We already got the license and your mother has arranged the preacher. He's a lawyer too so he knows how to do all the paperwork legal."

Dad suddenly said, "Willingham! Is his name Willingham?"

"Something like that. I met him. Nice looking older man. He'll do the paperwork."

Dad said, "Ginger has roped you into this so she can get this farm and sell it. She asked for the divorce so she could marry Willingham. He's a lawyer and she's worked for him for about fifteen years. I didn't know he was supposed to be a preacher but anybody can get ordination papers these days. I heard you can even do it over the internet."

Job said, "Granddad, she is getting you into a mess. In order for her to get away with this, I think someone is going to die. Have you thought all this through? If Grandpa is dead, it would be much easier for her to get this farm. She'll let your son take Mom away somewhere and I think he'll eventually kill her. And I know very well you could not keep me quiet so I'd have to die too. Think, Granddad! You're not a murderer. Think this through!"

I thought, *Job, my intelligent son, had thought it through - and he was right.* Everyone was quiet and I was silently praying fervently.

Robinson's phone rang and it was Mother saying the sandwiches were ready. Robinson told her Dylan would be down after them and could she see if she could find some potato chips and cookies.

Then Robinson said, "Another thing I want to know is about this farm. How much is it worth?"

Again I could hear a little but all I really caught was "lies."

He hung up and I heard Dylan coming in with the food.

Jim

I stood paralyzed with the phone in my hand.

Faith was not going to marry me!

A black pit of despair opened and I was at the bottom. It closed over me and I was sealed in a grave with no light and no way out.

I closed my eyes and knew I wanted to die. I had never thought Faith would love me and when she said she did, I had been incredibly happy. I had thought she was a woman who understood love. She had accepted her son and loved him in spite of how he happened.

How he happened? I remembered her obvious trauma, her nightmares, her fervent desire that Job never know how he happened.

Faith would never marry Job's father! Not only had he raped her years ago, he had kidnapped Job.

Kidnapped! Was it possible?

Suddenly I knew. If Dylan Robinson had kidnapped them, Faith would do anything to protect her son, maybe even marry Dylan. But she had been sending me a message. *She had called me Jimbo!*

"Oh, God," I said out loud. "Dylan Robinson has got her."

My mother was still standing by the phone and she said, "What!"

"Thursday evening I heard they transferred Dylan Robinson to St. Louis and he escaped from custody. I didn't tell Faith and I should have. I think he's kidnapped her and Job."

"Why do you think that?" Mom asked.

"That phone call. Faith told me she had changed her mind about marrying me and was going to marry Dylan Robinson. She would never, ever do that. And she called me Jimbo which she knew would tell me something was badly wrong."

I saw Mom turning pale.

I pulled out my own phone and started punching numbers. I started with Mrs. Voden. She had not heard from Faith. She said, "I'll check with Pastor Carson."

Next I got Sheriff Conners. I said, "They may have left the area already but can you post someone where the county road comes out? They have to go that way to leave unless they do it by boat."

Sheriff Conners said, "I can call and get someone posted where Indian Creek runs into the river. They've already been working on that marijuana business."

My family was organizing themselves to go after a kidnapper. I heard them rounding up their guns and ammo, binoculars and cell phones, and discussing who was staying to answer the phone. My family is not a bowl of wet noodles and they warmed my heart and gave me hope.

I called Vernon Chilton and as we were talking, Mrs. Voden beeped in. She said, "Faith's mother called Pastor and canceled the wedding. Pastor thought what she said was weird and he tried to call Faith but no one answered the phone. He and his wife are on their way out there."

I said, "Call him back and tell him to be careful. Dylan Robinson has escaped custody and I think he's kidnapped Faith. Warn him. Tell him maybe he shouldn't go in and if he does, set it up with him to call you back as soon as he looks."

My family and I loaded into my pickup and Mom's car. It was John, Jenny, Joan, Mom, and Dad. Esther was staying at Mom and Dad's with her kids so she would answer the landline. Everyone had their cell phones.

I called Jason Elfrink and he said Vern had called already but we discussed the possibilities and what the sheriff was doing. Elfrink said, "I'm on my way. Your sheriff is good."

While we were still on our way, Sheriff Conners called and said, "Pastor Carson and his wife went in and have come back out. They said Faith's mother answered the door and told them Faith had decided to marry Dylan Robinson and she and her father and Job had all gone with Dylan and his father over to Branson for the wedding. Pastor says he heard the dog in the barn barking and asked who was taking care of her and Faith's mother said she was. Police trained dogs will only respond to their handlers so you know that's a lie."

Then the sheriff asked, "Do you think Faith's mother has agreed to help the kidnappers to protect her daughter? Could they even be hiding in the house?"

I thought about it. "Maybe," I told him. "Faith isn't close to her mother and she and her father are divorcing but if Faith, Job, and Nathan are all being held by a kidnapper, she might would do what ever the kidnapper wanted."

When we reached the place where the county road meets Highway 106, we found a cluster of vehicles, most of them law enforcement. One of them was Pastor Carson and his wife. He said, "I'm glad you had Mrs. Voden warn me. I would have known something was wrong and argued and that would probably have been dangerous. The dog being shut up in the barn was not normal at all and you know that dog is trained and won't even eat unless given the right command and there is no way Faith's mother could be taking care of it."

My mind had been busy. Now we planned. One of the vehicles in the bunch was the Coopers who lived on the road on past Indian Cave Farm. They had been on their way to church. Mrs. Voden was there also with her son-in-law. Pastor had called one of the church deacons explaining where he was and asking the church to pray.

I pulled the sheriff aside and said, "I know that farm inside out now and I can sneak in and check around. I have a listening device so I can hear conversations while staying hidden."

I laid flat in the bed of the Cooper's truck while they started for home. I banged on the cab of the truck when we reached the place where I wanted out. I had a small backpack but I was out and into the woods within seconds. I was heading for the place where Dylan Robinson had watched the house. Screened from the road, I found a large pickup truck. I knew my guess about kidnapping had been right.

I scanned the house, greenhouse, barn, and the surrounding area with care. Faith's old truck was parked in its usual place with Job's scooter. Nathan's truck was beside the house and behind it was a silver Grand Marquis which I knew belonged to Faith's mother. Nothing else. No movement anywhere, not even one of the cats.

I used my binoculars and still saw nothing. I worked my way through the woods and around to the back of the barn. Ginger knew I was there, standing in front of a back door. She whined but quit when I said quietly, "Ginger, still!" It was the Dutch command for silence.

I opened the door and she looked at me eagerly. I said at a whisper, "Ginger, ghoodzo," affirming her good behavior, trying my best to give the harsh, breathy Dutch "g" its proper clearing-the-throat sound. I wasn't sure how she'd ended up in the barn but I found some rope for a leash and took her back in the woods, saying, "Ginger, follow." I began a careful circuit through the woods around the house area. I wormed as close to the house as I dared and listened with the sound enhancer but all I heard was the TV. I moved around to the place where Faith and I had watched her house that first day. It was a good vantage point to see the whole house area.

I said to the dog, "Ginger." She looked up at me and I said, "Ginger, Faith, zook, zook Faith. Faith, zook spoor. Reveerin."

I untied the rope and she didn't even reach the front door before she picked up something. I expected her to go over to the driveway but instead, she came back toward me and entered the woods nearby. I realized it was where the path went up to the cave and quickly called, "Ginger, zit. Ginger, blyf." I could not see her and moved quickly toward where she had disappeared, calling again, "Ginger, blyf."

She was there, sitting, waiting for me. I said, "Ginger, ghoodzo, ghoodzo." She whined with pleasure and I hugged her. I used my listening device and couldn't hear anything. I retied the rope leash. I didn't want her running out ahead of me and getting shot. We moved slowly toward the cave and Ginger let me know that Faith's scent was everywhere. From behind a screen of shrubs, I inspected the path up the steep mountainside to the cave entrance which actually was not visible from down here. I could see clear signs of the recent passage of people – dislodged rocks, even tracks when I looked closely. I studied what I could see of the tracks. There were a lot of them and different sizes and treads. At least four people had gone up the path to the cave. And Ginger was sure one of them was Faith.

I went back into the woods and had Ginger track Job and then Nathan. All three of them had gone up to the cave. They would never have done that early on a Sunday morning unless forced.

I moved back near the house and listened again. I heard Faith's mother talking to someone on the phone. She had silenced the TV which made listening easier. She said, "I know we said we'd wait until dark but I can't stand these people. Mr. Robinson ordered me to pack them up food like I'm the hired help!"

After a silence, she said, "I know, I don't like it either and now we may have to pay them off but all that Dylan wants is Faith. I think they'll take her and run to Mexico like they were talking."

Again there was a gap and then she said, "The boy is really quite sweet." Then after a brief silence, she said, "Are you sure that's true? Last night he and I talked over dinner and he was a darling."

After a longer silence, she said, "I know. The money. You have it all set up for tomorrow. The title company will file the papers and as soon as they hear it's done, that corporation will send the money to the account in the Caribbean. You and I will fly to Miami and board your yacht. I know it's all set up. Foolproof."

Then she said, "I know. You have to go. Until tonight. Kissy-kissy."

I wanted to laugh. I would never, ever have suspected Faith's mother of using "kissy-kissy" as a private lover's code.

After a few minutes of silence, I heard the TV come back on and I moved back behind the barn, taking care to stay hidden under the trees.

Faith had told me about her mother and Willingham so I was putting facts together. I called Sheriff Conners. I told him I thought Dylan Robinson was being helped by his father and they had taken Faith and Job and Nathan into Indian Cave to hide. Also Faith's mother was working with someone, almost certainly Willingham, the lawyer from Fredericktown, and they were planning on a major move tonight. I told him, "Faith's mother and the lawyer are scheming to get Indian Cave Farm and sell it, probably to that corporation. The papers are being filed tomorrow and the money is being sent to the Caribbean somewhere. They are planning to fly to Florida where he has a yacht."

The sheriff said, "In that cave? That's difficult. The entrance can be easily defended by one person." Being local, the sheriff knew the Civil War stories. "If something's on for tonight, we can get them when they come out. It'll have to be then. You didn't see any signs of anyone in the woods. We'll feed our people and give them provisions for a long watch and send them into the woods. We'll get all these vehicles out of sight."

I made another suggestion. The sheriff said, "That's a good idea. My dispatcher, Janice Dunbar, will know how to get a hold of the county recorder and warn her about shenanigans over the ownership of Indian Cave Farm."

I talked to the FBI agent, Jason Elfrink, and then to Vernon Chilton. Vern said, "I'll put my cousin on to Willingham. It's

Sunday and she's available. She'll check out that corporation too. If they do a money transfer, she might can follow it."

I knew what I was going to do but I was not going to tell the sheriff. Faith kept life jackets in the barn. I put one on Ginger. I could get into the largest one by loosening the straps. I was going to try to use others to float my gun, phone, and listening device but then I saw a plastic tub. To keep it stable, I tied two life jackets around it. I found knee pads and gloves to add to the tub.

I tried picking Ginger up and carrying her slung around my neck, like a shepherd carrying a sheep. After her initial surprise, she seemed okay with it and I thought I could do it. If Ginger was willing to enter the water, then I would need to carry her up to the back entrance into the cave. I worried about her swimming ability but she followed me into the water without hesitation. She tended to move at an angle to begin with but I helped guide her and she figured it out. Police dogs are never timid or stupid.

The creek was much lower than the first time I was here and I could mostly wade. I found the place with no trouble. It was not an easy climb with Ginger but "blyf," the Dutch command for "stay," seemed to work. Either that or she's smart enough to understand what I was doing.

I lay in the end of the long tunnel which had to be done on hands and knees and used the listening device. Only as I got it out, did I remember to silence my cell phone. I took time to pray, asking God's help and imploring him to make me clear-headed enough to do this. A ringing phone would have echoed through this cave like a siren.

Chapter 15: In the Cave

Faith

Dylan brought in a plastic bag with food. It contained a small bag of tortilla chips, a baggie with a few cookies, and sandwiches. Robinson said to Dylan, "Take some food and go back out on watch."

Dylan took out a sandwich and complained, "These sandwiches got almost nothing in them! I could eat this whole bag of food by myself. And there's no drinks."

I suspected Mother was showing her resentment at being forced to prepare food by being stingy.

Robinson investigated the bag, took out a sandwich and said, "You take the rest of this and go back out to watch."

Dad and Job and I were all extremely uncomfortable and while Robinson was eating, Job asked, "Granddad, can I wiggle around a little? My legs are starting to cramp." Job had wiggled and twisted and then turned over onto his face and started doing push-ups. Dad and I both also started doing some stretches and wiggles but none of us stood up.

Robinson watched us but mostly Job. When he finished eating, he said, "Tell me about this farm. Why is it worth a million dollars?"

Dad answered. "The main part is 640 acres and it has been in my family since before the Civil War. When all this area was logged over, they didn't allow the timber men to log their land so at least 500 acres of this farm is virgin timber. Later my family bought the land to the south and then the farm to the north. Altogether it's 898 acres. Undeveloped land here is worth at least a thousand dollars an acre. The house, barn, and greenhouse are all in decent shape and then there's this cave. A corporation which owns other caves wants to buy it. Their other caves have a hotel, cabins, campgrounds, and some even have ziplines. Here they could also have canoe and tube rentals. A few years ago they offered my mother a million dollars for it but she said no. They might give even more now."

"Why did your mother say no?"

"Roots. Family. We've been here a long time. That sense of belonging is more important to us than money."

"So you didn't plan to sell either?"

"I had my mother give it to Faith rather than to me because I knew my wife would sell it if she could. When my mother died, she thought I was getting it and when she found out I hadn't, she was very angry. She wants a divorce and she wants this farm. Her and Willingham had it all planned."

The silence sat for several minutes and then Robinson asked, "What about this Willingham?"

"After Faith came here, my wife wanted to move from Pine Bluff and I got a teaching job at Fredericktown. Right away she went to work for Willingham as a receptionist. My wife is a nice looking woman and has a way of coming across as really upper class. Willingham had a wife but she died last fall. I had no idea why my wife suddenly wanted a divorce but I found out the reason was Willingham. Now that he's involved with this, I suspect his motivation is more money than my wife. Did my wife contact you?"

Robinson said, "Willingham called me and said he wanted to represent Dylan. He said he knew from Faith's mother that all the allegations Faith and her son had made were false. Then when Dylan was being transferred to St. Louis he told me his investigations showed my son was being railroaded. He told me he was real sorry because he was sure my son was innocent. He asked if I could use my police influence."

My dad said, "You helped him escape."

"I checked through my channels and discovered everyone was totally convinced Dylan was guilty. Then I got a phone call and the man said if I wanted to help my son, I should be at a certain place at a certain time. Dylan has a friend or two in the St. Louis police department."

The silence sat for another minute or so before Job said, "Granddad?"

Robinson said, "Yeah."

Job said, "Granddad, I'm sorry all these people are lying to you. They've gotten you into serious trouble."

Then Robinson said, "All you people got a story. Maybe all of you are lying."

He punched numbers in his phone and said, "Mrs. Johnson, I need to talk to you. I want you to come up to the cave." I could hear Mother objecting. Then he said, "Put on some tennis shoes! And bring us more food and some drinks." He shut his phone while muttering, "Fool woman."

Then he punched numbers again and said, "Son, I called that woman down there and she's bringing more food. I want to talk to her. When she gets here, you come in and watch these people while I talk to her."

We sat in silence until we heard Dylan coming. Dylan was already drinking a can of soda. Robinson gave him his taser and said, "Keep an eye on them."

As soon as Robinson moved off, Dylan set the soda down and with a taser in each hand he walked toward us. I knew what he was going to do and as he tased Dad and Job, I was on my feet and running. When I reached the big room, I saw light coming from behind me and knew it was Dylan. I began yelling, "Help! Help!"

But I didn't stop. I ran toward the entrance, still yelling, but then took the right hand path that led to the Indian pictographs. I had no light but I knew the cave well and I hoped I could hide.

However, I heard Dylan behind me. He must have had a flashlight in his pocket because I saw light coming from behind me not from one of our lanterns. I tried to move faster but with my hands cuffed, I was having difficulty not falling. I knew what would happen if I fell.

I couldn't move fast enough and he grabbed my shirt from behind. As I tried to turn and hit him with my cuffed hands, he dropped the flashlight and yanked the bottom of my t-shirt up so it covered my face and penned my arms together. He laughed and jerked up on my bra. I fell and he was down on top of me, penning my hands over my head. His other hand was fumbling with my sweat pants, trying to pull them down. I was trying to kick him but wasn't accomplishing anything. I started yelling again but my voice was muffled by my t-shirt.

Then I heard Robinson yell, "Dylan, what are you doing?"

Dylan replied, "Just a little fun. She's marrying me tonight anyway. We're just getting a head start on the fun."

I yelled, "He's raping me!"

Robinson said, "Get off her."

Dylan said, "No."

Then suddenly Dylan shifted his weight and a struggle started over me. I managed to roll over and I tried to get my t-shirt back down off my face. I scrambled to my feet and took off down the path again while trying to pull my clothes back into place. I heard the fight going on behind me and then the gun went off. It startled me so bad I fell but I wasn't hit and I kept moving. If I could just get some distance, there were places to hide.

Jim

When I reached the end of the long tunnel which had to be crawled, I listened but heard nothing. I remembered that beyond this open area was a narrower passageway, another open area, and another narrow place before the big room where the two main pathways into the cave split. Beyond that was the passageway which led to the cave entrance. I left the lantern at the end of the first open area, afraid it's light would be seen if I took it further. I was moving silently but Ginger's gimping was making noise so I picked her up again. I had a small flashlight and used the light only in brief shielded flashes. As I neared the front big room, I listened, then began a pattern of moving only a short distance before stopping to listen again.

At the entrance to the big front room, I finally began to hear something. Then as I contemplated further exploration, I saw light across on the other side of the big room and I froze. The light was being reflected on the upper sides and roof of the large room. It moved and I knew it was one of the lanterns Faith kept in the cave being carried by someone walking but the convolutions of the cave floor kept me from seeing the lantern or who was carrying it. The light disappeared and I moved out further, listening.

Faintly I heard a man say, "Keep an eye on them."

I waited and the light reappeared and then disappeared again along with the accompanying footsteps. I concluded that whoever was carrying it went into the passageway leading to the cave entrance.

Then suddenly I heard running footsteps and Faith yelling, "Help! Help!"

I heard Faith turn toward the entrance but then she took the path which led to the part of the cave with the Indian pictographs and someone was running behind her! He had a flashlight!

I put Ginger down, saying, "Follow," and started running, no longer worried about sound. I saw the lantern light come back into the room from the entrance and it turned into the other path. When I reached the turning point, I saw the light reflected ahead of me but the person carrying the lantern was already around a bend. I still had the listening devise on and further away, I heard a scuffle start and Faith's muffled voice crying, "Stop! Stop!"

Then I heard Robinson asking his son what he was doing and Faith telling him that Dylan was trying to rape her. Robinson told him to stop but I clearly heard Dylan refuse.

I was moving fast while trying to move quietly but I could hear Ginger gimping along behind me. I heard more scuffling and someone running on further into the cave. As the fight continued, I clearly heard Robinson yelling, "Dylan, quit!" Then I heard a gunshot. Was Dylan shooting at Faith?

I did not take the time to stop and get out my gun but ran, intending to tackle Dylan. When I rounded the last bend in the path, I saw Robinson kneeling over Dylan who was lying on the cave floor. Faith was gone and when I stopped to listen, I heard someone moving on down the path deeper into the cave.

I pulled out my gun and watched. Robinson was checking Dylan. I saw the slump of his shoulders and guessed that Dylan was beyond help. How had that happened? It must have been Faith I heard running away as the scuffle started.

Robinson stood and I saw the gun in his hand. He looked off down the path where I had heard Faith go. He bent and picked up a flashlight. He started down the path after Faith, gun ready.

With a quick prayer, I picked up Ginger and began following as quietly as possible. As I passed Dylan, I looked.

It was ugly. The light was poor but I could see a bullet had gone into the bottom of his chin. I knew the wound was fatal and I noted that although there was some blood, he was no longer bleeding.

Ahead of me, Robinson had moved around a bend but I could

still see reflected light. Faintly further away, I could hear Faith moving slowing. She had no light. With my small flashlight, I hurried, praying as I went.

Then I couldn't hear her. I thought she was probably hiding somewhere. I moved on and stopped several times to listen.

I had my flashlight off and I followed Robinson. He was not moving quickly but searching every nook and cranny with his flashlight, gun ready. Was he just trying to recapture Faith or did he intend to kill her?

I didn't think Robinson was a killer but in his grief over his son, he might become one. I moved closer. He was not turning around to look behind him but if he did, he would see me. I had my gun ready.

Then he reached a place which I remembered from my tour with Job. A ledge came down on the right side of the passage. Ahead of us, it would reach the passage floor and it was easy to turn and go up it. It eventually reached a height of about ten feet and up there was a series of incredible pictographs. Faith would know that ledge and it was a place she would recognize in the dark. Up at the top, she could lie flat and not be visible from the passage below.

When Robinson reached the point where the ledge was about five feet above the floor, he noticed it. I saw him shining the flashlight back and forth and then moving on down where the ledge descended. He kept shining his light up the ledge and I knew he planned to look. Somehow I was sure Faith was there. What did he intend to do? Was he just trying to recapture her or would he kill her?

He looked carefully at the soil at the bottom end of the ledge, squatting for a better look. Job and I had gone up there so if the soil was suitable, there would be footprints. Robinson stood and started up the ramp.

I set Ginger down. She was watching Robinson as intently as I was. I prayed Robinson would not turn around. Then when he was half way up the ledge, he stopped and said, "I see you! Stand up! You're the reason my son is dead!"

I didn't wait. "Ginger!" I yelled, "Stellen! Stellen! Gun ahport! Gun ahport!"

As I begin yelling, Robinson started turning to look down at me. I turned to ran back toward the cave entrance hoping Robinson would watch me, not Ginger. Robinson fired at me but he missed and I kept running. He didn't fire again because Ginger had him. I stopped and pressed myself against the wall, my gun ready.

But who came after me was Ginger, carrying Robinson's gun in her mouth and wagging her tail like a boy's pet bringing him a stick. I knelt and hugged her saying over and over, "Ghoodzo! Ginger, ghoodzo!"

Then suddenly it occurred to me Robinson might still attack Faith!

But I found him setting half way up the ledge, looking old and tired. I called Faith and she came rushing into my arms. She was hugging me without reservation, full body contact that promised a lot for our future.

I marched Robinson ahead of me back down the passage to his son's body. The lit lantern was still there and I said, "Stay here with your son's body until someone comes." He just stood there looking down at the body of his son. I took Faith and moved on, Ginger limping along with us.

Near the passage going out to the entrance, we met Nathan and Job. We took time for explanations and were not surprised to find Faith's mother waiting at the cave's entrance.

She looked at us and demanded, "Where is Mr. Robinson?"

I answered, "Sitting by his son's body."

She looked at me with shocked eyes and I knew she assumed I had killed Dylan. I didn't explain. I just opened my phone and called Sheriff Conners.

As we waited, Faith's mother demanded, "Who are you?"

Her physical resemblance to Faith was unsettling but her body language and tone of voice were totally unlike Faith. I said, "I'm Jim Willis."

"You can't be!" She exclaimed. "Jim Willis is half Negro."

I deliberately smiled at her and said, "Yes, ma'am. My father is black but my mother isn't. When I'm here in this area, I pass as white."

She was staring at me in disbelief and I knew later Faith and I would laugh about it.

Sheriff Conners appeared with others and I took them into the cave. He cuffed Bob Robinson but was was gentle with him. Eventually Dylan's body was bagged and carried away. The gun was placed in an evidence bag.

We moved back down to the house before the sheriff started taking official statements. Ginger Johnson was setting in a chair on the front porch with Sally Ann guarding her. My family was waiting in a knot with Mrs. Voden and we moved toward them while the sheriff turned toward the porch. When Faith's mother saw him, she started with, "Sheriff, what is the meaning of this outrage?"

He responded with, "Sally Ann, has she had her Miranda? I've got some of those forms in my car. Get her to sign one and then I'll have Dewayne take her into town. I want you here taking notes while I take statements from everyone." He turned to the two deputies who were leading Bob Robinson and said, "John, there's some chairs in the back yard. Take Robinson around there to guard him."

As Robinson started toward us, Ginger moved and growled. I said, "Ginger, still!" She was quiet but she watched intently as the deputy took Robinson around the house.

Then Faith's mother demanded in icy tones, "What did you call that dog?"

I said, "Sorry, Mrs. Johnson, but she's a retired police dog. She was already named Ginger when your daughter got her. You can't change a dog's name after it's been trained like Ginger has." Then I smiled at her and said, "She's a great dog, very intelligent."

Sally Ann led her away to one of the sheriff's cars with her outrage expressed with every step.

My family was giving out hugs and so was Mrs. Voden. They had all been getting acquainted. I introduced Faith, Job, and Nathan to my sisters. Jenny said, "Job, I can't believe Faith is your mother. She looks far too young to have a son as big as you."

One of the deputies asked, "What was that you told the dog?" and we started a discussion about the use of dogs by law enforcement.

Later when we were in the kitchen producing iced tea, Job asked, "Mom, do you think I should go out and talk to Bob Robinson?"

She looked out the window where Job had been looking and said, "Dylan was trying to rape me and his father told him to stop. When he refused, I think his father meant to hit him with his gun but Dylan tried to take it away from him. It's ironic that Dylan died in the same way he claimed you shot him in the leg."

Faith and I had talked briefly about Robinson's search for her in the cave. Both of us thought he probably meant to kill her but possibly not. Now Faith didn't tell Job about it.

Job said, "He was crying. We don't want him committing suicide or something. I thought it might help if I talked to him."

Faith looked at Job and said, "Job, you're amazing. Go talk."

I was concerned and put on my listening device. Job went out and sat down and said, "Granddad, I know you didn't intend to kill him."

After a silence so long I thought he wasn't going to respond, Robinson said, "I told him to stop and he said no. He was pulling her clothes off and she was trying her best to fight him. He even had his pants open already."

Job said, "I know. Mom guessed what he was going to do and was up and moving before he even tased Grandpa and me."

After another minute of silence, Robinson said, "When that woman in Pine Bluff alleged rape, he told me she offered and he took. I told him he ought to have had better sense. They threw the case out of court but Dylan had done other stupid things and the Chief asked him to resign."

He sighed and said, "Now those women in St. Louis and that Indian girl out in Colorado are all yelling rape. You and your mother too. When I saw what he was doing, I knew it was all true."

Then in the following silence, Job got up and hugged the old man. Robinson had started sobbing and Job held him while he cried. When he calmed down, Job said, "He was your son and I know you loved him."

When everyone was gone and Faith was feeding us all chicken stew, homemade biscuits, and fruit salad, Jenny said, "Faith, you have nice people here. Not a single person all day asked us in which cabbage patch we found Jim."

The cabbage patch was a family joke. Whenever anyone commented in any way about me not looking like the rest of the family, they always said they found me in a cabbage patch. Jenny claimed she was 12 years old before she learned it wasn't true.

Jenny went on, "So can we do this wedding tomorrow or do you need more time? I do have a job."

We called Pastor and rescheduled for 4 o'clock Tuesday afternoon. We needed Monday to pick up the pieces from this mess. Willingham had not been located and they wanted Faith at the courthouse when the title company people showed up to record the land transaction.

Monday afternoon, the sheriff told me that our county prosecutor was only charging Bob Robinson with involuntary manslaughter and if Faith was willing to testify in his behalf, he might not even be convicted on that. Robinson had called his chief in Pine Bluff and arranged to retire. He would be facing charges for helping Dylan escape but Sheriff Conners said he thought it might not be all that serious if he was willing to tell the St. Louis people who helped Dylan escape.

So Tuesday morning, I did my morning prayers with joy in my heart. Today was the day.

❦ Chapter 16: The Wedding ❧

Faith

Tuesday morning, we had time for the normal watering and greenhouse work. About 1 o'clock Mrs. Voden appeared and we loaded up flowers and greenery for the church. She had come in a pickup with her son-in-law and we loaded our truck as well.

While we were doing this, Patty arrived and on her heels came Jim's mother and both his sisters. After everything that had happened, we felt like old friends. I introduced Patty. She was looking nice, definitely slimmer and wearing a new hair cut.

Job left driving our pickup with Mrs. Voden aboard, following her son-in-law. The men were getting dressed at the church.

As we entered the house, our phone rang and thinking it might be Jim, I went all the way back to my office to answer it. Instead it was Simone Oliver asking, "Faith, do your parents live in Fredericktown? Is your mother named Ginger?" It was so out of my present context that it took a minute for me to understand. His mother lived in Fredericktown and knew my parents.

Simone was panicking about an awful mess and it took me a while to sort out the gist of it. His mother had come for a visit. She had never come before. What's more, she did not know about Simone's sexual orientation.

I demanded, "How could she *not* know?!"

Simone then told me his mother thought he just pretended to be gay sometimes because it helped his business as a decorator. He told me, "All male decorators are gay."

I was so befuddled, I actually voiced my thought out loud, "Surely not!"

Simone responded with, "Well, all the good ones, the important ones. It's part of the mystique, dear. And it's so practical for my work. It's always the wives I work with and this way, the husbands never worry about me being around and I have a good excuse for not responding to advances."

At that point, I wanted to laugh but Simone was so wildly distressed about something that I controlled myself.

I was still confused over why Simone was calling when he dropped the bombshell. "My mother says your mother is one of her best friends and she wouldn't miss your wedding for anything. She is demanding I call and get an invitation!"

I sidestepped. "How did she even hear about it?" I really did wonder.

"Albert Kranks," he told me. "He does those wooden sculptures and I had ordered two of them. He delivered them this morning. He grew up with your father and he's going to your wedding. He was talking about it and my mother said she knew a Nathan Johnson."

"Can you tell her it's a small private affair?" I asked.

"No. Albert told her it's going to be at the church at 4 o'clock and afterwards the church is having a potluck. He told her everyone from the church was invited. She nattered on about how quaint country customs were and she's upstairs producing one of her special cheese cakes right now."

"Simone, my mother's in jail."

"What!" he said. "Why?"

"She was part of that incident Sunday. Not the shooting part, but she had a scheme in place for selling Indian Cave Farm and getting the money."

"My mother!" Simone exclaimed with the exasperation clear in his voice. "She has no common sense! She chooses the oddest friends!" Again I wanted to laugh.

I thought. My mother did not know that several people knew she had been part of the conspiracy and she had asked the sheriff to let her attend my wedding in order to keep up appearances. He had called me before agreeing. I had talked to Job who said, "I'll stick with her during the reception and try to deflect anyone saying anything to her. Mostly I don't think people know she was involved."

I explained to Simone. I said, "Bring her and park her with my mother. It should help keep other people from talking to her so much. I'll talk to Job."

Simone said, "Tell that boy I apologize for leering at him and I won't do it again. Honestly, Faith, I knew he'd be shocked and tell everyone, so it was more a prank than anything else."

"I'll talk to him," I said.

I had directed Patty, Jenny, Joan, and their mother upstairs. I joined them and Jim's mother asked, "Do you want me to play mother of the bride as well as the groom?"

I laughed and hugged her. I said, "I'm not sure how I feel about this but Mother is attending the wedding. The sheriff called me and said she asked to attend because she wants to keep up appearances. She doesn't know everyone knows about the kidnapping and Dylan's death. I'm thinking that mostly they don't know about her involvement. I hate to admit it but I think her attending has its funny side. She will be elegantly dressed and coolly polite with everyone."

Jenny said, "I could not believe how much your mother looks like you. I can see why those title company people didn't realize she wasn't you."

Joan said, "What surprised me was Jim pointed out that if she had just been content to sell the farm and run, she and Willingham would probably have gotten out of the country before anyone realized what was happening. Why was she so determined to stop you from marrying Jim?"

I shook my head. "I knew she would have a fit if she found out about Jim's ancestry but I don't think that was all of it. She never believed I was kidnapped and I think she thought she would be fixing an irregular situation. Mother has never been normal. Looking back, I know that now. Dad always wanted her to be happy and so he often protected her from realities which she did not want to face."

Jenny said, "But if they had succeeded with their scheme, it would have delayed anyone finding out about the sale of the farm but how did they think they could keep all of you quiet forever?"

I said, "When we were up in the cave, we did talk some to Robinson. Robinson did not know about the farm until we told him. Mother had told him the rape story was not true and he thought I would just marry his son and we'd have a normal marriage and he'd get a grandson. If the rape story had not been true, that would not have been a totally crazy idea but of course, it was true. Job told him that. He told Robinson that if they tried to go through with it, he and Dad and eventually me too would probably all end up dead."

Patty said, "When I heard it all, it sounded horrible but Faith, you seem okay now."

"Yes," I said. "It's awful really but also a relief he's dead. I ended up feeling sorry for his father. The man really did not believe his son was a rapist until he saw him trying to do it. I suppose that when it came to dealing with reality, he and Mother made a pair."

Joan said, "I think someone has to be a bit mental to do what they tried to do."

"I don't know but when he saw Dylan actually trying to rape me, he did try to stop him. He didn't mean to shoot him. That was an accident but he did intend to stop him from raping me."

In the end, neither Jim nor I had told the sheriff about Robinson searching for me in the cave, possibly intending to kill me. The man had been out of his head with grief and we decided he would not come after me again.

I changed the subject by telling them about Simone and his mother. We did all laugh over the absurdity of the situation. Jim's mother said, "I'll keep an eye out and give some help if needed."

The talk turned to dresses and Jim's mother asked if I knew what Mother would wear. It's a real social *faux pas* for the mothers of the bride and groom to show up wearing the same outfit. I looked at the purple ruffled midi which she planned to wear. It went perfectly with the what we were wearing and I told her I was sure Mother would wear a suit.

Jenny, Joan, and their mother enthused over my dress and I raved over the cleverness of Mrs. Voden's daughter and granddaughter. Jim's mother said, "It's lovely and suits you perfectly."

I had already showered so Jenny went in while Patty did my hair. She chatted. "Faith, you were right about moving. No one down at West Plains knows my past and I'm not telling them. My daughter and I have started to church and I'm working hard on cleaning up my language. If I use a bad word, you're supposed to pinch me. But don't do it where the bruise will show today. I want these people here to see me with no bruises for a change."

Joan and her mother were puzzled. Patty explained, "My husband used to hit me. I divorced him last year but he kept bothering me. Faith said I should move and she was right. I love not having everyone gossiping about me."

I got into my petticoats and Jenny came out of the shower

and Joan worked on her hair. Patty went in and Jim's mother said, "These old farm houses are great but usually short on bathrooms."

I said, "We have another one downstairs but with all the men gone, we can manage up here."

Joan came out of the bathroom and said, "You must have a decent hot water heater. Being third, I figured I'd get a cold shower but it wasn't."

I said, "Fourth actually. Job took a shower before he left."

Joan said, "He really is a good-looking young man. Has he started dating yet?"

I said, "No, but he's attracting attention. All of us including Jim have talked to him about girls." There were a few chuckles over that.

Patty had sat down on the bench in front of my dresser and I was going to help her with her hair. Joan moved over and said, "I'll help her. You finish getting dressed."

Patty said to me, "I see you even did toe nail polish. I haven't met Jim yet. He must be tall if you're wearing those platform sandals."

"Six foot five," his mother said.

"Wow!" Patty said. "Can I talk about the fight with Roger or is it too much?"

I said, "It's okay."

She said, "My ex was a deputy sheriff. He was after Faith – kept asking her out. After a dozen 'no, thank yous' he still hadn't got it so she ticked him off. Mrs. Voden and Jim Willis were both here. My ex started cussing at her and she told him to leave. Then Jim also told him to leave. My ex hit Jim and I heard it took him less than a minute to get him down and handcuffed with his own cuffs."

I shook my head. "That isn't exactly how it happened. It may have taken two minutes and Jim held him down while Mrs. Voden and I put the cuffs on him." Everyone was laughing.

Patty started asking what exactly she was supposed to do in the wedding.

It was lovely. Our small church was full but all the windows were open and the ceiling fans were gently stirring the air. Mrs. Voden and her helpers had done a great job with the flowers.

They looked beautiful and lightly scented the warm air so the church smelled fresh even with all the people.

Jim stood down front with the minister while John escorted his mother in with his father in tow and seated them on the front row on the groom's side of the church and joined Jim. The rest of his family were already seated except for Jenny.

Job escorted my mother in and seated her in the front row on the bride's side. She had chosen to wear a tailored suit, as I had guessed. It was silver-gray with a sheen and her purse, shoes, and small hat matched as did her gloves. She was the epitome of the elegant lady but the thought went through my mind that she would have dressed the same if she had been attending my funeral.

Jenny went down the isle first, tall and willowy, flowing blonde hair with her garden hat. She had the same long face as Jim and her mother but had chosen her hair style and makeup well. She was an attractive woman with an interesting face.

Patty went down the isle next and she looked lovely. I heard later that many of the people present did not recognize her. She joked about it and said, "They'd never seen me without bruises."

Then everyone stood while Dad walked me down the isle. I saw Jim waiting for me and he looked elegant in his navy suit. I knew Mother would approve of his looks, if not his ancestry.

At the end of the ceremony, Jim kissed me sweetly, almost shyly. We neither one are exhibitionists.

We greeted everyone as they exited and we cut the cake and started the picnic. Tables had been set up and chairs provided. Everyone talked. I knew that before it was over, everyone attending would probably get told everything. The sheriff was there in his uniform.

Mother was seated in the shade with Sally Ann in attendance, dressed up for the wedding. Simone had arrived with his mother at the last possible moment and now she was ensconced in a chair talking to Mother. Simone and Job were taking food and drinks to the party and I saw Sally Ann's date, another deputy, hovering about. Jim's mother was keeping an eye on things.

Jim and I were called back in to do the paperwork. When we finished, Dad and the sheriff were waiting. The sheriff said he'd give Mother a few more minutes before Sally Ann and another deputy took her away.

I was introduced to the FBI agent, Jason Elfrink, who is six foot two with red hair and freckles. He asked, "Who is the that lovely tall, blonde bridesmaid? Is she married?"

I met Vernon Chilton and his wife, Elsie, and a black couple, George Brown and his wife Shanika. Jim shared an apartment with them in Springfield. He and Vern and George had all been in the army together. I saw people were being polite and thought that in general people are nice.

Now, I heard musicians tuning up. Some of the local churches disapproved of dancing but Brother Carson considered square dancing an acceptable social activity if engaged in at locations where no alcohol was served.

Jim

As the wedding started, I told myself to keep my mind on the ceremony and off everything else. When Job escorted Faith's mother into the church, I saw she was dressed in a formal gray suit. It had a sheen but still, who wears gray to a wedding? especially if you're the mother of the bride and therefore going to be on display? She even wore a small hat and gloves. Other than things like the garden hats being worn by Faith's bridesmaids, I'm sure the church had not seen a hat in forty years, maybe fifty.

But with Faith's appearance on her father's arm, I forgot everything else. I had never seen her in a dress and this one was dreamy – romantic with ruffles and lace. From the moment she appeared, I couldn't take my eyes off her. When John handed me the ring, I groped around and he grabbed my hand and I heard him chuckle as he passed it over.

When we stopped outside the church door, I said to her, "We did it!" I heard the satisfaction in my voice. She laughed and said, "We did." It might sound like a silly exchange to someone listening but we understood. We were both committed, totally and completely.

The rest of the wedding party followed and we began forming a reception line. Faith's father escorted her mother out and I was formally introduced, along with my parents. She looked at my parents and as Faith had predicted, she made appropriate, if somewhat stilted, conversation with no hint of questioning how two blonde, blue-eyed people could possibly have produced me.

What she said to me was, "You are an attractive man, especially in a suit." My mother had worked on my hair and I knew I looked white. Faith's mother approved of my appearance, if not my parentage. But I knew it didn't matter. She was not part of her daughter's life and hadn't been for sixteen years.

We cut the cake and the party began. I saw Faith's mother seated in the shade talking with another lady. Nearby were Sally Ann and her date, another deputy. Job was dancing attendance. Faith had told me about Job's snow job. I might ought to keep an eye on that young man. Faith had also said, "Mother thinks none of these people know what happened out here Sunday!"

Then I noticed Simone bringing food and drinks to the lady sitting with Faith's mother. Faith filled me in, laughing. I said, "Now I'm wondering about that Simone. He certainly admired your looks. Maybe it's all a charade."

Faith shook her head. "Maybe," she agreed. Then said, "You know everyone here who wasn't out here Sunday is going to want to talk to us about what happened."

I said, "We're ducking out early so they won't have much of a chance to interrogation us."

We went back into the church for the paperwork and when we finished, Faith's father was standing with the sheriff. He said, "I'm giving your mother enough time for her to feel like she's made her proper appearance and then Sally Ann and Dewayne will take her back to jail."

I said to the sheriff, "Nathan knows where we're going for our honeymoon but no one else. We'll be back Sunday evening."

༄ Chapter 17: Honeymoon ༄

Faith

We had rented one of the cabins at Big Spring which had originally been built by the Civilian Conservation Corps during the Depression. Jim had asked me if I wanted to go somewhere exotic like Hawaii but I had said no. I wanted to spend time with him, not explore a new environment.

I had decided Jim would make a good father and I was going to do my part, even if I didn't really enjoy the process much. I got a big surprise. I had heard it described, read text books, and waded my way through a few steamy novels but I was still unprepared. Some things you really only learn about by doing.

Afterwards, I lay cuddled in Jim's arms and said, "I didn't know it could be like this."

Jim said, "I had began to suspect you didn't. God intended for this to be enjoyable. It bonds two people together in a way that is deeper than any other relationship."

I thought about it. Jim had told me rape was not about sex. Now I knew it was true. But how could couples like my parents stay together for years and not really bond? Maybe it only happened if the people were normal. My mother was not normal. I had known that for years. But Dad was. Maybe that was why he had not divorced her. She had initiated the divorce.

Then Jim said, "I was not sure we'd get this far tonight. I thought it might take you a while."

I forgot about my parents. Jim was here and now and very real. I felt love swelling in my heart and I heard it in his voice.

For the next five days, we hardly mentioned unpleasant recent events. We discussed Jim's job. He said, "My family is finding surveillance systems are a hot item. Rural people are having more and more trouble with thieves. I've been helping them some. They have hired, and fired, several people. Each of them was either unreliable or did sloppy work, or both. They hired a woman to run the office and then caught her stealing. They have dropped back to only family and just telling customers they'll have to wait. Mom has hired someone to help her with the house and she's going out on jobs as an assistant. Esther is running the office. They are losing business because they can't get to jobs fast enough. They've asked if I would consider coming back to Ellington."

"Do you like living in Springfield?" I asked.

"I like being able to move around looking either black or white without people remarking on it. In Ellington I have always passed as white and now with what's happened, everyone knows I'm not. I'm not sure if it will be a problem. I think some people have always suspected. When we had games and the other team had black players, I could tell they always knew. Sometimes it bugged them but they never told. I got to where I always made jokes so they knew I knew that they knew. It was fun. We'd make these jokes right in front of the white players and they never got it."

He was smiling. "When I started applying for college, we discovered there were a lot of scholarships for black kids and I got one so I let my hair go back to an Afro. But I ended up dropping out at the end of my first year."

He stopped and then said, "I told you I once had a girlfriend I wanted to marry. I was really broken up over her and I joined the army. It took me a while to pull myself together again. That's when I got serious about my relationship with God so maybe that bad experience sent me in a good direction."

"Do you want to pass our children off as white?" I asked.

He said, "I don't know. I do want them to know who they really are."

"Yes," I agreed. "If I had told Job the truth about his father, he would never have gotten into the truck with him."

Jim said, "Maybe not but Job told me he saw later that he had a handgun and Job thought he would have used it to make him get in the truck if he had not done it on his own. That might have attracted the attention of other kids but who knows? We can play the 'if only' game forever."

Jim moved the conversation sideways again. "During the reception, George was getting his jokes in."

"Was he?" I said.

"He and Shanika thought it was funny that none of those white people could see I was black but I told them that a lot of them did know. They were surprised because everyone was being nice."

On another day, he said, "You've never asked me how I happened."

"I'm the last person in the world to ask anyone where a kid came from. When I met your mother, I saw you look like her."

Jim said, "When she was 15, her mother moved in with a man who started trying to molest her. When her mother wouldn't protect her, she ran off. She was tall and lied about her age and started working as a waitress. She met my father. She says he was tall and handsome and she didn't care if he was black. They moved in together and he told her they'd get married when she was 18.

"When she turned 18, he still didn't marry her and she let herself get pregnant thinking it would get him to do it but instead he abandoned her."

"That's sad," I said.

"She says she had worked at this same cafe for a couple of years. She said there was this tall, blond white man who came in often and had asked her out. When someone else who worked at the cafe told him her boyfriend had dumped her, he started asking her out again. She said he didn't harass her but he joked and kept letting her know he was interested. When she reached the point her co-workers noticed she was pregnant, she told him. She says he told her he didn't care. They got married only about two weeks before I was born. He put his name on my birth certificate."

"Your parents appear happy together," I commented.

"They are," he agreed. "Dad claims he prayed about her and God told him to wait for her."

"Wow," I said.

"After I started working in Springfield for Guardian Security, I located my biological father and looked him up."

I looked at Jim and he was looking at me. "He's a professional gambler."

It was such an unexpected profession, I said, "What!" and Jim laughed.

"Mom had told me so I knew already. That's partly how I found him. He has several aliases but a handsome six foot five light-skinned black man with hazel eyes is not like trying to find an average looking five foot ten white guy with brown hair and blue eyes.

"When I found him, he was in New Orleans. I waited outside a private gambling club and when he came out, I moved in and said I wanted to talk to him. He looked around and said, 'Not here,' and asked me to get into his car. He looked at me and said, 'I should have married your mother.'

"I laughed and said she was probably better off that he didn't. Then he asked me if we wanted money. I told him no, Mom didn't know I had looked him up and I was just curious."

When Jim was quiet, I finally asked, "What was he like?"

He smiled, "Handsome, much better looking than me, intelligent, successful, and not terribly honest. Professional gamblers are not very welcome in a lot of gambling establishments. Most people don't know that. Poker is a game of skill and a really intelligent person can win often enough to make it worthwhile. Gambling establishments just provide the place and take a percentage of the pot so they don't really care who wins. However, consistent winners are not welcomed by other players. A successful professional will work in a large area where he hits each club only until he gets a big haul and then he moves on. They normally try to have some sort of cover. People think my father is a high-level drug dealer but most professional gamblers claim they're in real estate or something respectable. He will work an area for a while and then move on to another city. He never stays in one area long enough for anyone to suspect."

I said, "Not a very stable life."

"No," he said, "and I think rather lonely. My father took me somewhere to eat and asked me about my life. He asked about my mother but I said she was happily married and I didn't plan to tell her I'd looked him up. I think he was serious when he said he should have married her. He told me he bought a place in the Caribbean and retired once but he was bored. He said maybe when he was old, he'd go back. I told him there were other interesting things to do besides play poker but he said he thought he was too old to take up another profession. He gave me a cell phone number and I call him once in a while."

Then Jim said, "I noticed you don't keep any cards in your house."

I said, "Grandma didn't allow them. She said gambling was a sin rooted in covetousness."

"She was right. Also it's addictive. After looking up my biological father, I learned to play poker. It's true if you have a keen memory and are good at figuring odds, you can mostly come out ahead. But it gets a grip on you and you find yourself scheming where to find a good game. I didn't like having that desire controlling my life. I quit playing."

Jim and I hiked and canoed and swam in the Current River. It was a lovely five days away from everyone with only us and time to talk.

One day we met a black couple down by the spring and Jim told me later the husband had asked if I knew. He said, "Black people always know."

He liked for me to put sunscreen lotion on him and I discovered I liked him putting it on me. This touching business is fun.

As the days passed, I also knew something else was happening. I thought about it and then talked to Jim. "Jim, I'm changing. It's marriage. I can sense that who I am is changing. I think this is what the Bible means where it says 'the two shall become one.' It's . . . it's a little bit scary but also exciting."

Jim looked at me solemnly and then nodded. "Yes," he agreed. "I'm feeling it too. I've wrestled a lot over the years with my self-identity but this, this is different. It's a growing thing. I'm changing but it's a positive thing, a becoming something new but bigger somehow." He gave me one of his smiles that lit up his face and I kissed him.

On Sunday we somewhat reluctantly packed our things and headed back to Indian Cave Farm.

Jim

Our honeymoon was like a time out of time. I would always remember it later as a wonderful time, carefree and filled with contentment.

My only agenda for our honeymoon was to hopefully get Faith to enjoy the traditional honeymoon pass-time.

That girl I had wanted to marry was experienced and had

easily seduced me but looking back now, I knew how shallow and immature it had been. My insecurities about being wanted had made me an easy target. I was now grateful because the woman had dumped me.

I loved Faith and now I approached her with caution, not wanting to scare her, but the first night things went well, much better than I expected. Afterwards she had lain in my arms, clearly pleased and I was over the moon.

The next day, I asked for her help with sunscreen and she happily put her hands all over me and I put mine all over her. She had looked around and said, "We should only do this in private." She liked touching me and I liked being touched.

We talked a lot. I told her about my biological father. For me, passing is a game I play. I do it a lot because it makes my work easier but I have a big Afro wig I use when I want to be obviously black. I put it on one day for Faith and she said, "I like the look. It suits you."

I said, "Maybe I should let my hair do its own thing. It isn't as kinky as this wig but if I let it get longer and work with it a little, it'll do a decent Afro."

She said, "I can just see the shocked looks on people's faces at home." But she was laughing about it.

When she asked me, I said I was fine with our home being Indian Cave Farm. I said, "Job needs stability and you love the place. I can live there and still work for my family."

Sunday morning we took some time for one last session before we showered and packed. Our honeymoon was over and I suspected we would be returning to a world which was not going to give us enough time together.

❧ Chapter 18: Grandparents ☙

Faith

We were welcomed home by Job and Dad. Job's soybeans were up and growing rapidly. Fredericktown had hired a replacement teacher for Dad. He said, "I can sit out a year but I've applied to other towns in the area."

Jim and I were going to use the downstairs bedroom which had been Grandma's. I moved things down from my room. Grandma had used an old-fashioned double bed with wooden head and foot boards where Jim had been sleeping diagonally. It was disassembled and taken upstairs to the guest room with the twin beds. We carried the mattresses down from the twin beds and put them on the floor for a temporary solution. They were too short but extra pillows could be added to the foot.

On Monday after the incident at the farm, a young clerk from a title company in West Plains had shown up at the courthouse to record the sale of Indian Cave Farm to the corporation which owned other caves. They told me the ruckus went on for several days. The deal had closed on the previous Friday and somehow Willingham made the corporation think it was recorded and they had sent the money to his account on Grand Cayman.

He didn't know about Vern Chilton's cousin whose regular job was for a bank. The money was returned and they even paid the cousin a fee which they promptly tried to recover from everyone and anyone involved, starting with Willingham and eventually reaching me.

Jim called them up and told them we were the ones who put someone onto watching the situation and that alert had led to the recovery of their money. They said they thought it was the FBI and Jim said, "We were who alerted the FBI. Check with Agent Jason Elfrink."

After I had been home a few days, Dad got a phone call and I caught a few words and went out to the greenhouse to give him some privacy. Later when he came and found me. He said, "Your mother is now trying to stop the divorce."

I saw the look on his face. It was the wounded look of the betrayed – dismay, grief, pain – and indecision. I took his hand and said, "Dad, we'll survive this."

Willinghan had been arrested but now Dad told me, "Willingham was released on his own recognizance and he's skipped the country."

I said, "I know how you feel, Dad. You took responsibility for her when you married her and you were never a person to run out on your responsibilities. But this time, I think you need to quit. If you don't do it, she will keep on scheming against all of us."

"My lawyer says that with what has happened, it should be no problem for me to get the divorce, especially since I'm willing to give her half of what the house brings."

I thought. "Dad," I told him, "I know your marriage relationship was never really good and now you will never have back what you even had before."

Dad sighed. He said, "I know." I knew he still was having trouble letting go. Then he said, "I was thinking about the Biblical injunction to forgive. I should forgive her."

"Remember how you arranged for me to see a therapist years ago. That therapist told me I should forgive my rapist but she also explained if I ever found out who he was, that forgiving him did not let him off. I should testify in court and put him behind bars. She said she told battered women all the time that forgiveness had nothing to do with love or trust. She said you can love someone you don't trust and to protect yourself, you may need to cut off relationship. She also said that forgiveness, even from God, did not erase the consequences of sin. Mother was willing to trade her marriage for money and the status of becoming Willingham's wife."

Dad was quiet, thinking about it. Then he looked at me and said, "I can forgive her for that. What I have trouble forgiving is her treatment of you. She basically was willing to sell you to Dylan Robinson for this farm."

I saw his anger and I understood. What Mother had done could have resulted in all of us being murdered, including my son, Job. I said, "I have been praying and asking for the grace to forgive Mother. It isn't easy. But the broken trust is another issue. Broken trust has to be re-earned and I suspect Mother has no understanding of that. She is blaming it all on Willingham and taking no responsibility for her actions. If she again had the opportunity for wealth and social status, she would do the same again."

Dad looked at me and saw him thinking it through. He sighed. "I'll do my best to forgive her but with no trust at all, how can I stay married to her?"

I hugged him. I knew it was not easy.

In the end, he went through with the divorce. The house sold and everything was settled.

As the summer progressed, Jim was busy helping his family install surveillance systems. He had quit straightening his hair and discovered a lot of Ellington people saw the situation as a good joke. Successful pranksters are generally liked.

He also discovered his basketball coach had guessed back when he was in high school and so had a few other people. He said the old man told him, "I wasn't going to say anything. Some of these fool people around here would have had a fit. I noticed you never dated. That time they had the Sadie Hawkins dance, I know you got asked but you said you were going to be out of town. That was really the only thing about it that concerned me. And I heard that woman you married says she knew right from the beginning."

Jim said he'd had seven girls ask him to that dance and John had teased him unmercifully. "I think he was jealous. He only got asked by three girls."

Then someone in Ellington wanted him to check on a man he was thinking about going into partnership with and it didn't take Jim very long on the internet to find out the man was a rascal. He charged the client fifty dollars and suddenly he was in business as a security consultant.

Job was busy. Dad loved working in the greenhouse so Job took care of his soybeans and started helping Jim with his work. Jim told me Job was great, learned quick and was good with people. Somewhere along the way, he asked me if I minded if he asked Jim if he could call him Dad. I could tell Jim was deeply touched by Job's trust and respect.

School started and we had to readjust. Dad got a teaching job but it wasn't high school. The teachers had three preparation days before school started and before noon on the first of those days, James Hillis called Dad and asked if he was willing to take a sixth grade class. They had hired a girl just out of college who didn't show and when they checked, they discovered she had left the area with a boyfriend. So Dad had a job.

Dad had a lot of prep work so Job was off on his scooter every morning and home as soon as school was out. After a week he said, "Mom, everything is a little strange. I pay attention in class because I need good grades to get a scholarship and mostly it's interesting but . . . ."

He trailed off and I said, "Are they teasing you again about being a bastard?"

"No," he said. "it's partly the opposite. They want to hear all about what happened and girls are all hanging around but they all seem so childish. I don't know how else to explain it. I feel like an adult with my mind on adult problems and they are all kids talking about childish nonsense. Every day I can't wait to get home and work on serious things."

I sighed, "What happened has changed all of us. None of us see things the way we did before this all happened. That affair out in Colorado forced you to become an adult. It's . . ." I paused and then said, "It's like what happened to me when I got you. I had to became an adult. I think once you've made the transition to taking on adult responsibilities, then there's really no going back."

"You never went back to school, did you?"

"No, I got some books and studied and then took the GED. Now you can do schooling at home over the internet but if you want a scholarship, you probably need to go the traditional route. Have you joined any clubs or signed up for any sports? Some scholarships consider extras like that."

Job grinned. "I've joined the noon prayer group. That's why I've started packing my lunch. We're not really official. We meet outside for now but when the weather's bad, the janitor lets us meet in his room."

"Do any of the other activities interest you at all?"

"I'm going to the first FFA meeting but other students have told me the meetings are boring. They said it is mostly just hype about how great it is to be a farmer. If you really are one, you know it's just a lot of hard work. I don't mind doing that. It's real, not just a lot of talk. I like working with Jim installing surveillance systems. That's real work too."

I looked at my son who was no longer a child and remembered what I had told Jim about letting him grow up. It had happened.

With Dad teaching, Job in school, and Jim working, I was home alone. We were still a little concerned about me being here alone but the greenhouse was in fall mode now which meant I was not nearly so busy. In the fall we had always sold fall bulbs, mums, and houseplants – pots of African Violets, coleus, spider plants, and cacti. We only really took a break in January. In February, we started seeds for tomatoes and perennials. I had the surveillance system and Ginger had now learned her job and could be relied on to not attack customers who acted normal but if they strayed, she would stop them with growls. We had been told she would not attack without an order from one of us and so far she hadn't. I kept the shotgun loaded and handy.

Then one Sunday, Bob Robinson showed up at our church. I found out later he had come in right after the service started and sat in the back but we didn't see him until the service was over. When we exited the church he was waiting.

He took off his hat and then looking at me, he said, "I come to apologize."

I was so surprised, I just stood there, staring at him. He looked old and gray – sad. Discouraged?

He shifted, showing his discomfort, but then he looked me straight in the eyes and said, "You never told anyone about me coming to find you after Dylan was dead. I was totally out of my mind and I intended to kill you. I know saying I'm sorry doesn't make up for that but I really am glad that dog stopped me."

I said, "We weren't sure you really meant to kill me."

He looked down and then off into the distance and back to me. He sighed and said, "It was what I had in my mind. I thought that if it weren't for you, Dylan would not have been dead. It was crazy thinking. I see that now."

I nodded and said, "I accept your apology. Even my own mother believed the story about me faking the kidnapping. I love my mother but I've realized she isn't normal. I understand how you loved your son and it was hard for you to accept that he was a criminal."

Robinson took a deep breath and then exhaled sharply. I wondered if what I had said was too sharp but then he nodded.

He looked down and turned his hat in his hands and then looked at Job, at Jim, and then back to me. He said, "I wanted to ask . . . ." He stopped and we waited. He looked again at Job then back to me. "I wanted to ask if maybe I could see the boy some."

I looked at Job. I thought about how as his mother, I wanted to protect him, but he was in many ways an adult now. I looked back to Robinson and said, "We would need to discuss it."

He nodded and said, "I'll wait in my truck."

We silently watched him walk back to his truck. Then I looked at Job and asked, "What do you think?"

I had forgotten Pastor, standing by, waiting to see if he was needed. Now he asked, "Do you want me to call the sheriff?"

I looked at Jim who said, "I think it's okay."

We had a discussion and decided to invite Robinson back to the farm and talk some more. Job said, "I can talk to him on the front porch." He knew very well we could hear everything said there from inside the house.

At the house, Job took coffee out to the front porch.

We heard Robinson say, "I can't believe how much you look like him. I remember . . . ." After a pause, he said, "You look exactly like Dylan did at your age."

There was another pause and I realized his voice sounded choked up, like he was crying. "After – after that wreck that killed his mother, he was in the hospital for a long time and they told me he'd suffered brain damage and might never be normal again. When he came home and seemed perfectly healthy, I was delighted. He was physically fine and I didn't want to see anything else.

"That wreck is also when I started covering up for him. I had been teaching him to drive even though he was only 14. When that wreck happened, he had talked his mother into letting him drive. The wreck wasn't really his fault. A deer ran out into road and he swerved but a more experienced driver would not have, not there. The car rolled three and a half times. Back then not much was said about seat belts and neither one of them was wearing one. My wife was thrown out and the car rolled on her.

Dylan hung on to the steering wheel but he had a serious head injury. I never told anyone that he was driving.

"Dylan was all I had. He lost a year of school but he started high school and wanted to play football. He was a year older than the other boys and big for his age anyway so right from the start, he was a star football player."

Again he paused and I heard him sigh. "I had some trouble with him drinking and getting into trouble. I covered up for him, paid the bills and talked people into dropping charges. He was running a lot with Riley Ellington who was trouble. I tried my best to get Dylan to drop him but I think he just started sneaking around. When Dylan graduated, I knew he wasn't college material so I encouraged him to join the police force. He barely passed the academy but they took him on at Pine Bluff, mainly because of me."

He stopped again and I thought, *The poor old man just needs to talk to someone.*

"Looking back now, I see he lacked common sense. I thought he was just young and it would pass but I tried to keep a close eye on him."

He went on. "When that deal with your mother happened, as soon as she was found, he came and told me she had faked the kidnapping and he was one of the people who helped her do it. He said he'd been having sex with her and he was afraid the rape kit would find his semen."

Jim reached over and took my hand. I scooted over and he put his arm around me. Robinson when on. "I believed him then. I did." Then he said, "There's nothing I can say now." I heard the grief in his voice.

"If I'd known there was a baby, I'd have done something even if I did believe him. I think partly I believed him because your mother never named anyone."

Job said, "Mom didn't know who it was. She only figured it out last winter when I started playing basketball. I was growing up and when she saw me in sports clothes, she remembered who I looked like. She still didn't tell me because she didn't want me to know I was the result of rape. When I came home from Colorado and told her who took me, she fainted. Mom has never fainted before."

I buried my face in Jim's shoulder and he whispered, "Are

you okay? You don't have to listen to this."

I whispered back, "He's a lonely old man with no one left."

Robinson went on talking. "Your sheriff up here gave me an earful after he arrested me. He said after your mother had you several men around here thought she'd be interested in some fun but he says she let them know in no uncertain terms that she wasn't. He said just recently, he'd had a fire a deputy who kept bothering her." Again he paused but then said, "I saw it myself. Your mother was trying to fight Dylan off."

In the following silence, I heard Job get up and then I realized Robinson was sobbing and Job had moved over to hug him.

After a few minutes I heard Robinson blowing his nose. Job said, "Granddad, I don't mind us visiting some but Dylan is a sad thing to talk about."

Robinson said, "Uh-huh." He sighed again and asked, "What do you do? You mentioned playing basketball."

So they discussed basketball and then farming. After farming they moved on to Job helping Jim install burglar alarms and surveillance systems.

Robinson commented, "You've been a busy kid. Don't you ever just have fun?"

Job laughed. "Of course. We've been canoeing several times and we picked blackberries when they were in season. We saw a brown bear and her cubs. Grandpa said his father told him there were a lot of bears here when he was growing up and every fall, they'd watch and when the weather was turning cold, they'd get one for meat."

"Your Grandpa's family has lived here a long time?"

"Since before the Civil War," Job told him. "They bought this main part of the farm then and later added another farm to the south and then one to the north."

"That cave is big, isn't it?"

Job said, "Oh, yes, but we don't let anyone go in it. Grandpa told me way in the past, some Indians came every year two days before summer solstice. They would camp here and have a three day ceremony and stay through blackberry season."

Then I heard Bob Robinson say, "Your mother kept you and her family helped raise you. I wish . . . ." He stopped and then he said, "Did they all pretend your father died in the middle-east war?"

"Not really. We just didn't talk about it. Mom's mother had wanted her to put me up for adoption but Mom wouldn't. That's why we lived here with her grandmother."

"Your Mom's mother. She was a problem, wasn't she?"

Job said, "I never met her until she came for Mom's wedding. No one talked about her and I had wondered if maybe she was an alcoholic. She's blaming everything on Willingham who's skipped the country. It looks like she's just going to get probation."

The silence lasted a while and finally Robinson said, "Looking back now I see Dylan was never completely normal after that accident. He just didn't think things through. I didn't want to believe it was more than that but up there in the cave, I saw what he was doing. Your mother was yelling for help and trying to fight him off and he was laughing."

There was another long silence and then I heard Job get up. I had to look. The old man was crying again and Job was hugging him.

When the talk had moved to what Job did with his time, I started ducking in and out to the kitchen. I had a pot of beans for dinner and I put cornbread in the oven. It was nearly done.

I went out and Robinson looked at me and said, "They've just give me community service and put me on probation for a while. It ain't enough considering what I done."

I looked at him and said, "Losing your son was punishment enough. You loved him. You had hopes and dreams for him that are now also dead. What your son did to me years ago was terrible but God gave me Job to love and watch grow up." I looked at Job and then told Robinson, "With all that's happened, Job isn't a child anymore. He's been forced to become an adult. He can decide about seeing you."

Then I said, "Dinner's ready. It's only beans and cornbread but you can eat with us."

Jim

It was only a few days later that Faith come back from the doctor saying, "Not only am I pregnant but it's twins." Her father then told us her mother's mother had been a twin and had produced three sets of twins along with four other children. He had maintained some contact with his mother-in-law over the years but kept it secret from his wife. He told us Ginger's parents had been unable to read and write and she had grown up with the pigs living under the house and chickens running in and out. Once she left home, she'd wanted no contact with her family. Her mother was now living in senior housing in Piedmont and we went to see her.

I had called my biological father on the phone and told him when I got married. Now I phoned him again and told him I was becoming a father.

The next Sunday when we came home from church, a big silver Cadillac was sitting in front of the house. Ginger was on duty so the driver was still inside. I knew who it was before he got out. Faith got Ginger settled and she looked at him and said, "Your father. He has to be."

I introduced him all around using his real name, Buck Williams. Faith invited him to stay for Sunday dinner. He and I sat on the front porch and talked while dinner got organized.

I asked him, "Is it curiosity?"

"Partly," he replied. "Also I wanted to give you a wedding present." He handed me a small box and said, "Don't open it until I'm gone."

When we were seated and the blessing had been given and food passed around, Job said, "So can we discuss playing poker or is that off limits?"

Buck smiled at him and said, "We can discuss it inside these walls but it's not to be mentioned outside."

"I didn't know it was possible to make a living playing poker," Job said. "Mom said you have to be really smart."

I watched Job do to Buck what he had done with his Grandmother only somehow he felt more sincere. Later I asked him and he said, "I liked him. I suspect he isn't totally honest but he's not a villain either and . . . . " he paused and then said, "and I think he's lonely and would like having some family."

That day when Buck left, I walked out to his car with him and he said, "When I left your mother, I left her some money and a note telling her to go get an abortion." I felt a tremor run through me and then he said, "She never told you."

"No," I said, "she told me you left her some money but not about the note."

He sighed and said, "I'm glad she didn't do it."

When Faith and I opened his present, it was a huge roll of one hundred dollar bills and a note saying, "Consider this an inheritance. Your wife's family gave her a farm and it's only right for your family to give you something too."

I told Faith what my father had said as he left. "She's a good woman and a good mother. You two will raise some great kids together."

Faith shook her head and said, "What a surprise! This whole business has been one odd thing after another. I've been thinking about how ironic it is that it's Job who was really the cause of Dylan Robinson being brought to justice."

I nodded. "Remember you said it was like Joseph in the Bible. His brothers sold him into slavery but then God used it to put him in a position later of saving his whole family. What Dylan Robinson did to you was inexcusable but out of that, God gave you Job and in the end he has been such a blessing to you and others."

Faith nodded and looked at me and said, "All these years, it was like the only people really in my life were Grandma and Job and sometimes Dad. Now I've got you and so many others." She smiled at me and said, "I like it."

I smiled at her and she hugged me and I said, "Population explosion."

She snuggled in my arms and said, "Prepare yourself. Mom's mother said every time her husband even looked at her, she got pregnant."

I laughed.

Points to Ponder

1. What about interracial marriage?

2. Is homosexuality a sin? If so, how far is it right to go in expressing this?

3. What about divorce? Is it ever justified? If so, on what grounds?

4. What about animals? Do they have souls that survive death? Do they also go to heaven?

5. What about the use of marijuana? Should it be allowed for medical reasons? How about just for recreation?

6. What about forgiveness? Does forgiving a criminal for his action mean the victim should not press charges or testify against the person?

7. What about abortion? Is it ever justified? Why or why not?

OHP

Ozark Heritage Publishing was set up to publish books reflecting Christian morals and values but often containing non-traditional elements.

E-mail: ozarkheritagepublishing@gmail.com

Books by Mary Cambron-Collard

The Points to Ponder Series

Family Secrets
An Odd Soul
Survivor's Guilt
Incident at Indian Cave

The Bigfoot Tales

McDugal's Kirk: Book 1
Redemption: Book 2 of the Bigfoot Tales

Coming Soon

Feud: Book 3 of the Bigfoot Tales

Printed by CreateSpace, An Amazon.com Company.

Made in the USA
Middletown, DE
12 July 2020